Praise for

ORANGE WINE

"From the opening sentences, I fell under the spell of Esperanza Hope Snyder's enchanting heroine. Inés is talented, passionate, resilient, and a sublime storyteller. Unlike her sisters, she wants a larger life, and gradually, weaving her way between town and city, husband and lover, Colombia and Europe, she finds her way to making fragrant soap and gorgeous paintings. *Orange Wine* is an absorbing and delightful novel."

—Margot Livesey, *The New York Times* bestselling author of *The Road from Belhaven*

"*Orange Wine* transports you back to early-twentieth-century Colombia, then spreads its magic across themes of sisterhood, betrayal, love, loss, and—most importantly—hope. This is a delicious novel."

—Ann Hood, *The New York Times* bestselling author of *The Knitting Circle*

"*Orange Wine*, like its extraordinary heroine, is at once charming and gritty and undeniably compelling—a fable of femininity suffused with love."

—Robert Cohen, author of *Amateur Barbarians* and *Inspired Sleep*

ORANGE WINE

ORANGE WINE

A Novel

ESPERANZA HOPE SNYDER

Published by Mareas Books, an imprint of
Bindery Books, Inc., San Francisco
www.binderybooks.com

Acquired by Marines Alvarez
Edited and designed by Girl Friday Productions
www.girlfridayproductions.com

Cover design by Charlotte Strick
Cover illustration of orange tree branches by Anna Coleman

ISBN (paperback): 978-1-964721-34-7
ISBN (ebook): 978-1-964721-35-4

Library of Congress Cataloging-in-Publication data has been applied for.

First edition
10 9 8 7 6 5 4 3 2 1

Printed in China

For my beloved John, thank you for saving all my paintings after I moved to Italy. I guess you knew I would return.

Like the best wine . . . that goeth down sweetly,
causing the lips of those that are asleep to speak.

The Song of Solomon

Author's Note

Orange Wine was inspired by my grandparents.

FALLEN CATHOLICS

Chapter One

While I was giving birth to Lucy, my husband, Alessandro, was lying in bed with my sister Isabel.

I spent three weeks recovering after Lucy's birth. I slept, ate, fed my child, combed my hair, and looked at my dark circles in the mirror while lying on my wide mahogany bed. Like my mother, Aura, I had always looked forward to watching the world from my mattress, but three weeks were long enough. I wanted to join Isabel, Alessandro, and Julio in the downstairs world of meals and mundane conversations. Yet on this sunny morning in May, no one came to call on me.

I sat on the bed as my daughter slept in the crib next to it. The linen sheets were rumpled under my legs, my nightgown stained with evening sweat. I turned my attention to the bowl of water and the sponge the maid had laid out for me, added drops of my cologne to the water, and sponged my skin until I was certain I had transformed my salty sweat odor into the rose fragrance that later made me famous all over Paipa. I then discarded my cotton nightgown for a silk one. After brushing my long hair, I gathered it as best I could, looked in the mirror, pinched my cheeks, and tried to get up. The toilette ritual had exhausted me. It was the first time I had conducted it alone, and I felt sorry I had sent the maid away. After two attempts I sat down and decided to rest. I dozed off and was awakened by footsteps.

"What is it?" I asked Mariela.

"I was wondering if I should start cooking lunch."

"I thought you had already started."

"Doña Isabel never returned from the market this morning."

"She probably went to see the seamstress with the new material I gave her."

"I don't know, Madam Inés, it's getting late." Mariela's voice sounded strained. "I have enough ingredients to make soup. Should I start? You must be hungry."

"Go ahead."

"Would you like some juice?"

"What fruits do we have?"

"Oranges."

"That's fine. Is Alessandro downstairs?"

"I haven't seen him since dinner."

"Did he sleep in the study?"

"The door is locked."

"Get started on the soup. I'll be going down for lunch. Call me when it's ready."

The maid hesitated at the door. "Madam, are you sure you are strong enough to make it down the stairs?"

"I'll call you if I need help. Now go get my juice."

I sat on the bed and glanced over at my daughter, snugly wrapped and sleeping in her crib. Then I reclined back on my pillows and fell asleep. Half an hour later the maid's footsteps awakened me, and I had enough time to finish my juice before the baby cried for food.

Chapter Two

Mariela gently tapped on the door. "Lunch is ready, madam. Should I bring you some soup?"

"Are Isabel and Alessandro here?"

"No, madam."

"I'll have a bowl."

When the baby's cries roused me, it was dark outside. I took Lucy in my arms, placed her on the bed, and lit a candle. I kissed the baby, changed her clothes, and held her until she fell asleep. Then I handed her over to the maid.

"What time will dinner be served?"

"Whenever you want it."

"When does Alessandro want to eat?"

"He hasn't been back."

"That's unusual. Are you sure he's not in the study?"

"I don't think so, madam."

I glanced at Mariela. She was rocking the baby back and forth. I waited, but she did not return my glance.

"Tell Isabel I want to see her."

"She's not here either."

"Where could they be?"

The maid shrugged and looked uncomfortable.

"Go down and get everything ready. I'll be down soon."

I combed my hair and grabbed my robe from the armchair by the door. I was certain Mariela was wrong and had decided to go down and look for myself. Surely Alessandro was somewhere in the house. He might be taking a nap. I knew that the pregnancy had been hard on him, accustomed as he was to getting all the attention, but I was feeling better, and things would soon go back to normal.

As I tied my robe, I remembered Julio.

"Mariela! Mariela!" I screamed. "Come here right away."

Mariela climbed the stairs as quickly as possible.

"What is it, madam?"

"Where's Julio?" I asked for the first time that day.

"This morning before she left, Miss Isabel said she was taking him to the neighbors' house to play."

"Go get him right away."

I lit a second candle, glanced at my sleeping baby, and turned toward the door, determined to go downstairs. As I took the first step, I felt my stitches pull, ready to burst. I had to grip the banister.

I stood in the dim light, glancing at what seemed to be an endless stairway. I thought about the times I had rushed up the flight of steps to get to my room.

One night, Alessandro, after a glass too many, carried me all the way up and gently placed me on the bed. He dashed downstairs to get his guitar from the study so he could serenade me.

On another occasion, I took Isabel's hand and led her up the flight of wooden steps to my room. She placed her hand on my belly and felt Lucy move. Many times I chased Julio up those stairs and tickled him until he cried with laughter.

I took a step and stopped to rest. I had never cared to count them before. After thirty I touched the landing. All was quiet and still except for my hand holding the candle. In darkness and total silence, I felt alone in the house and in the world.

I held the candle in front of me and walked toward the living room slowly. The door to the study was locked. The key was missing.

As I turned toward the dining room, a tearing pain went through my body. I had to grab a chair and barely managed to keep myself up. I rested the candle on the dining room table and eased myself onto a rocker. Lucy cried, and although I wanted to run up to her, I remained seated for a long time. Mariela's scream woke me up.

"What is it?" I asked, barely lifting my head off the table.

"I'm sorry, madam. I thought you were dead."

Julio stood by the maid with a terrified expression on his face. I opened my arms as wide as my weakness would allow and mustered a smile. My son hesitated a moment before running to hug me. Then he pulled back and touched my forehead.

"What's this?" he asked, waving a bloody finger.

I glanced at the maid. "Mariela, go get some hot water."

I buried my face in Julio's hair and cried. "From now on it will be the three of us. You, Lucy, and me," I told my son. "You'll be the man of the house."

"What about Father?"

"He's gone away—far, far away." Alessandro would not be coming back.

Chapter Three

I had no choice but to admit that my husband had left me for Isabel. The first few days after I realized neither of them was coming back, I had trouble reconciling to that new reality—a consequence of what, I did not know.

During the walks I took, during the endless nights I lay awake wondering why this had befallen me, the same memory came to torture me.

I remembered a day during our honeymoon in Italy when Alessandro and I had stood arm in arm at Piazzale Michelangelo and glanced at Florence down below. My eyes had filled with tears when I had realized that our lives would be over before we could stand in the same spot again and observe the profile of that noble city. A sense of loneliness and despair had overtaken me, and I had cried while I looked at the Duomo far off in the distance. I shivered at the thought that Alessandro would not be mine forever and at the certainty that he would ruin my life.

~

Years after my mother remarried, I was born in a small town by the name of Paipa, located in a part of Colombia that few people visit more than once. It was in January, with the sun in Capricorn and Leo rising.

My mother's first marriage had been to a much older man whose relatives had fought in the War of Independence side by side with Simón Bolívar, the liberator of the country and the dreamer of La Gran Colombia.

General de La Rota was twenty-seven years older than Mother. She had been a child when they married. They had a daughter, Isabel, but the general died before she was born. He never had the chance to hold her in his arms.

My mother's life with the general, a wealthy and accomplished man of the world, was a privileged one; the land and the mansion were but a sign of it. They had Massimiliano, the general's great-grandfather, to thank for it.

Massimiliano della Ruota traveled around the world for five years in order to nurse his ego after a failed political career in Milan. Once he convinced himself that there was no future for him in his homeland, he changed his name from della Ruota to de La Rota to symbolize his broken fortune and tried to get as far away as possible. Within months he settled his affairs, moved his family to the New World, and settled in Bogotá.

During a card game with some of the wealthiest landowners in the city, Massimiliano won thousands of acres in Paipa. Not wanting to pursue a political career, he moved and set about building the largest mansion that the town would ever see, with marble from Carrara and Venetian glass. The house took ten years to complete, and on the day it was finished, he cried.

While they were married, Mother and General de La Rota enjoyed the mansion and gave outstanding parties; people traveled from Bogotá to attend their soirees. Politicians, economists, and military men all sought to be invited to the general's mansion and to meet his lovely wife.

The general died of a heart attack, and with him went the soirees and Aura's peace of mind. But then she met Father, who inspired in her all the passion that her first husband had not.

Chapter Four

My father, Rodolfo Camargo, who worked as a scribe in the only lawyer's office in Paipa, had failed to complete his law degree.

He and Mother fell in love as she sat on the couch, clutching her linen handkerchief, while a partner in the firm read the general's will out loud. Rodolfo marveled at Aura's green eyes and her porcelain skin, unaware that she was carrying her husband's child. She didn't know she was pregnant either, and she attributed the malaise she felt to her husband's death rather than to her body changing. By the time she gave Rodolfo the news, he couldn't bear the thought of living without Aura.

"We will marry, and I will raise the child as my own," he told her. "I will speak to Father Luis." The next day Aura went to see the priest.

Aura's second marriage was blessed with happiness and with four daughters, Rosa, Helena, Chata, and me. Chata's real name was Ofelia, but when she turned four, Father noticed her wide nose and started calling her Chata. Everyone in the household followed his example, and for the rest of her life, my sister answered to that name.

My childhood in the largest mansion in Paipa was a joyful

one. I was the youngest child. Mother said I was lively and healthy from the start.

"All children possess some degree of beauty," she told me, "but you are by far the most attractive of my daughters. Yet it's not your beauty that draws people to you; your sweet disposition has something to do with it as well. As a baby you ate and slept and only fussed when you had good reason to and continued to flourish until the age of one and a half, when you nearly died from food poisoning."

Mother always managed to conclude her appraisals of me with the nearly fatal illness that struck when I was a child. I could not help but wonder if my illness had in some way made my mother love me more. She did not leave my bedside until I recuperated, and once she had nursed me back to health, she never stopped feeling protective toward me.

Long after I had learned to read and write, I continued to have dishes prepared especially for me.

On Sunday afternoons Father took me to the rose garden. While he sat for hours in the shade and diligently copied Mother's roses on small wooden surfaces, I memorized her poems. Father was a quiet, gentle man. I never saw him angry, and I never heard him shout. He spent his time reading and watching my mother move about the house beautifying rooms with flower arrangements.

When I turned ten, Mother hired a seamstress to teach us all how to sew. My sisters and I made puppets and set up a theater at home to perform plays.

As a child I spent hours listening to the maids narrate scary tales. My favorite story was about La Llorona, the woman who cried all night after losing her children. Many nights I thought I heard her cry.

One day while I was outside reading with my nanny, I glanced at the cornfields and saw a small figure hiding. He was dressed in green and swung back and forth on one of the stalks. Speechless, I pointed a finger, but the little man had gone.

The next time I saw him, I was walking through the cornfields and noticed him swinging from another cornstalk, smiling. He brought his finger to his lips and beckoned me to come closer. I felt nervous but so fascinated by this creature, hypnotized by his swinging. For a while, I stood still, staring at him. Then I noticed a woman behind him, the most beautiful being I had ever met. When she spoke, her voice sounded like bells inside my head. Even though she never opened her mouth or uttered a word, I understood what she was saying.

"You have a gift," she said. "The gift of seeing . . . you see the future, see into people's hearts and minds. This will help you in life, but it will also bring you suffering."

Inside my body, the optimism and the suffering she mentioned came and left as suddenly as birds flying by. She smiled. "Use this gift to help others and to protect yourself." A warm feeling enveloped me as if she were putting a blanket over my shoulders.

Then a scene flashed before my eyes. I saw a circle of women dancing and playing tambourines, dressed in orange robes, their hair gathered loosely. They wore ankle bells and made beautiful music. I felt I knew them, even though I couldn't explain why. . . .

"You've been with them before," the woman said, "and they'll join you again during this lifetime, as your daughters." Then a man's face appeared. "You'll meet him too," the angel added. "He's your destiny. Remember everything I showed you today. You may not understand it now, but it will become clear one day. I'll be looking over you," the angel said before disappearing.

The little man was also gone. I sat by the cornfield repeating everything I had heard and seen, trying to memorize every detail, whispering, "Don't forget, don't forget."

The general's house and its surroundings were fertile ground for ghosts. As long as the de La Rotas could remember, strange events had taken place in the mansion. Paintings were often turned upside down.

On one occasion, we returned from a trip to find the large mirror in the parlor crushed into tiny pieces on the floor. The general's portrait had been taken down. When Father questioned the maids, no one was able to provide a feasible explanation. He gave up and attributed the event to a ghost, believed to be Massimiliano de La Rota.

It was said that after Massimiliano became a widower, he fell in love with a young woman. He had to compete with a landowner for her affection and was driven mad by jealousy. Massimiliano went about courting the lady and trying to win her over with lavish presents; he ordered jewelry from Milan and even went as far as buying a painting that, according to the dealer, was an original Botticelli. The girl looked at it for a while, sighed, and took it home. Massimiliano's fortune won. She married him. Several months later he found her in the arms of his stable keeper. Enraged, Massimiliano used his sword on both and hanged himself.

~

General de La Rota had left his widow without much knowledge about how to manage the land, and Father accelerated the decline. He quit his job at the law firm and dedicated his time to learning, exploring, and assimilating the pleasures of life.

Mother had never known how to manage money, and she and Father whittled away at the fortune that Massimiliano had brought from Milan and that his children had preserved almost intact in the New World.

My mother was an artist and a lover of beauty, and she passed her days minding her rose garden. She was proud of her collection of roses, which included the common as well as the exotic. We had yellow, red, white, and salmon-colored roses, as well as the infamous black rose.

Every day I woke to find fresh flowers in the house. Mother's work of arranging them began at ten and, with a pause for lunch, took until five o'clock. The last flower arrangement, done in a nineteenth-century Rockingham bone china vase brought from England by one of the general's relatives, was placed in what had become the music room and tea parlor.

Mother knew about roses, and she knew their thorns cut deeply. But she also knew how to take care of those cuts; it was life's cuts that she was afraid to face. I believe she thought it was unfair that after dedicating so many years of her life to beauty and to the cultivation of beautiful things, she should be forced to face reality in its painful cruelty. On the day my father told her they were running out of money, Mother planted a new rosebush in the garden.

"Rodolfo," she told him, "God knows I love you. The first time I saw you, I could tell you were a sweet, kind soul that could appreciate beauty in all its forms. But I wish you had learned something practical while you worked for that law firm; I would like to think my husband has his feet on the ground so that I can levitate when I feel like it."

Father looked as if he were about to cry. I watched him as he took a handkerchief out of his pocket and wiped his forehead.

"Aura, all these years I thought I was making you happy," he said.

"You have made me happy," she insisted, "so please don't ruin it now. I'm working on a new poem. I need peace of mind."

Mother stood back to admire her new rosebush, and then she handed me a bucket and told me to fetch some water.

Chapter Five

General de La Rota had always lectured Mother about the importance of education, and she decided to invest the last pennies of her fortune on Rosa, Helena, Chata, and me. Isabel was dating a local young man from a prominent family of coffee growers.

"I will never understand how someone could make a fortune from a few miserable coffee beans," Mother commented on the day she met him.

But then she, who had always lived amid fine things and had the best of everything, never spent much time analyzing wealth.

Whatever Aura may have lacked as a mother, she made up for by encouraging us to engage in literary and artistic pursuits. Rosa practiced the piano every morning for three hours. Helena took voice lessons from an Italian master who had moved to Paipa to seek comfort in the thermal baths for his arthritis. Chata studied embroidery under the Italian master's wife and proceeded to embroider cushions with cherubs for the whole house. Father taught me how to play the guitar; the first ballet teacher in Paipa taught me how to dance.

Mother sent Rosa to school in Tunja, a small town not far from Paipa, to become a schoolteacher, but fell ill before she could do the same for the rest of us.

~

One day Mother called me to her bedroom. She was still in bed and looked like a queen, surrounded by embroidered pillows, her face soft in the sunlight. I sat on the bed and waited for her to finish brushing her long hair.

"Inés, I've had a recurring dream about you," she told me after putting her hairbrush down. "I see you dressed in rags and shivering from the cold, your hair all tangled up; your hand is reaching out as if to beg for alms. I wake up in terror and lay awake the rest of the night."

"You shouldn't worry about me," I told her. "I'll be fine."

"It's not your fault I have that dream. But I have decided to leave you the mansion."

No matter how much I protested, my mother would not change her mind. I thanked her, but I worried that my sisters would not understand.

~

When the last morsels of the general's fortune had disappeared, Mother became ill with tuberculosis. She died in her sleep after dividing what was left of the family fortune among us. It did not take her long to distribute the porcelain, the family portraits, and the jewelry. The roses, along with the house, went to me.

Just before she died, Mother called me to her bedside. She looked at me for a long time. Then she kissed my forehead, took a deep breath, and before closing her eyes forever, told me that much of the land around the house had been sold to pay off the debts.

On the day the will was read, Father became a tenant in the

house he had learned to regard as his own. He could not complain, though, because I told him he was allowed to stay as long as he lived.

Isabel sat in a chair in the living room, looking at Mother's roses out the window. I walked up to her and took her hand. She tried to talk, but I stopped her.

"You can stay as long as you like," I told my sister. She squeezed my hand and turned to glance out the window again as she wiped her tears.

Chapter Six

After Rosa completed her studies in Tunja, she left for Bogotá, saying she would send for us once she became established.

Mother had made the right decision concerning Rosa. Chances were that she would never find a husband, and she needed to be able to support herself. Mother often said this as we watched Rosa reading or playing the piano.

Rosa had a tall, strong body with wide hips and large bones. Her face was neither pretty nor ugly, but her strong character and her determination came across as she glanced around a room. She had thick eyebrows and long dark hair. Her nose was too large to be defined as delicate, but it was well placed on her face. Rosa's dark eyes were unsettling when her glance switched from harsh or impatient to sweet. It was amazing to think she would be teaching children to read and write.

Rosa was as strong and willful as Chata was weak and frail. Chata's body, which constituted a narrow line half of Rosa's width, was crowned by a perfectly round face. On the right side between her mouth and her nose, a large mole rested. Regardless of what Chata did or said, people always looked at her mole and not her eyes. She had straight, thin brown hair she kept in a chignon; her voice was as shrill as Rosa's was deep.

When Mother confided in me about my sisters' shortcomings, I protested. "They may not be beautiful, but they have many talents."

"Yes, that's true," she agreed, "but their talents will not find them husbands. I know this is unfair, but life, in all its complexity, is seldom fair."

"What about me?"

"You have the loveliness to captivate many suitors, Inés, but you are a dreamer. Prettiness doesn't last forever. That's why I love my roses, because they remind me of how fleeting beauty is."

~

Once Rosa found a job, a bus ticket arrived for Chata. Rosa needed an assistant, she wrote. Chata was thankful and left the next day. I'm sure she didn't know, as she climbed the bus steps, that she would be waiting on Rosa for the rest of her life.

Mother had been right—my sisters never married. They passed their days together among Rosa's furniture and in her house, eating her food and drinking her hot chocolate.

After her first year in Bogotá, Chata returned to Paipa for two weeks. She looked frail and tired. I took her to the thermal baths every day; she cried silently while I rubbed her back.

"What's wrong?"

"Rosa can be so cold," my sister answered.

"You don't have to go back," I told her. "You can stay here with us. You saw your bedroom; it is exactly the way you left it. I was hoping you would return."

"I promised Mother I would live with Rosa," Chata replied. "I'd be too much of a burden here."

"We could open an academy for girls. You could teach embroidery, and I would teach ballet and music."

Chata remained silent. When the two weeks were over, she packed her suitcase. I walked her to the station, and she climbed onto the return bus to Bogotá.

"Promise you'll write to me!" I shouted as the bus was leaving.

"I promise," she answered before her face became a blur.

During the time I remained in Paipa, Chata wrote to me often, sometimes twice a week. In her letters, my sister narrated everything she and Rosa did, from the most insignificant rituals to their church outings and frequent fights.

Dearest Inés,

Today Rosa woke up in a bad mood, and when I placed a cup of chocolate in front of her, she started screaming, "I wanted coffee!" Then she threw the cup across the room and almost hit me. I picked it up and made some coffee, but the truth is, Inés, that Rosa always drinks chocolate on Tuesdays. I don't know how she's going to have the patience to deal with her students today. She left in a hurry and slammed the door so hard on her way out, I got a headache. I've done nothing but cry since she left. I'm only glad I have you to write to.

Yours,
Chata

Chata may have cried for days, but in the end she dried her tears.

Chapter Seven

Six months after Chata's arrival at Rosa's house, Helena joined my sisters in Bogotá. Rosa signed her up for a secretarial school and started looking around for eligible bachelors.

Rosa's expectations were not unrealistic. Helena was tall and slender and had thick brown hair, dark-brown eyes like Mother's, and pretty legs. Helena was not a beauty, but she knew how to walk and how to carry herself. The class she had inherited from Mother made up for some of her slight imperfections.

Dearest Inés,

Helena has learned to type and to write in shorthand; it's taken her twice as long as it would have taken me. I'm afraid she's not very bright. Now Rosa is searching for a company where our sister will make a living and find a husband. I think it is the husband that interests her most. A European would be her first choice. Rosa thinks Helena will do very well in life. "I'll bet my salary on it," she told me during breakfast.

Yours,

Chata

Four months later Helena finished secretarial school; she

applied for a job at the central office of the Société Nationale de Chemins de Fer en Colombie, a Belgian railroad company in Bogotá. After an hour-long test and an interview, she was hired to type handwritten notes and memos from the company executives. She was also expected to take dictation in shorthand.

The following month Chata wrote to report the good news.

Dear Inés,

A week before Helena started her new job, Rosa took her out and bought her three outfits of the finest Italian wool. Upon Helena's protests, Rosa told her she could pay her back after she married well, with emphasis on "well."

I'm thrilled Helena does not have to follow in my footsteps. You should have seen the way I went about altering hems and changing buttons! I felt like a young artist working on a masterpiece.

I reminded Rosa the other day that she had promised to send for you after Helena found a job. She had not forgotten. Now the road is clear for your journey. Go to the station to see if your ticket has arrived.

I can hardly wait to kiss you.

Chata

I packed my bags, bid farewell to Father and Isabel, and left for Bogotá. Although I planned to live there permanently, I was on my way back to Paipa six months later.

~

The first time I saw Bogotá, I realized how small and provincial Paipa really was. From the moment I stepped down from the train, my black shoes and pink silk dress were suddenly out of place in a sea of brown, gray, and navy long skirts and overcoats. The hats were simple and stylish, not loaded with flowers and silk bows. As I looked around for Chata, I was glad to remember I had a little money I could use to buy a new outfit.

My sister and I rode to Rosa's house in a hired car. Looking out the window, I noticed the wide city streets and even wider boulevards, astonishing when compared to Paipa's simple roads. As impressive colonial buildings appeared, Chata informed me that we were arriving in La Candelaria, the neighborhood where Rosa's house was located.

"That's Plaza de Bolívar," my sister pointed out. Looking at the stunning plaza—with its neoclassical architecture and imposing buildings—and the mountains rising in the background, I wished, with all my heart, that I could paint that landscape.

"There's the cathedral!" Chata exclaimed.

"Impressive . . . neoclassical style, right?"

"Yes," my sister replied. "It was built in the last century between 1807 and 1823 in the same spot where three other churches had previously been erected. Ready for the name, Inés?"

"Yes."

"Catedral Basílica Metropolitana y Primada de la Inmaculada Concepción y San Pedro de Bogotá. Catedral Primada for short. What do you think?"

"It's a mouthful," I replied, laughing. "But a building this beautiful," I added, "deserves a long name."

"Wait until you see the interior," Chata commented. "My favorite building in the plaza is that tiny chapel over there," she added, pointing her finger at a small church not far from the cathedral. "It's called Capilla del Sagrario de la Catedral Basílica Metropolitana de Bogotá."

"A long name for a tiny structure," I said.

"Yes, but it's at least a hundred years older than the cathedral," Chata explained. We watched people rushing across the plaza.

"Señorita, would you like me to stop so you can show your sister El Chorro de Quevedo?" the driver asked Chata.

"Yes, please, if it's not an inconvenience."

"What is that?" I asked.

"Quevedo's Fountain," my sister explained. "Some claim it's on the same spot where Gonzalo Jiménez de Quesada, the Spanish conquistador, founded the city in the sixteenth century."

"And it's named after the Spanish poet Francisco de Quevedo?"

"No, after a Catholic priest who had the fountain built in 1832. Oh, by the way," Chata interrupted herself, "did you hear about our cousin Gustavo? He's moved to Bogotá to begin his studies for the priesthood. Rosa is very excited that we'll have a priest in the family."

"The last time I saw him was when he visited Paipa with his family years ago," I replied. "I barely remember him."

"Well, yes, none of us have seen him since then, but now that he's going to be a priest, we all want to be part of his life." My sister winked. "Rosa is planning to invite him over for hot chocolate and *almojábanas* one afternoon."

"She'd be better off serving English tea and European biscuits if she wants to impress him," I said. We got out of the car and walked up to the fountain.

Rosa's house was located close to a park, not far from the main town square. The first few weeks, I spent hours on the balcony watching the Bogotanos stroll in front of the cathedral and the presidential palace during the afternoons. I could understand now what my mother had meant when she told me people from Bogotá were more reserved, sophisticated, and cultured than those from Paipa.

From the first day, I longed to go out to the square and stroll as if my needs had been met and all that was left for me to do in life was walk around one of the prettiest squares in the New World.

But Rosa did not approve of idleness or of me going out unchaperoned. I got to go out with Chata to take care of the shopping; I was never allowed to go anywhere alone. Although I did help Chata around the house while Helena and Rosa were at work, I yearned to be doing more.

I had brought my guitar with me, so on days when the sun warmed the mountains surrounding the city, I would go out on the balcony and play. Once I felt comfortable, I started singing as well. People would gather below to listen. Sometimes they applauded. Ladies bowed and gentlemen lifted their hats to me. Chata would watch behind the door and jump with joy when she heard applause.

"If Rosa finds out you're doing this," Chata cautioned one day when she noticed a larger crowd than usual, "she'll send you back to Paipa immediately. We must never tell her. It will be our secret."

For all her meanness, Rosa was good to us. She housed and fed us, and occasionally she would take us out to a concert. We lived close to the Teatro Colón, and often at night we could hear people leaving the theater. Chata knew I stayed up to watch the theater crowd, all dressed in finery, walking out of the Colón after a play. I never tired of admiring the women wrapped in their luxurious velvet capes.

One day Helena came home with four tickets for a play by Calderón de la Barca and an invitation to the reception following the show. I could have kissed her feet. I had read the play several years before and had been struck by the playwright's ability to weave a plot about free will, fate, illusion, and reality. In Calderón's play, a prince, released after years of captivity, is able to change and to prove a prophecy wrong, thus altering his destiny. I was struck by Calderón's powerful message, by the struggles of his characters, and I couldn't believe my luck. I would get to see the play at the Colón on opening night! I did not know then that *Life Is a Dream* would become a motif in my own existence, and that, like Calderón's characters, I would have my share of joy and misfortune.

For a whole week, Chata and I worked on our outfits. We cut and she sewed; we cleaned, adorned, simplified, and ironed. Finally, we were ready.

The theater was beyond what I had expected. Sure, I had attended plays performed at people's houses, but never a performance in a real theater with velvet seats, chandeliers, and red carpeting. I could hardly walk straight as I stared at the grandeur about me.

A theater company from Spain was performing. I had read *Life Is a Dream* more than once, but I never fully understood it until that night.

During the intermission, we followed the public to the foyer and stood around while waiters in white gloves offered us champagne flutes on silver trays. Rosa would not let me finish my second glass, but it did not matter.

At the reception following the play, so many people came to introduce themselves, I could hardly remember any of their names. Perhaps it was the champagne.

Two days later, gentlemen started calling on me. They were all quite proper and brought me flowers or sent me small presents with their calling cards. It was nice to be the center of attention. I thought Rosa would be proud of me for having several suitors. I was wrong.

"I'm trying to get Helena settled," she said impatiently after I showed her the calling cards. "I don't have time to work on you. Do you realize," Rosa added as she tossed the calling cards into the fire, "we'll have to feed these men? We can't just offer them a glass of water. That will cost me money."

Rosa was right. It would cost us to entertain. I decided not to invite any of them to the house.

I thought my suitors would go away, but three continued to insist. When I refused them all, they started sending me love letters and then serenading me at night, long after the Teatro Colón had closed its doors following the evening show. Rosa read the love notes and burned them in the fireplace, but she could not tolerate the serenades.

One night, after several serenades, Rosa packed my suitcase at five o'clock in the morning. She put me on the first train to Paipa with a one-way ticket.

"You're going to ruin your reputation and Helena's chances of a good marriage," Rosa told me as she handed me the suitcase.

I tried to reason with her. "You're overreacting. A little music never did anyone any harm."

"You'll be surprised where a little music will lead," Rosa pronounced. "Father Gonzales told me he saw you walking with one of the Carrillo boys."

"I repented."

"Well, it's too late to repent," Rosa admonished. "You have forgotten about common decency, the reputation of your family, and the respect you owe me as your older sister. Ten Hail Marys won't change that."

I arrived in Paipa a day later with my suitcase, my throat dry from the dust. Father greeted me at the station.

"Your sister just wants to protect you," he said, taking my hand.

Rosa sent me back to Paipa to protect me, and it was there that I met Alessandro Scala, the man who would break my heart and change my life. I wish Rosa could have protected me from that.

Chapter Eight

I reunited with Father and Isabel at the mansion. On the third day after my arrival, I opened the pantry to get some flour for bread and found it empty. This discovery made me realize how difficult the situation had become for us. I understood then why Isabel was a nanny, and I decided to contribute to the household as well.

As I looked for ways to earn a living, I realized how useful a teaching certificate would have been. I did not know anyone interested in learning how to play the guitar, but I had been taught by one of the finest tutors in Paipa, and upon his recommendation, was hired as a tutor for the Diaz children. During the mornings we worked on math, reading, and writing. In the afternoons I played my guitar, sang to the children, and checked their schoolwork.

After Mother's death, Father became a train conductor. He spent a couple of days a week away from home and brought presents and news of faraway places.

"I have tickets for the Saturday-afternoon show at the new circus in town," he announced one day during lunch.

I had never been to a circus, but I remembered my mother's description of one she had been to as a child. The idea of seeing acrobats, lions, elephants, and clowns was an exotic dream; nomads going from one town to the next wearing beautiful, colorful clothes had always fascinated me. I envied their freedom, their passion, and their spirit.

Books were one of the few sources of entertainment in Paipa, and although I constantly searched for new reading material, no one in the household shared my passion. Isabel played Mozart on the piano for two hours every day but never finished a book in her life.

I did not sleep much that week thinking about the show, and all the fables I invented for the children were related to the circus. When Saturday finally came, I was exhausted.

The Diaz children, Father, Isabel, and I walked to the large tent, which had been set up ten blocks from the mansion in the first open field outside of town.

Red and white stripes could be seen from far away. There were animal cages, giants, dwarfs, and fortune tellers milling about the place. Food vendors had already set their stands up; they displayed an array of candies and peanuts that would give anyone but a child a stomachache. I bought peanuts for the children and took them around to see the lions and the elephant.

Standing by the third tent was a woman dressed in a flowing white gown. She wore a fuchsia turban and had dark hair, large hoop earrings, and too much rouge. When the children and I walked by, she smiled a toothless grin. One of the children stopped to stare.

"What do you do?" he asked the woman.

"I'm a fortune teller," she answered.

"And what can you do?"

"I can tell the future."

"The future of what?"

"Of people."

"And how do you do that?"

"By reading the palms of their hands."

"Show me," he said as he turned his hand.

I pulled him away and told him he was too young for fortune-telling. The woman looked at me in defiance.

"No one is too young to have a future. Give me your hand," she commanded.

I raised my right hand reluctantly and spread my palm wide open when the woman pressed on it.

"Hmm. I see," she whispered as she traced the contours of my hand. She grabbed the other one. "These hands will be forced to do things for which they were not born," she predicted.

I gave her some change before gathering the children to go into the tent.

We found Father and Isabel and settled into our seats. A rather large clown was unsuccessfully trying to stand on his head when a man carried a stool to the center of the stage and placed a guitar by it. Another man followed him out, sat on the stool, and picked up the guitar. People grew silent.

"Good afternoon," he said, "my name is Alessandro Scala. I'm here to entertain you before the show."

He wore a white shirt and black pants; his hair was combed back and his mustache, unlike the fashion in Paipa at the time, was thick. As Alessandro tuned his guitar, all the clowns abandoned the stage; his presence filled the tent.

Isabel pinched my arm and leaned over the children. "He's handsome beyond belief," she whispered in my ear.

Alessandro lowered his head for a moment before singing. I sat with two children on one side and one on the other asking for more peanuts as I listened to him play the most melodious music

I had ever heard and sing in a forlorn way that struck me with its melancholy.

That Saturday afternoon at the circus was unforgettable for me, not because of the dancing elephant or the lions, but rather because of Alessandro Scala.

With time I forgot about the participants of the shows and their costumes, but I remembered the way my heart became a feather when I saw Alessandro and how it turned as cold as stone as I sensed that our destinies were somehow tied.

During supper that evening Isabel asked Father about Alessandro.

"He came to our house when he was a child," Father answered.

"Why haven't we seen him until today?" she insisted.

"I believe he was living in the capital. Attending the university over there."

Father stopped eating and put his fork down. He looked at Isabel for a minute. "Now, young lady," he said, "don't forget you are soon to be married. I would not give Scala a second thought." My sister laughed.

Chapter Nine

One month later Amalia Rios, a childhood friend, invited me to spend an evening with her family at their estate outside of Paipa. I gathered my light-brown hair into a bun and chose to wear the old-fashioned lavender dress I had inherited from Mother. According to Isabel, it complemented my gray eyes and fair skin.

That day at Amalia's I was eager to recapture some of my childhood memories. At sixteen, I was too old to play with dolls, but I still felt too young to embrace life as an adult. I arrived early. Amalia and I went around to all our favorite hiding places. We found the large oak tree, the abandoned cabin, and the stables. Both of us ran around the fields with the frenzy that only our youth could fuel. When the bell rang for dinner, we had to straighten our sleeves and comb our hair.

I knew the Rioses' house as well as my own, and I followed Amalia up the stairwell with ease.

As I reached the top of the stairs, I glanced into the dining room. The table had been beautifully set, as in the mansion during the golden days. A vase of pink roses resting on it brought back the image of Mother gathering flowers before supper.

My mind lingered on this thought until I noticed a man standing beyond the table. He had his back to me and was looking out the window into the fields, oblivious of his beauty and of the world around him.

The man turned around as if someone had called, and I found myself looking into his green eyes. There was a moment of silence.

"My name is Alessandro Scala," he finally said. "Our grandfathers were friends. My mother told me we met at your house when we were children." He smiled and walked toward me. "You and Amalia can run," he said, pointing to the window. I felt my cheeks grow hot and lowered my eyes.

Alessandro sat next to me during the meal, and although we both participated in the general conversation, a private dialogue took place.

I did not dare look up at him, but from the corner of my eye I watched his hands reach for the wineglass, manage the silver fork and knife, and pick up the linen napkin from his lap to wipe his lips, which I could now define as full and sensual.

Alessandro spoke with ease to Amalia's father about the European companies that had just started investing in the capital, and every so often he turned to glance at me.

"You haven't touched your food," he observed as a maid removed my plate. "Are you not well?"

"I've lost my appetite."

Alessandro raised his wineglass and looked at me as if to toast. "Mine has increased the more today," he said before he drank.

"Alessandro has agreed to sing for us tonight," Amalia's father announced after dinner. "Please join us in the music room."

All the guests abandoned their places at the dinner table and strolled toward the music room. I took a seat in the front row next to Amalia. Alessandro sat comfortably on the sofa in front of us.

"I'll be glad to play after the young ladies read a poem," he said while pointing in our direction.

Amalia took a poetry anthology from the shelf and read a poem by Gustavo Adolfo Bécquer. She then handed me the book and I glanced through it, searching for a short poem. Alessandro came to stand by me.

"Are there any sonnets by Garcilaso de la Vega in there?" he asked while he glanced over my shoulder.

I could feel his warm breath close to my ear. The book felt heavy in my hands. I tried to hold it steady, but my trembling fingers could not keep it so. People sat in silence waiting for me.

"May I?" Alessandro took the book and glanced at the table of contents. He chose a page and returned the book to me. I read.

> If I am wax to thy sweet will, and hence
> Sun myself only in thy sight, (and he
> Who views thy radiance uninflamed, must
>   be
> Void of all feeling) whence, Señora, whence
> Rises a circumstance, whose strange
>   offence
> Against the laws of reason, had it been
> Less seldom proved on me—less seldom
>   seen,
> Had led me to mistrust my very sense—
> Whence comes it, that far-off I am
>   inflamed
> And kindled by thy aspect, even until

My melting heart its fervour scarce
sustains,
Whilst if encountered near by thine
untamed,
Untameably bright eye, an instant chill
Makes the blood curdle in my crimson
veins?

"Ah, yes!" Amalia's father exclaimed with delight. "A love sonnet by Garcilaso de la Vega, one of my favorite poets! Please read another one, Inés." I turned the page and kept on reading.

As, love, the lily and purpureal rose
Show their sweet colours on thy chaste
warm cheek,
Thy radiant looks, angelically meek,
Serene the tempest to divine repose,
And as thy hair, which for its birthright
chose
The opal's dye, upon the whitest neck
Waved by the winds of heaven without a
check,
In exquisite disorder falls and flows;
Gather the rich fruit of thy mirthful
spring,
Ere angry Time around thy temples shed
The snows of hasting age; his icy wing
Will wither the fresh rose, however red;
And changing not his custom, quickly
change
The glory of all objects in his range.

My eyes filled with tears. I could feel Alessandro's gaze studying me. Had I not known the poem by heart, I would have had to stop. But Mother had made me memorize it years before; it was her favorite poem and all her daughters had to learn it.

Later, when we talked about that evening, Alessandro would tell me what he had been thinking while I read.

"I looked at your hair, with strands falling softly around your face, at your small and narrow nose, placed perfectly between your mouth and eyebrows, at your gray eyes, and I was captivated; when they welled up with tears, I thought about kissing your eyes, your nose, your lips."

After I finished Garcilaso's poem, Alessandro picked up his guitar and started tuning it. People conversed while they waited for the music. Alessandro looked up and motioned me to move closer. I joined him on the couch. We talked about poetry while he chose what to play.

The sitting room was comfortable and warm. The candles created a soft light. Alessandro asked me a few questions and listened with attention as if I were the only person in the room. An awkward silence followed. I rose from the couch and moved to the other side. Silence reigned.

In time, I forgot many details about that evening except the way Alessandro looked into my eyes.

I often sat in the living room of my house in Paipa listening to my record player, humming to Mozart and Vivaldi while dreaming of my happy childhood; yet it was the second movement of Beethoven's *Seventh Symphony* that captured the intensity and the sadness of my love for Alessandro.

For many years, the memory of that encounter was the last one of the day as I lay in bed. Often, I thought about how a single moment in a person's life can influence the future irrevocably.

Before that evening was over, Alessandro invited me to his house for tea on the following day. His parents were out of town, and he was in charge of the household, but Amalia's mother was willing to chaperone and to bring her daughter along.

I spent the night at Amalia's house, and while the two of us lay in the dark, we shared our secrets well past midnight.

"I noticed the special attention Alessandro was showing you this evening," Amalia told me. "I think he's having us for tea so he can see you."

Chapter Ten

I did not have a dress for the tea party and Amalia loaned me one of her own, a sheer white silk-and-organza gown that fell above my ankles.

"It looks lovely on you," Amalia said.

My friend and I were ready long before the carriage came to fetch us. We left at four and rode through the fields of Paipa to Alessandro's house.

The carriage turned onto a dirt lane. Far off in the distance I saw the house with pine trees around it, a white dog barking, and Alessandro standing by the door waiting for our arrival.

The house was built in the style of a Tuscan villa. Amalia, her mother, and I got out of the carriage, and Alessandro held the dog while we approached. His boots still had dirt on them from the morning ride.

When I stepped inside the villa, I felt transported to a new and different land. The place was not elegant and majestic like the mansion, but there was an aura about it that invoked the uniqueness of an Italian world. The floors were covered with the finest terra-cotta tiles. The living room was spacious. To the left there was a chimney with sofas all around it. The wall to the right was made of stone, and at the end of the corridor there was a staircase.

Alessandro had laid out a feast with cheese, cured meats, wine, truffles, and pastries by the chimney.

He poured a glass of red wine. "Some Brunello for you?" He handed me the glass. "My father brought it from Italy many years ago; he told me to drink it on a special occasion."

"And what special occasion could this be?" Amalia's mother asked.

"Having all of you here today." Alessandro took a sip of his wine and looked at me. "A fine wine," he said, "must be savored. You need to take in the aroma, and then keep it in your mouth for a little while so the flavors have a chance to come forth and enrich your palate. Try it," he ordered me.

I closed my eyes and tentatively raised the glass to inhale the rich aroma; then I took a sip and kept it in my mouth as the flavor changed.

"Now swallow," Alessandro said softly.

As I sent the red wine down, I opened my eyes.

"Do you like Brunello?" he asked.

"It's warm, rich, and mysterious." I took another sip.

"A very sensual experience." Alessandro raised his glass to his lips. Our eyes met.

"I don't see any tea around here," Amalia's mother complained. "I was hoping to have a cup."

"Tea is for the English," Alessandro replied. "They will make you a perfect cup. Italians prefer wine. I have something you might like," he said as he left the room.

A few minutes later Alessandro returned with what looked like a bottle of champagne in his hand.

"This is *spumante*. Italian *spumante*. Have you ever had any?"

"No," Señora Rios replied in an uncertain tone.

"It's our equivalent of champagne. In my opinion, it's superior to the French stuff."

Alessandro proceeded to open the bottle and to pour Señora Rios a glass. "Taste it. I think you'll like it."

She took a sip. "It's delightful!" she proclaimed while looking at Alessandro mischievously. "You are not trying to get us all drunk, are you?"

"My dear Señora Rios," he answered with a gallant smile. "Why would I want to do that? I cannot imagine a worse fate for a man than to have more than one drunken woman in his house! Women are difficult enough when they're sober." Everyone laughed except for me.

I finished my wine and went to look at the portrait of a woman I had noticed upon entering. It was out of proportion and simple, almost childlike. And yet it was captivating. The woman wore a black dress with a white collar. She sat on a chair, her head tilted to the left. The hairstyle looked odd. In Paipa, no women wore their hair short. I studied the painting for a while before I noticed Alessandro standing behind me.

"It's titled *Woman with Red Hair,* painted in 1917. Beautiful, isn't she?"

"Who is the painter?"

"Amedeo Modigliani, an Italian who lived in Paris. He died of tuberculosis at thirty-five, three years after he completed this painting. My father bought it during his last trip to Paris. He purchased two other Modiglianis, but we have not hung them up yet. Mother thinks they could shock our neighbors."

"Why?"

"Paipa is a provincial town."

"I would have to agree with that."

"In both paintings women are posing nude," he continued. "One is reclining and the other one sitting on a chair. Nothing is more beautiful than the female body," Alessandro added. His boldness was surprising.

"Amalia told me you moved back into the mansion," he went on as we walked back to join the others.

"Yes. It's not far from here."

"I returned to Paipa three months ago, and I have never seen you," he commented.

"I lived in Bogotá for some time, and since I came back, I've been working every day."

"Working? What a novel idea!" Alessandro was amused. "And what is it you do?"

"I tutor the Diaz children."

"So your mother left you destitute?" he whispered while he took another sip of Brunello.

"I actually enjoy it," I replied. "What do you do with your time? Surely you do more than ride."

I didn't understand why I felt so much anger toward Alessandro. One moment he seemed vain and superficial, while the next he looked at me in such a way that I would have done anything he asked of me. I felt my cheeks flush.

"As you know," he answered, filling his glass with wine, "I play the guitar. Music and riding take up most of my time. I spent a year in law school at the capital, but the weather did not agree with me."

Amalia and her mother offered me a ride home in their carriage. Alessandro kissed my hand and held it for a moment.

"Now that I know we are neighbors," he said, glancing at me, "I will look for you during my morning ride."

From that day on, whether I was walking down the street

to the bakery or to the park, alone or not, I glanced at men that from a distance resembled Alessandro. Sometimes thinking about him brought me pleasure, but at other times I felt a heaviness in my heart that I couldn't shake. It was almost as if I knew this man was dangerous, as if I understood he would cause me pain, though at the same time I couldn't resist him. One day I remembered the words of the lady in the cornfield, and I wondered if she had been referring to moments like these in my life, when I felt torn—almost paralyzed by fear—by a premonition that warned me I was about to make a mistake that would cause me suffering, even though at the same time I knew I could not alter that part of my destiny. These confusing feelings had prevented me from writing Alessandro the customary note that one always wrote after being a guest at someone's home. Part of me did not want to see him again. Another part of me was dying to be in his presence.

After going over the evening countless times in my mind during one of my walks, I finally decided to send him a note thanking him for his invitation to tea. Upon my return, I sat down and wrote on rice paper from Pineider, a Florentine landmark and the finest paper boutique in the world. I chose a sheet I had taken from Mother's writing desk many years earlier, and I wrote my message with care.

After I mailed the perfumed note, I wondered what Alessandro would think. Would he hold the envelope in his hand, trying to guess who had sent it? Would the aroma of my perfume reach his senses upon opening it? Would he save it or toss it in the trash without further thought about how long I had pondered before writing each word? I imagined Alessandro's fingers tearing my letter open, his eyes reading the words on the page.

Funny that he, who was previously a stranger to me and unrelated to my personal happiness in any way, had become so important that the world prior to his existence no longer mattered. I did not know yet that the world after his departure would not matter either, not for a long time.

Chapter Eleven

A month after Alessandro and I met, he knocked at the walnut door that separated the outside world from the world within the mansion, offering a box of cigars for Father.

From that day forward Alessandro officially became my suitor. He gave me wildflowers and wrote songs for me, passionate songs full of promise. I fell in love with his stories, his imagination, and his beauty.

My boyfriend took his guitar with him everywhere, and everywhere he was asked to play. People tipped him at parties and invited him to dinners and luncheons so they could hear him sing. He was the most talented musician in Paipa, the handsomest man.

"Why are you still in Paipa?" I asked him. "You are a skilled artist. You could be working in Bogotá teaching or giving recitals."

"I spent a year in Bogotá," he answered. "I don't like the climate and I don't like the people."

After nine months of teas and suppers and midnight walks in cornfields, Alessandro took me to the thermal baths in Paipa, waited for me to come out, and then asked to have my hand in marriage. I fainted in his arms, perhaps due to the minerals in the water, the heat, and the wedding proposal.

The disheartening rumors concerning his behavior did not bother me. Still, I thought I ought to know.

"Are you sure you want to marry me?" I asked.

"Why would I ask you if I didn't?" I noticed a hint of impatience in his voice. "If you don't want to marry me, say so."

"Of course I do!" I insisted. "It's just that all of Paipa seems to want to marry you as well."

"Well, there's only one of me and so many of them," he said calmly. "But don't be silly; it's you I want, Inés."

"Alessandro," I continued, "are the rumors true?"

"What rumors?"

"That Luisa Ruiz killed herself because of you?"

"What?"

"They say you ruined her reputation."

"What else do *they* say?" he asked sarcastically.

"That you've fathered illegitimate children," I whispered.

I managed to avoid his eyes, but I could still feel the intensity of his furious glance.

"The rumors are true if you choose to believe them," he pronounced.

Alessandro and I never talked about his personal life again. When he pressed me to set the wedding date, I said I had to think about it. Four weeks later, Alessandro lost his patience and smashed a wineglass.

"How dare you make me wait!" he yelled. "Am I not good enough for you? There are plenty of women in Paipa that would be happy to marry me!"

I was taken aback by that violent streak, and I tried to soothe him. "I wanted to surprise you."

"Surprise me? You'll be sorry you kept me waiting for so long," Alessandro mumbled as he poured himself another glass of wine.

"Will you forgive me?" I did not want him to be angry, to stop loving me.

"For what?" He set the goblet down. "For shaming me? No, I can't forgive you for that."

I thought his answer was the result of too much wine. Years later I realized Alessandro had been dead serious when he said it.

Chapter Twelve

Two days after he got over his drunken spell, Alessandro took me to see the Catholic priest in Paipa, Father Rossi.

The priest seemed pleased to see us. He had known my family for a long time. Alessandro's parents went to church and made their contribution, but their son had not followed in their footsteps.

"The last time I saw you in church, my son," Father Rossi told Alessandro, "was for your first communion. I have been trying to think of ways to bring the hopeless sheep back into the fold," he added, winking at me.

"I have reason to be concerned, child," Father Rossi told me during our private session. "I'm the confessor for all the women in Paipa. I know their most intimate secrets and Alessandro's as well. He's not the right man for you."

My heart sank. When I told Alessandro what the priest had said, he was enraged.

"Father Rossi has been waiting for the opportunity to humiliate me!" he shouted. "The first time I went to see him to ask about marrying you in the church, he went on and on about me having to repent for my sins and go to confession, return to Sunday mass, and be prepared to attend counseling sessions with you. They would take ten weeks. Ten weeks! 'Once you've done all this, my son, I'll be glad to marry you,' he said with the most angelic smile. I was outraged. 'All I want to do is marry her!' I shouted. 'I'm not a devil and she's not a saint. I won't acquiesce to such nonsense. If you don't want to do it, I'll find someone who does.' 'You are welcome to do so, my son,' the priest answered in that self-righteous tone of his. 'But remember, the church is a big family, and the pope is not going to question my judgment.' Can you believe that?" Alessandro's voice was loaded with anger.

For a moment I sat quietly looking at my fiancé. The anger he was expressing seemed out of place to me. After all, we knew the Catholic Church had its rules and we were supposed to follow them. Why should we receive special treatment? What gave him the right to question Father Rossi's decision? Would he always be fighting against the world, angry if others didn't give him what he wanted?

"Inés!" he shouted. "I'm talking to you. What do you have to say?"

The anger in his eyes told me that he wasn't really interested in my opinion, that he didn't want to be appeased. I decided to be cautious.

"I think first you should calm down," I said. "Then we'll go to see Father Rossi together and reason with him, try to convince him."

Alessandro looked at me, shook his head, and slammed the door on his way out.

Chapter Thirteen

When he visited me at the mansion two days later, Alessandro had calmed down. I offered him a cup of coffee, and while he stirred the sugar in, he told me about his new plan.

"Yesterday I remembered hearing about a controversial Protestant minister in Bogotá. Reverend Minder has become famous for challenging the Catholic Church and for trying to convert disgruntled Catholics into Protestants. Minder would be the perfect opponent for Father Rossi," my fiancé concluded with a smile.

Alessandro did not have difficulty finding the reverend; he was the only Protestant in Colombia at the time.

"Minder moved to Bogotá from London twenty years ago," Alessandro told me. "He's fluent in Spanish and divides his time between the poor and his research on El Dorado."

"Are you referring to *our* El Dorado?" I asked. "The Colombian legend about the Muisca king who used to cover his whole body in gold during festivities and then dove into Lake Guatavita from a golden raft?"

"The same one. A friend of mine told me that the reverend has interviewed people, organized trips, read treaties, and written several articles about El Dorado for a local newspaper. He's working on a book."

"Still," I told Alessandro, "I don't know if he's the right person to marry us."

"Minder's well known in the country, and his articles have been published in our finest newspapers," Alessandro insisted while he filled his pipe with tobacco. "The reverend is in the right place to conduct his research," he continued. "The Chibcha Indians from the Andes were supposedly the initiators of the rite. I read an article about it in Bogotá, and it surprised me to learn how advanced their civilization was. They melted and cast gold and copper ornaments, mined emeralds, wove textiles, and made pottery. If you can prove that Father Rossi has done anything half as interesting as Minder, I'll surrender."

"I have no idea what Father Rossi does during his free time," I replied, "but I do know that in the Chibcha tribes, succession to office was passed down from mother to daughter."

"Matrilineal?" Alessandro sat back in his chair and exhaled. "I think it's wonderful that Reverend Minder dreams of discovering El Dorado."

"There's a reason no one has found it yet," I said. "When did he become obsessed with his quest?"

"According to my friend, as a child, Minder read every chronicle about El Dorado he could get his hands on," Alessandro explained. "One in particular fascinated him. It described a Spanish conquistador submerging in the lake and resurfacing mute three days later."

"Really?"

"Yes. On the day he finished reading the chronicle of the mute fortune seeker, Minder started writing down a master plan that came to fruition when one of his relatives died and left him with a modest income for life. Since he's been in Colombia, the reverend has done everything short of jumping in the water,"

Alessandro went on. "Unfortunately, he never learned to swim. Besides, some think he's afraid his weight will pull him down even if he has a rope tied around his waist."

I laughed.

"You can laugh," Alessandro exclaimed. "But I would like Reverend Minder to marry us, and I hope he agrees to do it."

"Then perhaps you should write to him," I suggested.

Alessandro finally wrote Reverend Minder a letter inviting him to Paipa and to celebrate our wedding. A month later he received a twenty-page missive from the reverend stating the reasons why he would be delighted to conduct the ceremony. Minder included detailed instructions for Alessandro, asked where he would be housed, and mentioned his eating preferences. Alessandro showed me the letter.

"Do you mind being married by a Protestant?" he asked.

"As long as I can lie in your arms."

"We'll be fallen Catholics and our children will be Protestants." Alessandro laughed.

My first communion came to mind. I had walked down the aisle of the local church with a lily in my hand, my white chiffon dress floating vaporously around me.

I wondered if Father Rossi would ban us from the church. Every Sunday for as long as I could remember, I had been to that church and sat in the same pew reserved for my family. Every Christmas, Lent, and Easter, I had prayed with fervor. And now all that was about to be swept away with the stroke of Alessandro's hand. I wondered if I could go through with it.

But, I told myself, faith has no boundaries, no nationality, and no official language. I was certain God would still hear my prayers and those of my children, even in a Protestant church.

Chapter Fourteen

Reverend Minder arrived in Paipa ten days before the wedding ceremony so he could get to know Alessandro and me, meet our families, and talk to Father Rossi. He had to convince Father Rossi to lend him his church, and Alessandro had told him it would be a challenge.

When the reverend stepped off the train with his suitcase, Alessandro and I stared in disbelief. Alessandro's friend had warned him that Minder was a large man, but my fiancé almost had a heart attack. The man was big . . . bigger than anyone in Paipa. He had a tiny suitcase, which in his hand looked like a child's, and he moved with surprising grace for someone his size.

"My poor horses," Alessandro commented under his breath. I shuddered. Minder stood on the platform, talking to the train conductor while he wiped his forehead with a white handkerchief. He then put on his panama hat to protect his fair skin from the rays of the tropical sun, which in Paipa seemed deceivingly weak.

Alessandro managed to get the reverend onto the carriage; I sat in front of him, and my fiancé sat next to the carriage driver. Minder panted all the way into town.

After he had rested his heavy body and fed his hungry soul

at Alessandro's house, the reverend took it upon himself to meet Father Rossi and ask him for permission to use his church.

"Now, my dear fellow," Father Rossi exclaimed, "why in the world would I want to do that? You know I risk being excommunicated! I'm sorry, but I won't be able to help you," he concluded with a sad smile fit for the most solemn occasions.

"I understand," Reverend Minder retorted. "You need an incentive."

The priest wrinkled his forehead with interest.

"I have heard you are Paipa's chess champion," the reverend went on. "Alessandro told me you've been undefeated for ten years."

"Yes?" Father Rossi raised his dark eyebrows.

"What if I were to challenge you to a game of chess? You win, I give up; I win, you lend me your church."

"On one condition."

"What?"

"That we start tomorrow. I'm eager to play a new opponent. I've been defeating the same crowd for too long."

Before the week was over, Reverend Minder became the new chess champion in Paipa, and a parade was organized to celebrate the event. Minder almost broke the chariot getting in, but he rode about with the dignity of a Roman emperor.

After the parade, the reverend called Alessandro and me to his side.

"I've done it," he told us. "We'll use Father Rossi's church."

Chapter Fifteen

"We should have a tea party with plenty of cakes and pastries at four thirty sharp on Saturday," Reverend Minder told Donatella Scala. "You must invite Father Rossi so that we can make all the necessary arrangements," the reverend concluded as he stuffed a piece of cake in his mouth.

Even though Alessandro and his parents had started serving tea daily for Reverend Minder, they decided the best way to go about the negotiations with Father Rossi was to invite him to dinner.

"That's the difference between an Italian and an Englishman," Alessandro's father told his wife. "One has a tea party; the other would demand nothing less than seven courses. You know how much Father Rossi appreciates your culinary skills. He'll never turn down a good meal."

Donatella looked at her husband and smiled. "Carlo, you are right," she said. "Father Rossi is a gourmet," she explained to Reverend Minder. "Wine is his passion; the last time we had him over for dinner, he drank a whole bottle of Brunello. By the end of the evening, he was ready to swear it ran through his veins instead of blood. 'I am convinced,' he told me, 'that red wine is the chosen drink in heaven.'"

Reverend Minder let out a hearty laugh. “Even though I do not drink,” he said after a sip of tea to wash down some puff pastry, “I feel about food the same way my heavenly colleague feels about wine.”

I watched Donatella and Carlo as they set about planning an elaborate meal for Father Rossi. My future mother-in-law consulted the recipe books and planned the menu. She decided to serve homemade spinach ravioli and lamb with rosemary and green beans, followed by a wide variety of local cheeses, all tasty and aromatic. “They go well with my homemade Tuscan bread,” she explained. For dessert, Donatella baked a Russian crepe cake with raspberry sauce.

Carlo brought several of his best bottles of wine up from the cellar. “This rich Chianti would be superb with the lamb,” he told Alessandro and me while he poured some for us to taste.

“Do we need a white wine as well?” Donatella asked her husband.

Carlo thought about it for a minute. “We should serve a dry *spumante*,” he said after swallowing some Chianti. “Remember the last time? Father praised the *spumante*. This is the perfect occasion to lavish as much wine on the priest as necessary. Don’t you think?”

“After the way he treated me, he shouldn’t get a drop,” Alessandro commented. His mother turned to look at him.

“I agree with your father,” Donatella pronounced. “This would be the wrong time to cut back. You can say what you will about Father Rossi, but he is a connoisseur of fine wine. I was even considering a Brunello, as long as you promise me you won’t drink a glass every time you serve him,” she added, looking at Carlo. “Thank goodness it’s not champagne. There should be enough left over for the wedding. Carlo, remember the time it took a year to receive our shipment from Europe?"

"That would be a disaster," he agreed.

Father Rossi's dinner seemed as important as the wedding, and when the day came, we were all nervous.

Donatella asked me to help her finish the crepe cake. "I hope the spirit of competition inspires Father Rossi to agree to marry you and Alessandro," she mused. "We could have a double ceremony." Donatella sprinkled plenty of sugar on the cake. "Anything would be better than a Protestant rite," she concluded as she poured more raspberry sauce on top.

"Have we decided who will bring the subject up?" I asked.

Donatella licked her finger. "After dessert, Reverend Minder will start discussing the wedding details."

The reverend expressed delight at every dish but fell asleep after the cheese and started snoring in the middle of a speech that Father Rossi, inspired by the wine, was giving about Lourdes. Alessandro prodded him gently. Minder raised his head, opened his eyes, looked around, closed them again, and snored loudly. Donatella started wringing her hands. She looked mortified.

"Why don't we let the reverend rest at the table and have dessert and coffee in the sitting room?" I suggested. Everyone agreed.

After dessert and before cognac, Donatella sat next to Father Rossi and took his hand.

"Excuse me, Father, for being so bold," she began, "but Reverend Minder was hoping to ask you something. Unfortunately, he fell asleep." She squeezed his hand. "Would you agree to conduct a double ceremony for Alessandro and Inés? I can't die in peace if they don't marry in the Catholic Church."

I don't know if it was the wine, the atmosphere, the hostess's sweet voice, or the dessert that softened Father Rossi's heart, but he acquiesced.

"As long as the ceremony is private," he pronounced. "I would not want the Vatican to get involved; we might all end up excommunicated," Father Rossi added before taking a sip of cognac.

"And what about all the things you told Alessandro he had to do?" Carlo inquired.

"I was just trying to bring him back to the church. I think it's more important not to let the Protestants take over, Carlo. Don't you agree?"

The evening ended with more cognac and cigars. On his way out, Father Rossi thanked Donatella and added, "I'll have a double ceremony with the reverend if he promises not to fall asleep."

Alessandro filled our glasses with Brunello. "A toast to my future bride," he said. As we drank, I remembered the first time we kissed. "Soon you'll be mine," he whispered in my ear.

Chapter Sixteen

Isabel and I were in the kitchen preparing a feast to celebrate Father's birthday when I decided to tell her about the wedding. I had been postponing this moment for too long. Something inside me resisted sharing the news with her, as if I feared it would upset her. I knew it was irrational and I couldn't explain it, but I also knew I could no longer wait. If my sister had already heard about it—gossip in Paipa spread faster than the plague—she had not said a word to me. I could feel the tension rising between us, though, and I could no longer stand it. Why had I waited so long to tell her, I wondered, as I stood next to her, kneading dough for French bread. It was true that I felt guilty about getting married before she did, since she was older than me. Also, my sister didn't seem to like Alessandro very much, and deep down I was afraid of what she would say. In fact, the way she looked at him sometimes made me wonder if she despised him. I took a deep breath and tried to calm my nerves.

"Alessandro and I are getting married," I finally said as I wiped sweat from my forehead.

"You're what?" Isabel asked, her eyes wide in amazement.

"He asked me to marry him."

"You cannot be serious!" My sister laughed. She wiped her

hands on her apron. "I need to take a walk," she said before leaving the kitchen. I followed her.

"What about Father's dinner?" I tried to keep up. "The guests will be arriving soon."

"The hell with them. The hell with everybody!" she shouted back.

I returned to the house and put the bread in the oven. Although my intuition had been right, as hard as I tried, I still could not understand my sister's reaction. I had told her about Alessandro from the beginning. She had always listened with what seemed like interest to me but had never expressed her opinion. Now there was no mistaking her silence. She had never approved of my relationship with Alessandro. But why? What had he ever done to her?

After Father's feast was over, Isabel seemed calmer.

"Are you sure you want to marry Alessandro?" she asked while we dried the china and put it away.

"Yes." I held a plate up to examine it more carefully. It had a blue flower pattern on it. "I wonder where Royal Copenhagen comes from. It's such exquisite china."

"Denmark."

"Massimiliano must have brought it with him from Europe," I said.

"When did Alessandro propose?" Isabel lowered her voice.

"Two months ago, after he took me to the thermal baths."

Isabel picked up the remaining cups. Inadvertently, she dropped two. We saw them burst into fragments as they hit the ground. My sister looked at the mess, sat down at the kitchen table, and started crying. I had never seen her so upset, and even though I knew the china was special, I could not believe that two cups would mean so much to her.

"Wouldn't you marry Alessandro?" I asked.

"Not in a thousand years," my sister answered as she got up, placed the remaining cups in the cupboard, and slammed the door with resolution.

As the wedding day approached, Isabel became more anxious. I figured it had something to do with the fact that her beau, the coffee bean expert, had not proposed. No one understood the reason.

Many men in Paipa looked upon my sister with desire. She ate little so that her small frame would not be burdened by extra weight, walked every morning until breakfast time, engaged in special exercises for her small waist, brushed her long brown hair every night without fail, and wore a corset even while she slept. Her dresses were made of the finest silks. Everything about her, from her movements to the way her brown eyes rested on men, was provocative.

Following Father's party, I moved into the Scala residence as a permanent guest. Donatella would not accept any excuses. I didn't mind. Living there, I could spend time with Alessandro and avoid confrontations with Isabel.

Chapter Seventeen

The preparations for the wedding got under way. Donatella went with me to dress fittings, ordered roses for the church, and talked to both Reverend Minder and Father Rossi. While we waited for one of the fittings at Madame Lucien's atelier, she told me about her family.

"Carlo," my future mother-in-law whispered as she helped me tighten my corset, "was the most handsome man I had ever seen." She pulled a string with all her might.

I held my breath and tightened my stomach as much as I could.

"I wonder why we continue to wear these torture instruments," Donatella complained as she pulled the other string. "Can you breathe?"

"Yes." I ground my teeth. "They've stopped wearing them in Europe. I wonder what it would feel like to be without one. Where did you meet Carlo?"

"In Bogotá. I used to go to Parque Nacional to feed the pigeons. One day he sat down next to me, and we started talking. As we talked, he took the loaf of bread, tore small pieces off, and passed them to me as if we had done it a million times before. That afternoon I had an appointment with Doña Leonor, a famous psychic in the city. 'You and this man, this Carlo,' she told me, 'have been together during other lives. You'll marry this time.'"

"I heard about Doña Leonor when I lived in Bogotá," I commented. "She's a legend. Did you consult with her regularly?"

"I used to go to the capital just to see her," Alessandro's mother explained. "She's dead now."

Donatella and Carlo complemented each other well. I never saw them argue or disagree.

"Don't think, child, that it's always been like this," Donatella told me. "After our first three years of marriage, Carlo wondered if he would ever be able to satisfy my thirst for social standing. I took it as an insult, and we didn't talk to each other for six months."

I was surprised. "How did you manage to make up?"

"I broke the silence to tell him I was pregnant. He was so happy! Everything went back to normal during the pregnancy, but a few years later Carlo started mentioning a second child. I had already made the decision, while pregnant with Alessandro, that I would only have one. I did not want a large family. Besides, every time I looked in the mirror I saw a disfigured whale. Carlo pressed me for an explanation. 'I won't be able to love any other child as much as I love Alessandro,' I told him.

"My husband resigned himself to showering his affection on Alessandro, and he did the boy more harm than good. We both spoiled him. There are times when I wish I'd had more children." Donatella sighed.

~

The Scala family had a trusted maid, Luisa, who took pride in cooking and keeping the household organized. Theirs was a monumental house located in the northern part of Paipa and surrounded by forests and gardens with statues, olive trees in the yard, and lemon trees planted in large terra-cotta vases that had no doubt been imported from Italy.

"When was the house built?" I asked Alessandro during one of our walks.

"Three years after my parents married. Father came to look at some property he had inherited here. He liked the place and hired architects to design the house of his dreams. When she realized she would be much more important in Paipa than in Bogotá, Mother warmed up to the idea. Do you like it?"

"It's beautiful."

It was an impressive house. The architects had traveled from Bogotá to help Donatella decorate it, but since they had never left Colombia, their ideas about Italian villas came from nineteenth-century books. As a result, there were too many marble columns. In the front yard Donatella had placed poor copies of Roman statues. They made the place resemble a small-town park.

Several days after one of my dress fittings, my mother-in-law's behavior changed from talkative to taciturn, almost despondent, as if a dark cloud had descended upon her. I didn't say anything in front of Carlo and Alessandro, but in the afternoon, while we were drinking our usual cup of hot chocolate, I asked her what was wrong.

"I'm sick," she replied. "Yesterday the doctor confirmed that the pain I've been experiencing is due to a rare illness that has spread all over my body." Donatella started crying.

"I'm so sorry," I replied. "Do Carlo and Alessandro know?"

She shook her head. "I don't want to upset anyone," she answered, "especially now, during the wedding preparations."

At that moment I understood why Donatella had fallen ill; the revelation upset me. My mother-in-law's mysterious illness would take center stage during my wedding celebration, a bad omen for my marriage. But then I shook the feeling off and told myself not to be selfish, to think of Donatella and her suffering. I handed her my handkerchief.

"Your health is more important," I replied. "You need to tell them."

As the days went on, it became more difficult to ignore Donatella's symptoms. She tired easily and had to spend whole days in bed. I asked Alessandro what he thought about her malady.

"It's simple," he answered while we sat under a tree in the field, our horses drinking from the stream. "Mother's illness is diminishing her body a little bit at a time," he explained. "She is not able to enjoy her surroundings because she doesn't feel well but also because throughout the years she has compared herself to wealthier and more successful people, and bitterness has gotten the best of her."

I had the feeling that Alessandro was oversimplifying the situation, but I didn't want to meddle or to annoy my future husband.

"Surely something can be done," I said. "There are excellent doctors in Bogotá. We could take her there for a consultation."

"Father already has. He's been so patient. They all say the same thing—that it's in her mind."

At that moment I felt a pain in my chest, around my heart, as if it were being squeezed.

"I know what's wrong with her," I heard myself say. "She's terrified of losing you, her only child, her son, to me, to another woman, and the only way she can express this fear is through illness."

Alessandro burst out laughing. "This is the first time I've heard that explanation, Doctor," he teased, "and frankly, it sounds ridiculous. Don't be silly. Mother adores you."

I didn't say anything, though I felt I was right. For a moment my whole body had experienced Donatella's pain, her sadness, her jealousy. I wished I could talk to her about it, reassure her, but I remembered what the angel in the cornfield had said, that my gift would allow me to see what others were thinking and feeling, and that it would help me protect myself. I didn't wish Donatella harm, and now that I understood the cause of her suffering, I would be more patient with her. But I also realized that she couldn't love me, because I was taking her son away from her.

A few days later, Donatella suffered a violent attack. For a week she was unable to leave her bed, and when she finally got up, Carlo improvised a wheelchair for her to get around.

"I'll never walk again," Donatella pronounced as she sat in her new throne.

Regardless of her failing health, my mother-in-law was adamant about being consulted on all matters relating to the ceremony and the reception. We did not have the courage to oppose her. But she was too weak to participate directly in the activities involving the rest of the planning and spent her days in bed trying different types of makeup and hairstyles, as well as writing the menu for the party and recipes for the wedding cake. Donatella was an artist at baking beautiful tortes and pastries, and she took great care in choosing the right cake for us. Her determination to find the perfect cake distracted her from the pain. I was glad to see she had found a way to escape from her own suffering.

Chapter Eighteen

Shortly after Donatella and Carlo had moved to Paipa, he went to court to represent his clients while she stayed at home and baked elaborate desserts.

"I was determined to become the best at it, and soon I had a following," Donatella told me. "Eventually, my fame spread around Paipa, and some of the ladies asked me to offer baking lessons," she said. "Even your mother wrote me a note about it."

"Mother did not like to cook," I commented. "She wrote poetry."

"Rosa was supposed to learn before she went to study in Tunja."

"I didn't know that."

"The town elite had never welcomed us," Donatella went on. "Overnight I organized my kitchen, polished my utensils, and opened my doors to Paipa's high society. It was a dream come true—teaching what I loved while making money."

Donatella used the infamous quote attributed to Marie Antoinette, "Let them eat cake," to advertise her business.

"Why don't you write it on your wedding invitations?" she asked me while we were considering paper. "It would be adorable! You could use gold ink. I can see it now, *Let Them Eat Cake* scribbled in the fanciest manner on top of the card," she said, closing her eyes and letting out a sigh.

"I was thinking of something simple," I replied. "Black on white. I'm not fond of ornamentation."

"Oh, well, if that's what you want." Donatella took her mirror out of her purse and applied red lipstick.

~

My mother-in-law's illness not only added a layer of complexity to the wedding preparations but also made Luisa's load harder to bear. The poor maid nearly had a nervous breakdown. The doctor gave her some herbs for infusions and put her right arm in a sling so it would get some rest. The house became run-down from the lack of dusting and sweeping.

Donatella eventually capitulated, and with her eyes closed, chose a recipe.

"This is the last cake I supervise or bake," she exclaimed. "I can't think of measuring flour when my body is in so much pain. Sugar and butter don't taste good to me anymore," she continued in a somber tone. "Let the ladies of Paipa bake their own cakes!"

As my wedding day approached, Donatella got out of bed less frequently. When she did, her legs would not support her; yet there were moments when she asked to be taken to her favorite little restaurant. She ordered *ajiaco*—soup with chicken, potatoes, and corn on the cob served with avocado, capers, and fresh cream—and ate it as if it were her last meal. She had always eaten that way.

Even in her misery, Donatella was thrilled that Alessandro was marrying me, "a fine young woman from an established family."

"I am determined," she told me when I talked about postponing the wedding because of her weak health, "to see it happen."

"But, Donatella," I insisted, "Alessandro could have any woman in this town. I'm not sure I'm the best choice for him. My family is no longer what it was."

Donatella took my hands and looked me in the eye.

"I don't mind that you're destitute," she said without hesitation. "Money comes and goes, but class you can never buy. Believe me, I know."

Alessandro and I continued with the wedding plans, but for the sake of simplicity, we chose to have the wedding reception at a restaurant on the outskirts of Paipa.

Donatella still wanted to pretend that the party would take place at her house. For two days maids cleaned and dusted; Luisa ran up and down the corridors trying to cook and to cater to Donatella, who continued ringing the little bell by her bedside table whenever she thought of something else, which was every three and a half minutes.

I went into the kitchen to check on the progress of the cake and found Luisa crying into the batter.

"This will never do!" I exclaimed, trying to control my anger. "What is the matter with you? Haven't you been drinking your infusions?"

"Every time your mother-in-law rings the bell and I rush to see what she wants, I come back and the batter has gone to ruin," Luisa answered, sobbing. "The last time, three people had spoons in their hands and were eating it right out of the bowl! I will never be able to finish this cake!"

"Slow down, slow down," I told her. "And make some chamomile tea."

I went to visit Isabel at the mansion to ask for her assistance.

Chapter Nineteen

My sister was in the back room dusting the family portraits. I sat down on the armchair beneath Massimiliano de La Rota's proud demeanor. Isabel turned around and waited for me to speak.

"I was wondering if you could take charge of Donatella until after the wedding."

She turned back to Massimiliano's portrait and continued dusting without looking at me. "Why does anyone have to take charge of that woman?" Isabel finally asked.

"She's weak and needs attention."

"Why don't you postpone the wedding, then?" my sister ventured. "Wait until she gets better."

"Donatella won't get better." I tried to sound detached. "She's dying."

"So am I," Isabel answered promptly. "We are all dying a little every day." She used a linen cloth to clean Massimiliano's mustache.

"Alessandro and I talked to her about postponing the wedding. She refused."

"And what do you want me to do?"

"You could keep her company, help her dress, and assist

her with hair and makeup. You are talented in those areas, and Donatella needs to see improvement every day."

Isabel turned to glare at me. She threw the dustcloth on the floor and rearranged her bun. Then she took her apron off, dropped it on the sofa, and tied the ribbon on her blue dress.

"Until now, you made your own decisions," she shouted. "You moved out of the house, chose the man you want to marry, took care of the wedding arrangements without even bothering to consult me, your father, or your other sisters, and now you come asking for help! Excuse me while I laugh!"

I stood up. My knees were shaking, but I was determined not to let her win.

"I'm sorry," I said in as steady a voice as I could muster. "This is not a good time to talk. I'll come back another time."

"Go!" Isabel shouted when I turned toward the door. "I wouldn't want Alessandro to worry. Get married; don't fret about your sisters or your father."

I stopped at the threshold, determined to face Isabel once and for all. "You already have a suitor," I said in a low and steady voice. "Set the date."

I heard Isabel's footsteps behind me and turned to face her. Compassion took over my heart at the sight of her red cheeks and eyes full of tears. Clearly, she was miserable.

"And you think it's that simple?" she screamed. "People like you go through life making it look easy. Well, it's not." My sister started sobbing.

I was baffled. "Why are you angry at me?"

"It's not you," she said impatiently. "Every night I lie awake and feel time pass until dawn. I fear I'll never have a husband, children, and a home of my own. And yet marriage is such a mystery to me; it seems so definite it scares me. I am angry at God for making me a woman and at the world for deciding my fate." Isabel wiped her tears with her sleeve.

I made the sign of the cross and turned to leave, but my sister walked in front of me and stood in the way.

"Now wait a minute," she said. "You hear me out. Until recently you were going around with Donatella, choosing bedding, flowers, and a wedding dress. You moved into her house. You allowed that woman to advise you. Do you know what her father did in Italy?"

"I don't understand why it matters." I tried to get through the door.

My sister barred the way. "Her father was a baker. It shows. And Carlo is not much better. Do you know what his parents did?"

"I see you're eager to tell me." I was losing my patience.

"They were farmers, poor farmers," Isabel said with satisfaction, like a child who has just delivered the right answer.

"How do you know all this?"

"Do you think Mother would approve of such a match for you?"

"She would want me to be happy," I answered.

Isabel sneered.

"I thought our families came to the New World to start over, to forget about the past," I said. "Why persist with the same values and standards for measuring that our ancestors did? Has history taught us nothing? Don't you think people should be judged according to their merits?"

Isabel smiled and placed her hands on her hips. "In that case, Alessandro would not fare well."

"Why do you hate Alessandro? Has he ever offended you?" I shouted.

Isabel moved away from the doorway and started pacing around the room. I no longer felt a desire to flee.

"He's a scoundrel," she pronounced, "and everyone knows it. But it's your life, and if you want to marry him, so be it," my sister concluded.

"Isabel, for our mother's sake," I said, "let's put this behind us. I don't have anyone else to turn to."

Isabel stopped in the middle of the room and turned to face me. "What else does Donatella need?"

"The day of the wedding, you'll have to dress her and keep an eye on her."

"Has she threatened suicide?"

"Of course not. I have an uneasy feeling."

"That comes from knowing that you're making a mistake," Isabel announced.

"What?" Rage welled up inside me.

"You'll never be happy with that man."

Her eyes were red, her face swollen from crying, and yet she had gone too far. I was furious and felt like grabbing her by the neck and shaking her until the strange notions in her head dissolved. I slapped her. Isabel stared at me with disbelief before retaliating. The screams woke Father up from his nap. He grabbed his Smith & Wesson, ran outside, and fired a shot.

That afternoon, I visited Amalia Rios and told her about Isabel's refusal to help.

"I don't understand what's wrong with my sister," I concluded.

"She's jealous of you," Amalia said. "She's had her eye on Alessandro and hates to lose."

I thought about Isabel's comments and her unusual behavior. "But she's had a beau for years."

"Still," Amalia insisted, "I would be careful if I were you." She took my hand. "I'll help you, but you know how Donatella is."

I knew Donatella well, especially now that we lived under the same roof. My mother-in-law was famous in Paipa for her impatience and arrogance. She had no friends except for the mystics, mediums, palm readers, and charlatans that depended on her generosity. During séances and weekly Bible studies at her house, people ate her cakes and drank her tea while laughing behind her back. "Amalia," I told my friend, "I'll always be grateful to you."

She smiled. "I'll bring Father's pistol to the wedding just in case." She straightened her skirt.

I hoped, with all my heart, that we wouldn't need a pistol on my wedding day.

Chapter Twenty

Father asked me to join him and Isabel for dinner at the mansion. During the meal, he insisted that my sister and I abandon our differences. He begged Isabel to assist me with the wedding preparations.

"That's what Aura would want you to do," Father told her.

Isabel put her fork down. "I don't think Mother would be thrilled about Alessandro."

"You don't know that," I said.

"And neither do you," she replied with anger in her voice.

In time, Isabel showed up at the Scala household offering to help.

"You look beautiful in your white dress," she told me on my wedding day as she put the finishing touches on my hair. I did not know what to make of her new attitude.

My sister gave me the mirror so I could see what she had done. "Your hair in a chignon and Mother's pearl earrings are all you need."

Donatella asked to see me. When I walked into the room, she cried.

"I can't believe you're about to be married to my angel," she managed to say between sobs.

Isabel carried my train and stood close to the door as Donatella continued to rave.

"You better get dressed or you'll be late," I told my mother-in-law. "You know how long it takes you to put on your makeup. Amalia should be here soon. She and Isabel will accompany you to the church at ten."

"I don't want to ride with those women," Donatella whispered in my ear. "I want to go with you. When I told you to use the carriage, I was thinking of riding in it myself."

"Fine," I replied, "but you still need to get dressed or you'll make me late."

"Brides are supposed to be late. You don't want to seem too eager."

"Donatella," I begged her, "please, don't make it more difficult for me. I'm already nervous."

"All right," Donatella grumbled before she started ringing the bell frantically for Luisa to come and dress her.

Isabel and I went back to my room. "How will I survive?" I asked my sister.

"This is nothing," she answered with a wave of her hand. "Wait until people start drinking."

I studied her face. As hard as she tried to seem happy, I could tell she was tense.

Isabel looked in the mirror, straightened her black velvet skirt and silk blouse, shut the door, and motioned for me to sit down in an armchair while she held the train. She pulled a silver flask out from her purse, took a drink of cognac, and passed it to me. I hesitated.

"I don't want Father Rossi or Alessandro to smell my breath during the ceremony."

"Oh, spare me." Isabel took another drink. "They should smell their own breath."

The cognac burned my throat. I studied the flask before passing it back to her.

"I've seen this before."

"It belonged to Mother."

"How is your wedding going to be?" I asked after taking another sip, which went down more smoothly.

"Small."

"And the dress?"

"Not a regular wedding dress."

"Why not?"

"Juan and I are not traditional. His mother asked me twice if I wanted to wear her dress. She even had me try it on. Imagine me in that vulgar tulle thing!" Isabel brought the flask to her lips and took a gulp.

"You don't seem to like Juan's family," I said as diplomatically as I could. "Have they been unkind to you?"

"They don't have class. They have money." Isabel emptied the flask. "But that isn't enough."

"You're not thinking about breaking up with Juan, are you?" I looked at her.

"Your father would never forgive me," Isabel answered as she tightened the lid on the flask. "He says Juan is a good match for me. The other day he reminded me that Mother gave her consent before dying. 'I won't be able to support you all my life,' he went on. Always the same story."

Isabel wiped her eyes with the tip of her silk blouse. I took her in my arms and held her for a long time.

My sister pulled back. "I wish I were like you," she said.

"What do you mean?"

"You're not ashamed of working. You're marrying the man all the women in this town desire."

"Isabel, the truth is I'm scared," I confessed. "I don't know what marriage will be like."

I didn't tell her about my fear of losing my way, of forgetting those things that had always been important to me. I wanted to paint, to dance, to play my guitar. And now I was marrying Alessandro. Soon I would be having children. Could I really be a mother? Love unconditionally? I wondered.

"You'll be fine," Isabel whispered while she put the flask away.

"I don't know," I said. "Alessandro told me I'll have to stop working after we are married."

"And what do you think?"

"I'm afraid one day I'll regret it."

"At least you don't have any regrets right now."

"Why? Do you?"

"I do."

"Such as?"

Isabel was about to speak when we heard a loud knock at the door.

"Who is it?"

"Darling, it's me," Father answered. "Let me see how beautiful you look." He fiddled with the locked door.

Isabel reached over and opened it.

"You look ravishing," he gasped.

"Have you been to see Donatella? Is she ready?"

"Is she ever!" he exclaimed. "She looks like the queen of Egypt."

"Could you take her to the church?"

"I offered to take her and Carlo, but she insists on riding with you in the carriage."

Father was still a handsome man. He studied himself in the full-length mirror and fixed the flower on his lapel. He wore his elegant suit and a European silk tie Mother had given him one Christmas. I wondered if he was reminiscing about his own wedding.

"Could you convince Donatella to go with you?" I begged him.

He wiped a tear from his left eye. "I don't know." His voice was shaky.

"Please, Father." I embraced him. "Think how odd it would look if she arrived at the church sitting between Alessandro and me."

"I hope that's not a sign of things to come," Isabel commented as she walked out of the room.

Chapter Twenty-One

Alessandro and I married in the Catholic Church in Paipa on a Saturday morning in June. For a long time, I saved the clipping of the newspaper article describing our wedding. I'm sure no one present at the ceremony could have imagined that our end would be as tragic as our beginning had been splendid. On our wedding day, it seemed as if the future would be anything we chose to make it.

Father Rossi stood at the altar in his finest robe and stared at Alessandro and me in silence for a few minutes. I thought he would never speak.

"Adam and Eve were beautiful," he finally said in a booming voice. "God created a splendid world filled with the wonders of nature. Man ruined it." Father Rossi pointed at me. "Eve gave Adam the apple, and with a single bite, changed their lot and ours. Humans should obey the law of God or be willing to live with the consequences. You must renounce the devil and his wicked ways!" The priest shouted at the top of his lungs while looking straight at Alessandro.

People shifted uncomfortably on the wooden pews. I felt the burden of all humanity fall upon my shoulders just as Adam and Eve must have.

When his turn came, Reverend Minder walked up to the altar in a striped silk robe. Devout women continued to blow their noses. The reverend placed his massive body in front of the congregation and in a voice every bit as loud as Father Rossi's, began.

"Let us remember, dear friends, that our God is the same God whether we call him Catholic or Protestant. These are but two faces of the same deity who, in his infinite wisdom, presents himself in whichever package is more palatable for us." He stopped to wipe his forehead.

"As I was saying, our God is also a kind God, a forgiving God. He wants his children to be happy, to enjoy life. We would do him a great disservice if we did not consider this as part of our destiny. Your ancestors covered their bodies with gold and tossed precious stones in the sacred lake of Guatavita before plunging into its depths to purify themselves. Let your offerings to God be kindness and generosity, patience and compassion." He wiped his forehead once more.

"The Chibchas knew that their cleansing ceremony was paramount to the continuation of life. Man is imperfect, and as such, he sins. But he also possesses the ability to redeem himself."

"I was wondering when he would get to El Dorado," Alessandro whispered in my ear.

After Reverend Minder and Father Rossi blessed us in the Catholic and Protestant religions, we all left for the reception, a half-hour journey from Paipa.

Alessandro and I were the first to arrive at the restaurant, which consisted of a colonial building with a veranda all around and a bullring in the center. Pink geraniums were everywhere.

We had reserved the entire establishment for the wedding party. Guests had appetizers and cocktails outdoors and then enjoyed the luncheon served in the rooms that circled the bullfighting ring.

I led Father into a room and placed him at Donatella's table. The rose had disappeared from his lapel.

"It takes a wedding to bring you out," Donatella said.

"Weddings and funerals," Father answered, "and not just any wedding. Riding with you this morning was a pleasure."

All the tables were full. Alessandro and I took our seats next to Father Rossi and Reverend Minder, and the luncheon got started. Our meal included empanadas, *ajiaco*, tamales, and other local dishes. Guests washed the food down with Italian and French wines, aguardiente, or fresh fruit juices. *Spumante* was served with the cake.

Father stood up, raised his glass, and waited for silence. "I would like to propose a toast," he finally said, "to Inés and Alessandro. May they be as happy as Aura and I were." Rodolfo emptied his champagne flute and wiped his eyes.

Isabel stood up. Her face was flushed. "To my sister and brother-in-law." She raised her glass. "May they be true to each other." She drank and smashed her flute against the chimney before leaving the room.

Alessandro laughed. People went back to talking.

"What's wrong with your sister?" Amalia Rios asked.

"She's had too much to drink," I explained. "Let's hope she'll be all right."

"I'll keep an eye on her." Amalia raised her skirt and showed me her father's gun tightly wrapped around her leg.

"Be careful with that," I managed to say as she danced away.

While Alessandro and I went around the tables to greet our guests, people decided to conduct mock bullfights in the ring. Jackets flew off, and someone seized a red tablecloth to serve as the matador's cape. A coin was tossed to see who would be the bull and who the fighter.

When the bullfighting began, Father bestowed his wedding present on me. It was a necklace with an emerald in the center and three beautiful stones for earrings and a ring.

"Aura asked me to give you this on your wedding day," Father said as he placed the necklace in my hand. "May this emerald preserve you from the evil eye, from envy, and from jealousy."

I turned to show Alessandro the necklace, but he was gone. I could not find him anywhere.

"He might be in the bullfighting ring with the others," Father ventured.

I found Donatella sitting on the bleachers, cheering the bull on.

"I'm looking for Alessandro," I shouted from the bottom of the ring. "Have you seen him?"

"He was here a minute ago," she shouted back. "Said he was going to get a drink. Why don't you come up here and sit with me?"

"I want to show him something," I insisted.

"You have the rest of your life to talk to him, dear." Donatella motioned for me to join her. I climbed the steps and sat down next to her.

"There he is!" She pointed.

I glanced up and saw Alessandro leaving a room in the posada. Minutes later, Isabel walked out, fixing her hair. She leaned on the veranda, and when she noticed me, she waved and smiled. I waved back. Isabel seemed happy. Perhaps she had had a talk with Alessandro and cleared the air. Perhaps she had told him about our fights and he had reassured her that everything would be fine. I decided I would ask my husband about it the next time we were alone.

Chapter Twenty-Two

Two days after the wedding, Alessandro and I embarked on a journey that would take us to Italy for our honeymoon. Enzo, a childhood friend of Alessandro's father, had written, extending an invitation to the whole family. When he heard about our wedding, he sent a shipment of wine. In the box, he included a key to his house and a note stating that we would have to travel to Florence to return the key.

Alessandro and I boarded a ship in Cartagena and traveled to Brindisi. Once on Italian soil, we went north to Rome and then to Florence, where we lived for three months with Enzo, who had become a fairly well-known sculptor in that city.

Enzo's house was located close to Piazzale Michelangelo on a hill that loomed above Florence and presented a breathtaking view of the landscape.

Mother had traveled to Florence after her first marriage, and her description of the city had always fascinated me. Listening to her stories, I had imagined walking across the Ponte Vecchio, the oldest stone bridge in Europe, and peeking in the windows of stores that had housed butchers, tanners, and farmers until the sixteenth century, when one of the Medici rulers had decided to offer the space to jewelry shops instead. More civilized, more attractive, more lucrative.

Strolling along the bridge with my husband, I often stopped to admire necklaces, earrings, and rings on display. There were gold and gems in every shop window, pieces that celebrated art, love, taste, and craftsmanship.

Alessandro and I went by foot all the way to the Ponte Vecchio and beyond to end up drinking a glass of wine at Caffè Rivoire in front of the beautiful fountain at Piazza della Signoria. It was there that I saw Pineider and bought some Florentine rice paper in memory of Mother. We often sat at Rivoire for hours, talking, admiring the medieval buildings, and watching elegant Florentines go about their daily lives. How different from Paipa and Bogotá, not only in climate and population, but also in its landscape. While Colombia's treasure was its natural beauty—the lakes, trees, and mountains—Florence boasted exquisite architecture and art that went all the way back to the thirteenth century. Dark, narrow medieval streets led to grandiose plazas and churches that took your breath away. Mother was right. Florence was the most beautiful city in the world, the most romantic.

Alessandro and I ate at local trattorie, visited the Uffizi Gallery, and strolled through the Boboli Gardens around Palazzo Pitti. Sometimes, after crossing the Ponte Vecchio, we walked *oltrarno* all the way to the Porta Romana and the San Frediano neighborhood. On Sundays we attended mass at San Miniato al Monte, a fifteen-minute walk from Enzo's house. In the afternoon we returned to Piazza della Signoria and watched Florentine society out for their Sunday stroll. I had never seen such elegance.

We both loved spending time around the Duomo and walking down the streets surrounding it. Often, during our walks, we glanced into courtyards and saw beautiful gardens, fountains, and flowers.

"I would love to visit the other Medici estates and gardens in Tuscany," I told Alessandro after seeing the garden in Palazzo Medici. "Mother told me they were beautiful."

My husband squeezed my hand. "We will, my love, we will," he said.

From Palazzo Medici, we reached the Duomo and stood outside for a while, admiring the geometrical design and the outside walls covered in white, red, and green marble. The building was just as magnificent inside. No matter where we went in the city, we could still see Brunelleschi's dome with its terra-cotta tiles.

One morning, in a street close to the Duomo, we noticed a group of people outside a building. One of them was giving a speech. We stood with the group, listening. When I heard "Dante," I turned to Alessandro. My husband was able to communicate with ease in the Italian he had learned from his grandfather. Alessandro nodded, came closer to me, and whispered, "They recently proved that this was the location of Dante's house. You are my Beatrice, but more beautiful."

One morning Alessandro decided that we should go to Fiesole, an ancient town on the hills beyond Florence. Once we got there, we walked around, visited the convent of San Francesco, and stepped into shops selling beautiful cloth, hats, and shoes. Alessandro spotted a small trattoria and stopped.

"I'm going to get us some water," he said. "Wait for me here."

I sat on the terrace and looked at the people going about their business—women with baskets filled with food for the day, children returning home from school for lunch. After a little while my husband came back with his own basket of food. I tried to peek inside it, but he wouldn't let me.

"Come on, Inés." He smiled playfully. "I'm going to take you to the best restaurant in town, with breathtaking views of Florence."

We walked up narrow streets until we reached a building at the top, a beautiful villa.

"Welcome to Villa San Michele," my husband said. "It used to be a monastery."

We walked outside the villa, taking in the view of the Tuscan hills, the cypress trees surrounding it, and Florence below. Alessandro found a spot under a tree, took his jacket off, and placed it on the ground for me to sit. It was a sunny day, not a cloud in the sky. He produced glasses, a bottle of water, a bottle of Chianti, bread, olives, prosciutto, and pecorino cheese. Sitting under that tree eating, drinking, talking, and admiring the city of Florence next to my husband, I felt happy and fortunate to have him.

After I wore the three pairs of shoes I had brought from Paipa down to the ground, I went to look for replacements. Until then I had never imagined that shopping could be an art. The salespeople measured my foot, looked at it closely, and even massaged it. I put on my first pair of Italian shoes and was lost forever. The shoes were a necessity, the hats a luxury. I tried on several hats and bought a pink one with silk roses that reminded me of Mother's garden.

Even though I had been brought up in a wealthy household in Paipa, I had no idea that there could be so many lovely things in the world. I had inherited my mother's aesthetic inclination, and although I did not cultivate roses, I had gotten into the habit of placing one on my night table every morning.

As I walked through the streets of Florence, admired the architecture, and studied the sculptures and the paintings of its Renaissance, beauty captured my imagination. I wished with my whole being that I could paint or sculpt like those artists who had produced such lovely things, objects that I could no longer live without, now that I knew they had a place somewhere in the world.

In every corner of that city, I caught glimpses of charm and a reason to believe in humanity's ability to overcome the humdrum of everyday routine and to express the essence of beauty in a painting, a fresco, or a sculpture. I was never as aware of the passage of time as I was in Florence. To think that human beings could produce such art during a lifetime was amazing.

Alessandro took me to see Botticelli's *Primavera*. To the left of the canvas I noticed the god Mercury, and next to him the three Graces in their transparent garb. Flora, Chloris, and Zephyrus—the spring wind—created a perfect balance on the right side of the painting; and there, alas, in the center I saw Venus, the personification of beauty and grace. The fruit, the flowers, and the beautiful Graces created the illusion of abundance, fertility, and harmony.

As I stood in front of the magnificent painting, partaking of the spirit expressed within it, I felt ill. With the custodian's assistance, Alessandro accompanied me to a chair. I apologized.

The custodian shrugged. *"Succede spesso,"* he said, it often happens.

"Really?" Alessandro asked while fanning me with his hand.

"Every week beautiful *signore* and *signorine* faint in front of the painting. Museum director don't understand. I explain. Foreigners not used to our way of life. Our rich food, our wines, our beautiful art. This special trip for you?" he asked Alessandro.

"Yes. It's our honeymoon."

"Ah. Sweet. In Italian we call it *luna di miele*, same thing."

I told Enzo about my experience. "You have the tourist's malady," he explained. "You've been exposed to too much beauty in a brief time. Rest is the best cure. A Frenchman named Stendhal wrote a treatise about the subject. Read it."

After reading Stendhal's piece, I remembered my mother describing a similar occurrence during her trip to Florence. That night I had a dream.

I was walking naked through the streets. As I strolled by a group of men, one of them said, "There goes Venus." I looked down at my body and realized I was with child.

When I told Alessandro about my dream, he took me back to the Uffizi to see Botticelli's *The Birth of Venus*.

Although Enzo warned me that I should get some rest, there were so many things for me to do. I had ten large diamonds that the general had bought from a jeweler in Paris as well as the three emeralds Mother had saved for me. The larger emerald weighed three carats, and I had thought about having a ring made from it. With the other two, similar in size and shape, I would have a pair of earrings to match the ring and necklace.

I planned to go to Buccellati, the most famous jeweler in Florence, to ask him for an appraisal and to discuss the ring and earrings.

"But my dear," Enzo said, "you'll be overcharged. Only the English can afford him. Italy is a country of craftsmen, and Buccellati will not do the work himself. I know someone who works for him. His name is Roberto Risi, and he has a shop, if you can call it that, on Via Romana between Piazzale Michelangelo and the Boboli Gardens. I'll introduce you to Roberto if you want."

After consulting with Alessandro, I decided to meet Roberto Risi and show him my emeralds.

Roberto made beautiful rings. The contrast between the beauty of the pieces he was working on and the stark, desolate place where he carried on his work was incredible.

"If Roberto were ambitious," Enzo said, "he could open his own jewelry store. All he wants is to be left alone and to have a glass or two of wine after he's done for the day. That and to smoke his pipe."

One day, while Roberto and I were talking, we lost the emerald destined for the ring. We searched the cubbyhole for hours but could not find it. Roberto lit his pipe.

"Come back in an hour," he told me.

When I did, he had cleaned the whole place up and found the emerald. "Something once lost is twice as precious when you find it," Roberto said as he handed me the stone. "Let me make the ring."

When I told the story during dinner, I remarked on Risi's kindness and generosity. Enzo agreed.

"Roberto is honest," he said.

"Well, he better be careful with my wife," Alessandro replied. "I wouldn't be so naïve if I were you, Inés."

Enzo laughed. "That's the Italian blood in you that's boiling," he told my husband. "But Roberto is a good man. Worry about the others." I sensed that something was amiss.

Since our arrival in Florence, Alessandro had become aware of the glances I often elicited. Florentine men rested their eyes on my face longer than on their own women, as if fascinated. *"Ciao, bella,"* some whispered. They had never seen someone like me.

"Your features are a mixture of the Old and New Worlds," Enzo explained, "an exotic blend of both elements. Your gray almond-shaped eyes, the light-brown hair, a nose narrow like a European's. Your lips are larger and wider than most. It's not your face, though. The way you carry yourself, your glance, your walk, are all a testament to another culture, to a world with different rhythms. I would like to make a sculpture of you, Inés," he concluded.

Alessandro found the attention bestowed upon me disturbing. "I can't help thinking that sooner or later I will lose you," he had told me before we left on our honeymoon.

"I'm the one who should feel that way," I said as I remembered him coming out of the posada room with my sister.

"What do you mean?"

"You have been the most coveted bachelor in Paipa," I said. "Even my sister is in love with you."

Alessandro looked at me for a minute before he burst out laughing. I decided to continue.

"Remember our wedding day at the posada?"

"What did you see?"

"I saw you both walk out of the same room."

"And what do you think we were doing?" he asked, raising his voice. "We were talking about you. That's what."

In Florence, Alessandro's jealousy increased. Once, after our usual trip to Caffè Rivoire, he turned to face me as we walked out.

"I noticed the way you were looking at the man in the corner," he said.

"What man?"

"Don't play innocent with me," Alessandro insisted. "He was looking at you too."

My husband stopped in the middle of the street. A horse carriage was approaching. I felt Alessandro's tight grip on my arm. He squeezed his fingers and brought his face close to mine. "If you ever do that again, I'll break your neck," he whispered.

I managed to get out of the way seconds before the carriage went by. My heart was throbbing. The man who had just threatened me seemed to be someone else, not Alessandro. He walked back to Enzo's house as quickly as possible while I struggled to keep up.

That night, my husband made love to me with anger. Afterward, he lay back on his pillow and started crying.

"I'm sorry, darling," he pleaded. "I should never have doubted you."

Sadness overtook me. I loved Alessandro and would do anything for him. But no matter how I tried to reassure him, I knew he would always doubt me. I couldn't sleep but stayed in bed for fear of waking my husband up.

With time, Alessandro's fits of jealousy became more frequent and his outbursts less controlled.

At night, and after many a drink, he kept me up, questioning my actions and accusing me of infidelity. *What about you?* I thought of asking him, and yet, there was a part of me that did not want to know.

Chapter Twenty-Three

Alessandro and I returned to Paipa with my jewelry, a few new dresses, hats, and shoes for me, and a new suit and a guitar for him. We settled in a small house in town. Since we had spent all our wedding money in Florence and Alessandro did not have a job, he asked his father for a loan and promised to start looking for some way to earn a living.

My husband often organized parties at our house. Even when money was running short, somehow he managed, and, at the last moment, people showed up to celebrate one thing or another. Some days I would have preferred a quiet dinner with Alessandro.

After everyone had gone, I cleaned up while he went upstairs to bed. We did not talk much. When Alessandro was awake, we made love. Most nights, he was already asleep by the time I joined him in the bedroom.

I sat on a chair by the window and thought about painting. I had started putting money away to buy supplies and was trying to decide what I would paint first.

More often than not, I stayed downstairs as long as possible so I would not have to feel the weight of his body on mine and smell cigarettes and liquor on his breath. Later on while I watched him sleeping, pangs of guilt kept me up for hours. How could I feel that way toward my husband, the man I had married? I had no answers, but a wave of love in the recesses of my heart would sometimes sweep over me, and I would love him again and momentarily forget my doubts.

After parties, Alessandro stayed in bed until late the next day. I did not mind his habits until I became pregnant with my first child.

~

Father tried to help Alessandro find a job, and when he thought the right opportunity had come along, he walked over to see us.

The front door was unlocked, the curtains drawn, and I was lying on the couch with a wet cloth on my forehead. All around there were papers, books, and clothing. The ashtrays were brimming with cigarette butts, and there were wineglasses on the table, some half full. Once morning sickness had taken over my life, I had stopped caring.

"Are you all right?" Father asked. He could not conceal his amazement.

"I have a terrible headache."

"Can I get you anything?"

"A glass of water, please." I turned to glance at him.

"Look at those dark circles under your eyes!" he exclaimed. "You seem thinner." Father went to the kitchen and found more dirty dishes. "Where's the maid?" He handed me a glass of water.

"Alessandro fired her last week. He said we could not afford her."

"He can afford his parties, though," Father commented with bitterness. I drank the water slowly.

"Where is he, anyway?"

"Sleeping."

"At this hour? It's two o'clock in the afternoon."

"He goes to bed very late," I explained.

"I can imagine," Father mused. "Can you call him?"

I was afraid to wake Alessandro. He would no doubt be in a bad mood.

"Why don't you go up?" I suggested. "He's in the bedroom."

Father started going up the stairs. "I wonder how things got to this point," he said, loudly enough for me to hear.

I followed him. Halfway up, the smell of cigarettes and alcohol overwhelmed me. I felt sick but continued climbing.

Alessandro was lying on the bed fully dressed, his face buried in the pillow. He did not move until Father called his name. Then he went into the bathroom.

Father sat down by the window and waited for his son-in-law to vomit. I stood by the door. Alessandro joined us. He had washed his face, combed his hair, and tucked in his shirt, but he still looked hungover.

"Rodolfo, what a pleasant surprise!" He shook Father's hand. "Sit down, Inés." Alessandro pointed at another chair by the window.

I walked in and sat down. My husband opened the window. The light breeze settled my stomach.

"I'm sorry," Father said, "I came without an invitation." He crossed his legs. "I haven't seen Inés in a while, and I wanted to make sure she was all right."

"Of course she's all right." Alessandro laughed. "What did you think? That I had sent her away?"

"Well, in her condition," Father insisted, "she should be getting plenty of rest. She seems awfully tired."

"That's because she fired the maid and insists on doing everything herself," Alessandro explained as he took a freshly starched shirt out of his drawer. "I told her it would be too much, but she wouldn't listen. Your daughter is a perfectionist, you know."

Father gripped the armrests on his chair. "I'm not sure that having parties is helping her any," he pronounced in a slow and deliberate tone. "Inés needs to sleep. Besides, there would be fewer cleanups. When her mother was pregnant—"

Alessandro interrupted him. "My friends come here to hear me sing." He walked over to where we were sitting. "I am an artist, a poet," he continued. "Inés knew that when she married me."

"Yes, but now you are about to become a father," Rodolfo said.

A sneer swept across Alessandro's face. I looked out the window so my husband would not see me crying. He didn't like to see me cry.

Alessandro leaned close to Father and looked at him with anger in his eyes; I had seen that look before. He seemed to be fighting back the urge to grab Rodolfo by his shirt collar and bang him against the wall. Instead, he stepped back and lit a cigarette.

"And you came here to remind me that my wife is pregnant and that I am about to become a father?" he asked sarcastically.

"No." Father started pacing around the room. "I came to talk to you about two job possibilities."

"So I need to go out and get a job?" My husband laughed. Father ignored him.

"I was thinking you could teach Italian. You have the right personality for it."

"What do you mean?" Alessandro took a long drag from his cigarette.

Father stopped in front of the window and inhaled. "I know

two gentlemen from Bogotá," he said. "They want to open a language school in Paipa. I talked to them about you."

Alessandro seemed interested. "Where do they plan to open the school?"

"At the old town hall."

"I'll go talk to them," my husband stated, "but I'm not making any commitments. We don't need the money. I want to work on my music." He put out his cigarette.

"If that's the case," Father continued, "I have another offer." My husband looked up at him with a sly grin on his face.

"Do you remember the café that opened a year ago in the main square?"

"I'm a regular customer." Alessandro smiled. "Don't tell me they need a musician."

Father took another deep breath, turned down the cigarette Alessandro was offering him, and watched his son-in-law light another one.

"Paco quit. They're desperate to find someone else. What do you think?"

"Paco was terrible," Alessandro exclaimed. "I'm not sure I want to play while people talk and eat. I have too much respect for my art."

Rodolfo undid his shirt collar. "Why don't you try?" he asked. "You don't have anything to lose."

"If it will please my father-in-law," Alessandro said as he blew smoke out.

Chapter Twenty-Four

My pregnancy felt like a journey without a final destination. I welcomed motherhood and the mystery of the process and watched my body change slowly to adapt to the new presence within it. With time my body and mind became used to it, but the pregnancy was for me what a first piece is for a painter.

Alessandro was hired to work at the language school. Everyone agreed he was a gifted teacher, but he had difficulty keeping a schedule. On those mornings when he did not feel like going to work, he didn't. The school director hired a boy to go and awaken my husband when he had a class waiting for him. Eventually, the boy gave up and so did the school owners.

Father then convinced Alessandro to play and sing at the local café. Since he did not start work until the evening, my husband found that job more agreeable. His late parties at home could continue, and he would still be able to sleep in every morning.

For a time, Alessandro expressed renewed interest in me. "You know, Inés," he told me one day during lunch, "the pregnancy makes you beautiful. Your skin is softer, almost transparent. Your cheeks have a healthy glow similar to those Renaissance paintings of women we admired during our honeymoon."

Alessandro passed his hand around my face, and a warm feeling took hold of me. I remembered when we made love for hours while we looked into each other's eyes. Sometimes Alessandro would blow the candle out, but I insisted that he light it again. I craved the intensity of his eyes, the dialogue between our souls.

During my pregnancy I found happiness in small things. Every morning I walked to the mansion and visited Father and Isabel. We sat in the rose garden. After a cup of tea, I trimmed the flowers, cleared their stems, and watered them. Before leaving I paused to fill my lungs with their wonderful, delicate scent. Isabel and I examined the bushes carefully, and she helped me cut those roses that were ready. When I got home, I took the petals and laid them on silk cloth.

In Florence I had bought a book about beauty and flowers. It had lovely illustrations, and turning the pages was a sensual exercise that elicited exotic scents and aromas. The book was in Italian, but I understood the gist of it. I took to making creams and potions and perfumes with my mother's roses during that year.

~

Every morning I was besieged by dirty plates and wineglasses. The loud company and the singing and drinking kept me up until late, but I was so immersed in my own world and in the child I was carrying, I barely noticed when people came or left.

I fell sick from fatigue, and the doctor told me that I was putting myself at risk. He prescribed an herbal infusion with chamomile so I could get some sleep. I decided to talk to Alessandro.

"Do you think it would be okay to postpone all parties until after the baby is born?" I asked him as I cleaned up after another late night.

"What?" Alessandro looked up from the couch.

"I'm not getting enough sleep," I explained. "The doctor told me I need more rest."

"You mean lying on the couch all day is not restful enough for you?" my husband asked.

"I don't lie on the couch all day," I shouted. "I don't mind cooking and cleaning. But having to clean up after your parties is getting harder!" I grabbed a wineglass and smashed it against the chimney.

"My parties?" Alessandro got up from the couch. "I thought you enjoyed them. I'm sorry if I have been imposing my friends on you." He rubbed his cigarette butt into an ashtray.

Alessandro went to the bedroom and returned with his jacket on. He took me by the shoulders and turned me around to face him.

"Look at you, Miss Aristocracy!" my husband shouted. "You stopped working, your inheritance was a joke, and you expect me to take care of you. Now you're pregnant. We'll have another mouth to feed. From now on, I'll be seeing my friends away from here. But I warn you. Leave me alone."

Alessandro backed me into the wall. He turned to the table and with a sweeping motion of his hand, knocked the bottles, glasses, and ashtrays onto the floor. He did not return that night.

Three weeks later while washing the dinner dishes, I went into labor. The midwife kept me company while Alessandro slept. Julio was born at five o'clock in the morning, but his father did not see him until the afternoon.

My husband seemed happy with the baby. "This boy is destined for great things," he pronounced.

Still, he went out drinking every night and brought friends over from the bars, played his guitar, and sang.

After our son's birth, it became clear that the house we were living in was too small for our family. Besides, Alessandro had not paid the rent for months, and we were about to get evicted.

I decided to approach Father and Isabel. My sister had been helping with the baby; she came to see us often. Father brought us eggs and vegetables and occasionally a chicken. Sometimes he left money on the kitchen counter. We never talked about it.

Isabel had just prepared a pot of tea, and we were sharing it in the living room while Julio slept peacefully in his crib next to us. I warmed my hands with the cup.

"Do you think the mansion is large enough to accommodate us all?" I asked tentatively.

Father was stirring sugar in his tea. "Of course it is," he replied. "It's large enough for three families. Don't you agree, Isabel?" He turned to my sister.

Isabel looked at me. "It's your house," she said. "You don't have to ask us for permission to move back in."

"I think it would make things easier."

My sister put her cup down. "Why? Is the honeymoon over?"

"Isabel, you stop that now," Father commanded.

I hired an old carpenter who had worked for Mother and set about fixing the nursery for Julio and Mother's room for Alessandro and me. When the work was completed, each room had a fresh coat of paint, working windows, and perfectly polished floors.

Six months after Julio's crib had been placed in the old nursery, Father suffered a heart attack. His death strained my relationship with Isabel. Neither of us had forgotten our altercations. I did not understand my sister—I did not know what her motivations were, and I felt uncomfortable. But Isabel had nowhere to go.

"I'm leaving," she said one afternoon after shutting her bag. "You don't want me here."

"You can live with us as long as you like," I said.

"But what if Alessandro doesn't want me to stay?" She sat on her bed.

"He doesn't seem to mind."

Isabel started unpacking. That year, I became pregnant with Lucy.

Chapter Twenty-Five

Alessandro poured a second glass of wine for himself. He filled Isabel's glass as well, but I covered mine.

"No more for me, thank you."

"Suit yourself," my husband answered. He brought the goblet to his lips.

My husband seemed more content living in the mansion without Rodolfo to watch over his shoulder; it was as if he had found a place where he belonged.

"Maybe I should not have any more either," Isabel whispered. She wiped her mouth with a linen napkin.

"Go ahead," I insisted. "If it weren't for my condition, I would."

"Are you sick?"

"No, I'm pregnant," I confessed.

My husband seemed happy with the news. He ordered the maid to bring out a bottle of champagne. "To Inés." He raised his flute.

Alessandro poured the last drops into his glass and turned to Isabel.

"To my wife's sister," he said. "May you be happy." He looked into her eyes.

"I am," she replied.

~

During the months that followed, Alessandro never ate at home. He left before dinner and sometimes did not return until the next morning.

One evening, Amalia came to visit me. Isabel greeted her politely and said she had to go out to see a sick friend. After my sister left, Amalia spoke.

"Maybe I shouldn't tell you this, in your condition and all, but I cannot stand it anymore."

"What is it?"

"Have you heard the rumors about your husband?"

I felt lightheaded. For a moment, the room went dark, and I feared I was going to faint. The intuition that a terrible premonition had just proved true would not leave me.

"What are they?"

"That he's a scoundrel. That he's never home. That he drinks and gambles and owes money to half of Paipa. Where is he now?"

"I don't know where he went."

"Everybody else in Paipa does. Inés, when are you going to open your eyes?" Amalia whispered as she took my hand. "I'll show you." My friend stood up. My heart started beating so fast I felt my chest could burst.

Amalia drove me to the café in her carriage. It was crowded. The smell of alcohol and cigarette smoke blended to create an acrid stench. I felt the urge to vomit and had to hold my hand over my nose. The music stopped. People abandoned the dance floor and stood around, whispering.

Only one couple was left on the floor. I could recognize my husband's back anywhere. The woman was difficult to see in the dark, but she looked familiar. I examined the dress, the shoes, and the head leaning on Alessandro's shoulder, a cascade of wavy long hair down to her waist. There was only one woman in Paipa who would think nothing of wearing her hair down in public—my sister. Could it be her? I ran out of the room. Alessandro did not notice.

Amalia held me while I wept. "I'm sorry I brought you here," she said. "I'll take you home."

I bent over with pain. "Alert the doctor," I managed to say. "The baby will be born any minute." Lucy was born prematurely that night.

Chapter Twenty-Six

Lucy, my second child, was the catalyst that forced me to think about consequences before I had fully realized the importance of my actions.

I would always remember my first pregnancy better than the second. Julio was the heir, the male that would carry on the family name and inherit any family fortune. His birth proved that Alessandro Scala had made the right choice, that I was fertile, strong, and healthy.

Julio was a piece in the evolutionary puzzle of the Scala clan. Yet no amount of love from Alessandro could make up for all the pain I went through to deliver him a son.

I felt betrayed. The pain, the long hours of suffering, the feeling of fear and death all came hammering down on me at once when I realized I had no control over my flesh.

Doubts were born. I remembered my husband and Isabel leaving the room in the posada on our wedding day.

Toward the end, when my body and my mind went their separate ways, while one watched the other squirm and suffer, I realized that men and women would and could never be equal. No matter what my mother had said. No matter what I had often thought. For how could they be the same if they could not share the torment of bringing forth a new life into this world? And if they were both necessary for the miracle of life, how could it come about if the woman did not carry the child for nine months and birth it?

Therefore, I concluded in my semi-frenzied state, regardless of what anyone said, that women were superior to men because they could withstand more pain.

I decided from then on to judge people by how much grief they were able to bear with dignity. Granted, I thought that much agony in life is fruitless.

My suffering had resulted in a privileged status. The matriarch. The heir's mother. The son's nurturer. The source of life, of food, the breastfeeder always there to fortify her children and to be watched in awe by a man who could not fathom what it was like to carry another being, give it birth, and nourish it.

God's punishment to women, I concluded, was not the torment of pregnancy and childbirth, but coupling these with the intellectual ability to question and to wonder. Eve's real punishment, I thought, was to be blessed with an inquisitive mind trapped in a body that would strive to perpetuate itself regardless of the pain or the consequences.

As I held Julio in my arms hours later, I forgot these doubts.

My second pregnancy brought them back to life. After a long labor and a difficult delivery, I looked at Lucy in my arms and wept. I knew that Lucy's gender could one day be responsible for her unhappiness.

Chapter Twenty-Seven

Soon after Alessandro left me, I ran out of money. I would have to sell the house as well as my mother's jewelry to survive. I was angry at my husband for being such a selfish fool and at myself for allowing him to treat me with disrespect, for letting him waste my inheritance and all our resources, and for making me a laughingstock all over Paipa. But what did I care about other people's opinions? Now it was about survival. I didn't have the luxury of wallowing in my suffering. *Alessandro will regret it one day,* I told myself. But Isabel's betrayal . . . I realized she had always been jealous of me. Now she had stolen my husband. How could I have been so blind? What kind of seer was I, when I couldn't even see what was in front of my very own eyes? I would never forget what they had done, but I wouldn't give them the satisfaction of knowing how much they hurt me. I would take my pain to the grave with me. I realized I was crying, and I remembered the angel in the cornfield.

Many people in Paipa were interested in the oldest mansion in town. When the rumor spread that I would be selling it, some found the perfect pretext to knock at my door and go through the rooms, glancing at our family portraits, our French Empire furniture, and our delicate porcelain vases. I was well mannered about it and gave the tours myself.

I had kept the study locked as a reminder that a certain part of my life was over, but people invariably wanted to see it.

"Isn't this the famous study where Simón Bolívar had a meeting with one of your ancestors?" Señora Ramirez asked.

"Yes, it is."

"The furniture is delightful. And look at that view! What do you use it for?"

"It was my mother's study. This is where she wrote her poetry. Lately my husband practiced his guitar in this room," I told her.

"From what I heard," another lady whispered loud enough so I could hear, "that's not all he practiced."

"And with her sister, of all people," Señora Ramirez added. "Is it true," she went on, "that Alessandro and Isabel ran off together?"

I paused for a moment before answering. "I wouldn't know," I finally said. "I've been so busy with the children."

"But wasn't Isabel supposed to be here to help you? A lot of help she turned out to be!" Señora Ramirez insisted after she blew her nose.

"Are you interested in the house or in any of the furniture?" I asked. "I'm expecting company fairly soon, and we haven't had lunch yet."

I had already decided to close the doors of the mansion to my prying neighbors when I was told that a foreigner wanted a tour of the house. He had been sent to Colombia by the Belgian government to investigate the possibilities of expanding the railroad, and Paipa was on the map for a new train station. Giles, as he was named, had heard about the mansion at the boardinghouse where he was staying.

When I received his request for a showing, I decided it would be the last one. I would rather shut the house and let it fall to pieces than put up with the vicious comments of my neighbors.

The next morning Monsieur Giles showed up promptly at ten o'clock. I had the maid prepare a late breakfast and served it in such a stately manner that no one would have guessed I had just spent my last coins buying the chocolate and the bread.

My guest ate and drank politely and then proceeded to examine the house. He went through all the rooms, observing the details and commenting on the furniture.

When he got to the study, he stopped at the entrance. "This is the room where the Great Liberator had his meeting with the *coronel*, isn't it?"

"Yes. They both sat over there."

"How long did Bolívar stay?"

"I'm not sure," I said. "But I do know he came more than once."

Monsieur Giles continued with the tour of the house. Once we were done, he turned to me decisively. "When will I be able to take possession?"

I was not used to the straightforward manner of the Europeans. "But you haven't even asked the price," I stammered.

"That's not a problem," he said. "I would like it furnished, though. Could you come up with a separate price for the furnishings?"

"I wouldn't know how to go about that," I confessed. "I inherited it all from my mother when she died."

"An expert could give an estimate. Would that suffice?"

"I suppose so."

He opened his bag and took a roll of money out. "Here's my down payment."

I reached out for the money slowly in an attempt to mask my desperation.

At that moment, I wished, with all my heart, that I would never have to return to Paipa. It would be impossible to recapture my youth in any other house in the world. The mansion represented my past, my mother's life, and my happy childhood. If, for any reason, it were to be annihilated, so would my childhood, the afternoons spent in a hammock under the trees, the walks around the lake with Helena, the dance and music lessons in the parlor, and the nursery where porcelain dolls sat side by side, waiting for the next schoolteacher to arrive.

After Giles's departure, I walked toward the study and tried to imagine the meeting between Simón Bolívar and Colonel Francisco de Paula Santander.

They must have sat in armchairs and discussed the future of La Gran Colombia while the women in the house scurried about, making sure they were comfortable. The two men probably shared an aperitif, delicate pastries from an ancient recipe, and a meal behind closed doors. After dinner came the decision. Peace or war. Unity or independence.

I stood in front of the window and looked at my mother's rosebushes. The flowers swayed with the wind, petals falling carelessly about. I closed my eyes and tried to imagine the view without the roses.

Bolívar would probably have glanced far off into the distance as he tried to assess the benefits of war. After all, the brilliant attack on Nueva Granada had taken the Spaniards by surprise; that victory had been well earned.

I opened my eyes. On a clear day, the Liberator would have seen the same mountains I was now seeing. What great plans he and the colonel had had for us. If Colombia, Ecuador, and

Venezuela had remained united, our territories would have expanded, our resources tripled. Bolívar was a brilliant man—no doubt a visionary. And to think he would have been murdered had it not been for the help of Manuela Sáenz, his lover, who distracted his attackers while he escaped through a window. Hers was a passionate love, a love of conviction. She was the liberator of the Liberator, as Bolívar himself aptly put it.

I thought about Alessandro and one of the last times we had made love. He had kept his eyes shut, and a feeling of loneliness had swept over me. I longed for a love like the one Manuela and Bolívar shared, a love without reserve.

Perhaps Manuela had accompanied the Liberator to Paipa. She may have had a cup of tea with the women in the parlor while they came up with their own agreement, as women often do. I could imagine them proposing it to the men during dessert. Without them, the peace treaty could have suffered.

Chapter Twenty-Eight

It took me one week to sort through my possessions and pack. I kept the linen sheets, the woolen blankets, my mother's books, and my father's pipe collection. Everything else was part of the agreement I had signed a few weeks earlier with Monsieur Giles.

"Let me know when you are ready to go," he said one afternoon after handing me another handful of bills.

"You are so patient," I replied. "Can I offer you a cup of rose tea?"

"I heard about your husband and your sister," Giles told me while we drank our tea.

"Everyone in Paipa knows."

"Where will you go with two children?" he asked with concern.

I poured more tea. "My sister Rosa lives in Bogotá. She's a schoolteacher. I thought I could stay with her until I find a job."

"Have you ever been to Bogotá?" Giles asked. "It's much larger than Paipa."

"I know. I lived there with my sister before getting married. At least," I added, "the Bogotanos won't be pointing fingers. They could not care less who Alessandro Scala is. Sometimes people here act as if it were my fault that Alessandro left."

"I'm sorry."

"Women are the worst," I continued. The bitterness in my voice surprised me. I grew silent.

After tea, Monsieur Giles and I walked around Mother's rose garden. I stopped in front of a bush that had just given birth to three rose buttons and held one of them in my hand. As I leaned over to inhale its aroma, the Belgian gentleman picked a rose and handed it to me.

"Inés, you are a beautiful woman," he told me. "I will never understand how a man could leave you."

I took the flower, inhaled its aroma, and remained silent.

"What are you thinking?"

"If I had not come back to Paipa, I would not have married Alessandro."

"I'm sure you had good reason to marry him," Giles said. "Besides, you wouldn't have your children now." He wiped the top of his boot with his walking stick before turning to me. "If you don't mind my asking you, why *did* you come back to Paipa?"

"Rosa grew tired of my suitors. She packed my suitcase and carried it to the station for me."

"Does she know you're going back?"

"No," I admitted. "I plan to show up at her doorstep. She may have gotten rid of me once, but it would be hard to turn the children away. Besides, before she died, Mother asked Rosa to help us if we ever needed it."

"Has she heard about your situation?" Giles asked.

"No." I leaned down to smell other flowers.

"You seem to enjoy these roses."

"Mother left them to me."

"You are welcome to take them."

"I would if I had a place to plant them, but they really belong here. My mother wouldn't want me to take them to Bogotá. She wouldn't want me to sell the house either."

"I'm sure you wouldn't if you didn't have to," Giles commented. "You are welcome to come visit your roses anytime. I'll hire a gardener to take care of them, although I doubt that he will manage as beautifully as you obviously have."

Back at the house, I offered Giles a brandy in Mother's old study. He left with the house keys in his pocket.

Four days later I took leave of the mansion by going into each room and recalling the happiest memory I had experienced there.

My last stop was the rose garden. I stood for a while, glancing at the colorful mosaic the flowers made, and I remembered Mother going up the steps with whole bunches of roses in her arms.

I had asked her once how she could carry the flowers without getting hurt by their thorns.

"The secret is to hold them tightly but not so tightly that they cut," Mother had replied. "The same is true about love." I now understood what she had meant.

As I knelt to smell the roses, their sweet aroma overwhelmed me. I saw Julio running toward me and struggled to tear myself away.

"What's wrong, Mommy?" he asked.

"Nothing."

"Then why are you crying?"

"I'm watering my mother's roses," I told my son as I embraced him. "Tears make them grow stronger."

That was the last time I saw the flowers in their full splendor.

Chapter Twenty-Nine

At nine o'clock, Monsieur Giles loaded my trunks in his carriage and drove us to the station. He found the train for Bogotá and supervised the railway employee as he took our tickets and our luggage.

When I was getting ready to board, Giles stopped me.

"Inés, if I were not married," he whispered in my ear, "I would not hesitate to ask you to stay."

After wiping a tear from my face, Giles stood, hat in hand, while we settled in our seats and then waved to us until we lost sight of him and of Paipa.

The trip to Bogotá was as long and weary as my return to Paipa had been years earlier. People on the train glanced suspiciously at me, a woman alone traveling with two children. Even those men who admired me did so from afar, as a traveler looks upon a distant shore that he will never reach. I was aware of their prying eyes, the curious whispers between husbands and wives as well as the look of pity that some could not manage to disguise.

"She must be a widow," I heard a woman whisper to her husband with disapproval in her voice, as if I were somehow responsible for my husband's death.

If only I were *a widow,* I thought. Then I would have a good excuse for living without a man.

I looked out the window. The countryside was clean and luscious, with few houses located miles apart and green everywhere, not a patch of dry land in sight. I marveled at the tall guava trees, banana trees with large stalks of ripened fruit ready to be eaten, farms with cows and horses, and pigs in sties and chickens and roosters. Now and then I would spot a person walking by the road or a child running in the fields. I leaned my head on the windowpane while Lucy slept in my arms and Julio rested his head on my lap. The train stopped in several towns between Paipa and Bogotá, including Tunja, Chocontá, and Guatavita. Passengers got on at every station. By the time we left Tunja, our compartment was full. The temperature went down as we climbed higher in the eastern ranges of the Andes. I closed my eyes and thought about the times I had gone to the hot springs in Paipa with Mother and Father, and later with Alessandro. I would miss those hot springs, my childhood home, and the peaceful atmosphere of my small town. I would miss the valley that had made Paipa famous.

As we got closer to Bogotá, the sky grew cloudy and rain seemed imminent. Soon it started raining. Going past the outskirts, I could see houses that had been built in a hurry, crowded next to each other, by people eager to live in the city and to work there. Recent economic reforms and the arrival of foreign capital invested to expand our railroads had created a boom. Poor campesinos who were struggling in the country decided to move to the city to look for work, though with little money, they had no choice but to live in temporary housing in cramped neighborhoods. As I watched the rain fall on those precarious homes, I wondered how long their inhabitants would be able to last in the city. It rained often in Bogotá. The rainy season was from March to November, and the capital was a bit colder than Paipa. I would have to buy the children coats. I already missed the sunshine in Paipa. The rain made the capital seem dreary. After we got off the train in Bogotá, I left my boxes and trunks with a station guard while I took the children and looked for a carriage.

As we arrived at Rosa's doorstep, more clouds appeared, and right after, a torrent of rain. I wrapped Lucy as best I could, grabbed Julio's hand, and ran for cover. The coach driver piled our trunks and suitcases by the door and watched us from the carriage as we got drenched.

I knocked on the door furiously. The lock turned twice, the handle moved, and I found my sister Rosa's eyes staring at me.

"I should have known it was you!" Rosa exclaimed. "You look like a wet rat. And what's all this?" She pointed at the wet trunks.

I pushed Julio forward as softly as I could manage and followed him in, shutting the door, the wet luggage, and the painful past out. It was only then that Rosa noticed Lucy all wrapped up in my arms.

My sister stood in the middle of the hallway and looked at me disapprovingly.

"What are you doing here?" she asked.

Chapter Thirty

I tried to assess whether or not Lucy had been drenched and helped Julio out of his overcoat with my free hand.

"Could you please get me a dry blanket or a towel?" I begged Rosa.

She called the maid, who went about helping me with the energy and zest that my own sister lacked or failed to show.

"What brings you back to Bogotá?" Rosa inquired again.

I handed Lucy to the maid, went back to the door, and carried the luggage in, piece by piece, while my sister watched, astounded.

Finally, Julio was dry. I breastfed Lucy while my son had some hot chocolate with cheese and soft bread. As I watched him eat, I felt hungry, but I thought better of requesting food.

"Could I please have a glass of water?" I asked Rosa. "My throat is dry from the trip." She ignored my request and continued to interrogate me.

"Is this a vacation? Where is Alessandro?"

"Please. I need a glass of water."

"You can't show up at my doorstep with two children and a bunch of old trunks and not expect me to ask any questions," my sister insisted. I let her know she should be quiet, but Rosa would have none of that.

"This may come as a surprise to you," she went on, "but I have never understood you." Rosa looked at me as if she were speaking to a foreigner who had difficulty grasping her language.

"Let me refresh your memory," she continued. "Last time you were here, I took you over to the bus station and bought you a one-way ticket to Paipa with the understanding that you were never to come back."

"Well, never is a very long time," I mused. "Besides, I had no choice."

"People always have a choice," Rosa said, raising her voice. "You leave, or rather, get sent away, get married, have two kids, and show up without your husband? What is wrong with you?"

I fought back the tears. Julio's eyes were resting intently on my face. He had never heard anyone talk to me like that, and he did not know what to make of it. I looked at Julio, my eyes two paper boats floating down a stream.

"Honey, could you please go to the kitchen and bring me a glass of water?"

Julio was reluctant to get out of his chair. He seemed to think that Rosa had to give her consent. She might turn and tackle him if he tried to leave the room.

My son stared at Rosa and waited for her to say something, but his aunt was too involved with me to notice him, so he went to the kitchen.

"Alessandro left after the baby was born," I informed Rosa.

"Where did he go?"

"I don't know."

"Why did he leave?"

"I don't know."

"Is there another woman?" my sister continued, her voice full of suspicion.

"Yes."

"There's always another woman," Rosa stated, as if she were an authority on love, marriage, and all the rest. "Do you know her?"

"Yes."

"Well? Who is it?" She was fidgeting in her chair.

"Isabel."

"Isabel," Rosa repeated after me, much like a Latin pupil recites the declension of a verb. "Isabel who?"

Suddenly, recognition swept across her face. She turned red, leaned over the chair, and looked me straight in the eye. "Not our sister?" Rosa's mouth opened in disbelief. "What an outrage! And you're just going to sit there and let her get away with that?"

I felt my cheeks get hot. Anger rose inside me. "What do you want me to do?" I retorted. "Go back to Paipa and expose her for what she did? Do you think shaming our sister would fix anything?"

"She's not the only one to blame," Rosa said. "He's just as guilty."

"Believe me, I know. I put up with Alessandro and his disgusting behavior because I wanted to save my marriage, to avoid a scandal. But she's my sister! Our sister! I never thought someone I loved and trusted could hurt me so deeply. I don't know if I'll ever be able to trust anyone again."

Rosa handed me a handkerchief. I sat quietly for a moment, wiping my tears.

"You could have stayed there and demanded that the scoundrel support you and the children instead of running away, making it so easy for him and Isabel."

"Yes, you're right, Rosa. But I chose to think about my children, their future," I said. "I can't afford to let Alessandro hurt them the way he hurt me. Because everything he touches turns to ashes. Believe me, I've seen it happen."

"But why run away like you did?" Rosa asked. "You made things easier for them."

"Rosa," I said in a conciliatory tone. "I was hoping I could stay with you for a while, until I figure things out."

"What about the mansion?" my sister asked. "What will become of it?"

Julio walked in and handed me a glass of water.

"I sold it."

Rosa stood up. I thought she was about to slap me. She started pacing around the room, hands on her wide hips. "I never understood why Mother left you the mansion," she said. "I can't forgive her for that. She betrayed the rest of us. What about the furniture?"

"I had to settle Alessandro's debts," I answered. "I sold the house furnished. Everything else I brought today."

"And my piano?"

"It went with the house. I had nowhere to put it. I sent you a telegram asking about it, but you never replied."

"Well, I didn't know you were getting ready to sell it! For Christ's sake!"

"I'll give you the money for it," I offered, hoping to appease her.

Rosa's hands formed into fists. She remained silent for a while.

"What good is the money?" she finally screamed. "That piano was an antique. It's irreplaceable."

Rosa calmed down. "You don't plan to go back to Paipa?"

"No."

"And what will you do here?" She pressed on. "You can't stay forever. I have Chata and Helena living with me. The house is small. My income cannot support us all."

"I want to contribute to the household."

"And after?"

"I'd like to find a job, become independent."

"Good, since you've already ruined your chances of a decent marriage," Rosa said.

Chapter Thirty-One

Chata, Helena, and Rosa had to adapt to sharing the house with the children and me. Lucy woke up often during the night, and even though I calmed her, my sisters had their sleep disturbed. I heard them talking in the morning.

"Did you sleep last night?" Rosa asked Helena as the maid served breakfast.

"That child cried all night. Please pass the butter. I have to be rested for work. I won't be able to concentrate today."

"And what about me?" Rosa asked indignantly. "I don't know where I'll find the patience to teach. Is Sleeping Beauty still resting?" Rosa asked the maid.

"Yes, madam. I was going to take her breakfast up in a little while. She must be tired after such a long trip."

"Don't you start giving her special treatment," Rosa said. "She comes down to eat like the rest of us." I imagined my sister shaking a finger at the poor maid.

I followed Julio downstairs. He stood at the entrance to the dining room, cap in hand, waiting for a sign to proceed. Rosa looked at him in silence.

"My, you're the portrait of a perfect gentleman, hat and all," Helena said. "Did you dress yourself?"

"My mommy helped," he murmured.

"Well, come over here and have some breakfast. You must be hungry," Rosa commanded in the nicest tone she had used since our arrival.

"Yes, and thank you, Aunt Rosa."

I watched Julio as he stared at Rosa with fascination. She did not look at all like me, so it was hard for the child to remember that we were related. To him, Rosa must have seemed like a foreigner with a different way of interpreting the signs of the world. Helena looked slightly more human; she was by no means beautiful, but she had a stately figure and did not seem as threatening.

Julio placed his napkin on his lap as I walked in the room.

"You're up early," Rosa said.

"I was trying to put Lucy back to sleep."

"Well. I have to get ready for work," Helena said, getting up from her chair.

Rosa patted her hand. "I'm glad to see you're taking your job seriously. When will you complete the French class you signed up for last year?" She wiped her mouth.

"In two months," Helena answered. "I can't wait to start typing correspondence in French. There's only one other girl at the company who speaks the language. I'm looking forward to earning more money and meeting a decent man."

Rosa nodded approvingly. She glanced at me. "We've had enough of poets and artists in our family, haven't we, Inés?" She smiled and turned to Helena. "What you need, my dear, is a businessman, a professional. We'll work on that."

Rosa followed Helena out of the dining room. While I buttered my son's bread, I wondered what the future would bring. Julio put his spoon in his hot chocolate and tried to find some cheese.

"I think it's going to be interesting, living here," I said.

VELVET SOAP

Chapter Thirty-Two

At the Belgian railroad company, Helena spent most of the day typing in a large room with thirty other women, talking when they had the chance, but still she dressed in tight-fitting suits and high heels.

My sister enjoyed her job but looked upon it as a temporary condition. Her real desire was to find a husband who could afford to support her so she wouldn't have to work.

"I'll be able to let my nails grow longer then," Helena told me one day while I was giving her a manicure.

"Would you like staying at home and thinking only about your house and children?" I asked her. She was so different from Mother.

"Who said I would have to stay at home all the time?" Helena replied. "There are plenty of activities for a woman in society." She held her left hand up to glance at it. "I could devote myself to pious causes."

~

Helena met Régulo Vaca Piñeros two days after his promotion at the railroad company. My sister told us the story during dinner that night.

"*El jefe*, the Belgian who oversees the operation, organized a reception in Régulo Vaca's honor. He had champagne and caviar brought in from Claudel and ordered Czechoslovakian dishes from the new restaurant around the corner, close to the train station—the one owned by an immigrant who was once a great chef in Europe. Remember someone told us about it?" Helena turned to ask Rosa but did not wait for an answer. "Everyone at the company was invited to the reception. I was among the first to arrive and to congratulate Régulo in person.

"'I'm glad to see that a Colombian can make it in this company,' I told him as we drank champagne."

"What did he reply?" Chata asked.

"He thanked me politely. *El jefe*, who was standing next to Régulo, eating caviar, interrupted our conversation. 'It's not a question of nationality,' he said. *'It's a matter of talent and hard work.'"*

"Why, of course," I agreed.

"'Don Régulo is here every morning at six,' *el jefe* went on."

"He sounds like a hard worker," Rosa interrupted. She seemed very pleased with Helena's story. "I bet Régulo would make a fine husband."

From then on, Helena patiently waited for Régulo to notice her. She spent whole evenings scheming to invite him to lunch, but every time she started planning the menu, she could not go beyond the customary soup that constitutes the first dish in a Colombian meal.

One night she thought Régulo would like to have *ajiaco*, but the following night it was vichyssoise, followed by all sorts of dishes with names she could not pronounce. I listened to her recipes, but secretly, I started to hate Régulo for creating such an atmosphere of disruption around us.

During that period Helena often dreamed about preparing a French meal for Régulo. She would come downstairs in her nightgown, her hair disheveled. It was the same dream, but I would listen to it as if I were hearing it for the first time.

"We were sitting at the table having dinner," Helena would say. "The table was perfectly set, the whole meal ready to be served, and, at a particular moment, I would notice that a key ingredient was missing." At this point in her story, Helena always cried.

After many sleepless nights, my sister mustered enough courage to tell Rosa about her desire to invite Régulo.

"Well, I'm listening. Tell me," she commanded.

Helena talked without pausing to breathe or to drink her coffee. She mentioned Régulo's looks, his personality, his station in life, and the nightmares.

Contrary to what I had expected, Rosa was sympathetic. In fact, she was enthusiastic. "That won't do. Will it?" she told Helena. "You need your beauty sleep now more than ever. We have to come up with a solution. I'll help you," she added before taking a large bite of bread.

Rosa went to see Régulo in person. "I am here to invite you to a surprise party for my sister Helena. It would give her great pleasure if you came," she added, handing Régulo an invitation.

When Helena returned home that evening, Rosa told her what she had done.

Helena was thrilled. "What did Régulo say when you gave him the invitation?"

"He told me he would consider it an honor to attend."

Helena danced around the room until she felt dizzy.

"I have planned a small dinner party, and I would like you to help with the cooking," Rosa told me.

"I'd love to do it. I miss the parties we used to have at the mansion."

"Well, this won't be anything like that," my sister admonished. "Whether we like it or not, our station in life has changed, at least temporarily. But we still need to make a good impression on our guests."

Chapter Thirty-Three

Chata and I cooked a sumptuous meal for the party. We brought out Mother's recipe books, washed the fine china and the crystal, cleaned and dusted all the furniture, ironed the tablecloth, and swept under the rugs. Helena was too nervous to help; after all the recipes she had memorized, she let us take care of everything.

Rosa thought it was a good idea. "You concentrate on making yourself beautiful," she told Helena. "We will take care of the rest."

"You know what Rosa means," Chata told me as she swept. "You and I will take care of the whole affair."

Rosa's only contribution was to buy roses for the mantelpiece. I suggested adding a bouquet of lilies to be placed on a side table, but Rosa said lilies were too common.

Earlier that week, Helena had asked me to send Julio and Lucy somewhere else the evening of her party.

"I hope you don't mind, Inés," she said. "The truth is, I don't want to have to explain anything to Régulo."

~

On the day of the party, I fed the children an early dinner and prepared to take them to the neighbor's house.

As I strolled down the narrow corridor, I noticed someone by the front entrance. The dark frame was in sharp contrast to the sunshine beyond the door. I walked toward the sun, holding Julio's hand and carrying Lucy in my right arm.

Julio slipped away and ran to the door, screaming "Papá! Papá!" His patent leather shoes echoed with every step. Lucy started crying. I tried to catch up with my son, but by the time I reached the threshold, Julio was holding on to the stranger's legs.

Julio's grip made the man lose his balance and knocked his hat off. He moved backward into the sunshine so the boy could recognize his mistake. I picked up the hat with my free hand, reshaped it as best I could while holding Lucy, and handed it back to him.

"I'm sorry," I told the stranger. "My son made a mistake."

Julio looked up and let go of the man's legs and trousers before hiding behind me.

"It's all right." The man put his hat on.

"Are you lost?" I asked. He looked familiar, but I could not place his face. Had I met this man before? But when? Where? A voice whispered in my ear, *He's your destiny.* All of a sudden, I remembered the face of the man that the angel in the cornfield had briefly shown me.

"I cannot find one twenty-four," he said. "The numbers stop at one nineteen."

"You're in the right place," I told him, pointing to a small tile on the other side of the door. He lifted his hat.

"Régulo Vaca Piñeros, at your service."

"Inés Camargo de Scala."

He glanced at me for a moment and then moved so that I could get by.

"If you're looking for Helena Camargo's house," I told him, "the door is at the end of the hallway. I'm her sister. I'll be back in a minute."

"Thank you," Régulo replied, lifting his hat once again. I looked at him and paused briefly before turning to take Julio's hand. As I moved, I sensed Régulo's eyes following me. Under his scrutiny I felt underdressed in my knit burgundy skirt and matching suede shoes; I tightened the fox wrap around my shoulders and walked into the sunlight feigning indifference, though my heart refused to slow down now that it knew our destinies were somehow tied.

Chapter Thirty-Four

When I returned from dropping the children off at the neighbor's house, Chata grabbed my hand and took me into the kitchen.

"What do you think about him?" she asked eagerly. "Isn't he handsome?"

"I've seen better," I replied.

"Of course, of course you have," Chata agreed while she ran around the kitchen looking for dishes. "The first thing he did when he walked in was to inquire about you!"

"We met outside. I pointed him in the right direction."

"Yes . . . yes, I know," Chata continued. "He told us. But what I mean is—"

"Chata!" Rosa called from the living room. "Where are the empanadas?"

"I'm coming!" Chata walked over to the counter to get them.

"What are you trying to say?" I asked my sister as I took a platter from the cupboard for the empanadas.

"That it's not Helena he likes, it's you."

"How would you know?"

"I just know. Helena has been laboring at pleasing him since he walked in, but all he did until your return was look at the door. Régulo will never marry her," Chata concluded as she took the platter from me and walked into the living room. I followed.

Régulo spent the rest of the evening talking to me, and when Helena coaxed him into dancing, he asked me to join him. We danced a tango. It was the latest rage just arrived from Buenos Aires. I did not know the steps, and Régulo offered to teach me. He placed a hand behind my back, put his cheek next to mine, and clutched my hand in his. I felt a tremor as we moved. His hand was shaking. His words mingled with those of the singer, and the plaintive love song became one with Régulo's voice. I felt my face flush. My knees weakened when I looked around the room. We were the only couple dancing, and all eyes were trained on our bodies as we moved to the melancholy rhythm. I closed my eyes and dreamed of making love to Régulo, while he whirled me around the floor with ease, as if he had done so endless times before.

When the song was over, I sat down between Rosa and Helena.

"I can see now why the tango got started in the bordellos in Buenos Aires," Rosa said in a condemning tone.

"Régulo," Helena called him over. "Will you teach me to dance the tango too?" He took her hand and looked at me.

After the last guest left, I went to fetch Julio and Lucy from the neighbor's house. When I returned with the children, I found Helena in the kitchen, drinking and crying into her glass.

"What's wrong?"

"You want to know what's wrong?" my sister screamed.

I handed the children to the trembling maid and asked her to put them to bed. Rosa walked in and glared at me. She threw the dishes in the sink. Many broke.

"Wait," Rosa said with a resolute tone in her voice. "Let me guess. You want to know what's wrong."

I sat down. Helena wiped her tears, blew her nose, and drank another shot. Rosa grabbed the bottle.

"You'd better stop that," she commanded. "You won't be able to go to work tomorrow. Don't think I didn't notice the way you were drinking that expensive wine he brought. You're a lady. Ladies don't get drunk."

Helena turned to face our sister. "What would you have done?"

"I would've fought for him. That's what I would have done." Rosa pointed at me. "By God, she didn't even have to find him!"

"Are you talking about me?"

"You seem surprised," Rosa sneered. She walked around the kitchen, trying to control her rage.

I turned to Helena. "All I did was talk to Régulo."

She started crying again. Rosa approached me. I thought she was going to slap me.

"All you did was talk to him, the one eligible bachelor we invited to the party so that your sister could get to know him. Couldn't you stay out of the way?" she shouted.

"What's the harm in talking?"

"What about the tango?" Helena screamed. She stood up and tried to reach for me but lost her balance and fell.

"You danced with him too," I told her.

"You call that a dance?" Rosa asked in a somber tone. "Mother should've never signed you up for ballet lessons."

"I'm glad Alessandro left you for Isabel. You deserve it!" Helena managed to say before passing out.

Rosa and I carried Helena up the stairs and put her to bed. Once we left the room, Rosa turned to me.

"You better stay away from him," she threatened. "I'm warning you."

My anger made me bold. “It’s not my fault he prefers me to Helena.”

“When are you going to stop being so selfish?” Rosa insisted.

“What do you mean?”

“Can’t you see? Régulo may want you, but he can’t have you. You’ve already ruined your life. Let Helena marry him! It’s an order.” Rosa walked into her room, slamming the door behind her.

Chapter Thirty-Five

The following day, Régulo asked Helena to deliver a note inviting me to lunch. After giving me the note, Helena took what was left from the liquor cabinet and locked herself in her room with Rosa's cigarettes.

"Go," Chata said. "Don't miss this opportunity. I'll look after the children."

Régulo hired a driver, and we went to the north just outside the city to enjoy a country luncheon. We drove past fields with cows grazing and stopped at a restaurant close to a lake.

We chose a table by the window and ordered beef and potatoes with plantains and fried yucca. Régulo produced a bottle of wine and poured a glass for me.

I inhaled the aroma. "Do you always travel with your own wine?"

"Often." Régulo poured wine into his glass. "We are not a nation of wine producers. Chances are we won't find good wines in restaurants."

"Have you always had such an interest in wine?"

"I grew up seeing it on the table, but I didn't start learning about it until I worked at Claudel and made the wine deliveries."

I took a sip. "This is superb," I pronounced. "I'm not a wine connoisseur, but my mother was very fond of it. She served it with every meal. One tradition from the past worth preserving."

"You know what they say. . . ." Régulo held his glass up to the light.

"What?"

"In vino veritas. Wine brings out the truth."

"In that case," I replied, "I'd better stop drinking now."

Régulo smiled and lit a cigarette. "You could look upon it as an opportunity to get the truth out of the way," he said in a persuasive tone. "Tell me about growing up in Paipa. What is your fondest childhood memory?"

"My first communion."

"Why?"

"I remember walking down a red carpet in my new leather shoes, wearing a beautiful chiffon dress and veil. Having communion was a mystical experience for me."

"Not for me," Régulo mused. "The only time I went to church, someone stole my hat while I was praying."

"What, then, is your fondest memory?"

"I used to enjoy lying in bed early in the morning and looking forward to my sister Fidelia bringing me a cup of hot chocolate and warm bread."

~

After lunch Régulo and I went to his house and made love for the first time. One moment we were having a conversation about the new building designed to accommodate the main offices of the railroad company and the next we were in his room, lying on his bed. It may have been unexpected, but we both knew it was meant to happen.

"My mother always said that there are no accidents," I told Régulo as we were getting dressed.

He embraced me. "I agree. Things happen for a reason," he added. "I wish my mother had had the chance to meet you. She would have loved you."

"Do you really think so?"

"Yes, and my grandmother too. In fact, when I was a child, my grandmother often said that one day I would meet a woman who would bring magic into my life. . . ." He looked into my eyes.

"You're teasing, right?" I smiled.

"No," Régulo protested. "I'm serious! Whenever she made a prediction, you listened. The women from that side of my family have all been clairvoyants. My great-great-grandmother became famous because of her gift. People would travel far to visit her in Somondoco, to ask for her advice and to benefit from her healing powers." I felt a chill down my spine.

"How do you know all this?" I asked Régulo.

"Because she left a notebook filled with notes and predictions, recipes for healing, and advice for her descendants," he replied.

"And where is that notebook?" I asked. "Could you show it to me?"

"It's in a box of books somewhere in the house. I have to look for it," he replied. "When I find it, I'll show it to you." He embraced me once more. We stayed that way for a long time.

That day we walked back to Rosa's house arm in arm as if we had been married for many years and we were out for our afternoon stroll. As I studied the colonial architecture that made Bogotá famous, watched children playing in Plaza de Bolívar, and listened to Régulo talk, I felt happy. We stopped to admire the National Capitol, which was built in the same neoclassical style as most of the other buildings in that plaza.

"Can we stop by the cathedral so I can light a candle?" I asked.

"Yes, of course," Régulo replied. We walked in, and I knelt and said a prayer. In that sacred space I marveled at the passion that had sprouted deep down inside my being. My greatest surprise was that I felt no remorse. I expected to feel guilty; after all, I had just committed adultery. And yet, I felt no guilt, no fear about the future—only a profound calm and the recognition that I had, after a long search, found a home.

As we were leaving, Régulo asked me if I had been inside the small church close to the cathedral.

"No," I replied.

"That little baroque church is my favorite one in the city," he commented. "I want to show it to you."

"Chata likes it too," I replied. Walking in, I could see why they both liked it. The church was small in scale but very beautiful.

After leaving the church we walked past Simón Bolívar's statue. It was a beautiful day with a clear sky. We stood for a while, arm in arm, watching as the doves flew around the Great Liberator and landed briefly on the ground to get the crumbs children were tossing.

When Régulo and I arrived in front of the house, we found my belongings lying in the street and Julio sitting on the front steps, looking confused.

"Where's Lucy?"

"Inside with Aunt Chata."

Régulo placed his arm under my elbow to support me.

"I'm responsible for this," he said. "I'll find a solution."

I thought I could faint and had to lean on Régulo. How could something that felt so right, so pure and special, be wrong? Why would my sisters, who were among those I loved most in the world, be angry at me for finding love? Wasn't that what Mother had wished for all of us? Wasn't that what life was all about? I had suffered plenty with Alessandro. Didn't I deserve happiness? I couldn't make Régulo love Helena any more than I could make Alessandro love me. And where was Rosa's compassion, the charity that she spoke so often about? I sat down on the step next to Julio and remembered what the angel had said. I was meant to learn, to experience joy, but also to suffer. *What will you do,* a voice inside me asked, *give in to Rosa, or choose your own path?* That day I began a new life without my sisters' blessing. It broke my heart, but I had made my choice.

~

Rosa and Helena shunned me. They thought it was disgraceful that I was living in sin with a man whom either of them would have been proud to marry.

"You're taking the wrong path," Rosa said before shutting the door one last time. "I'm going to write a letter to the Vatican. You don't deserve to be a Catholic."

Régulo set the children and me up in a house not far from his and became our provider and protector. Since I was a married woman, we had no choice.

"I'll never forget the first time I saw you," Régulo told me one night after we made love. "The shape of your long legs, your high-heeled shoes, the way you looked at me—everything about you captivated me from the start. The minute you turned to walk into the street, I knew that I belonged by your side, and that I would do anything to be next to you."

"Even if I had two children?"

"Even then."

"Even though I had a husband?"

"Even so. I'm not telling you it was rational," Régulo explained. "It felt more like the recognition of something inevitable. Without hesitation or knowledge about what I was doing, I loved you with a passion I had never felt before."

Chapter Thirty-Six

The president of the Belgian railroad company had given Régulo a three-story villa in an elegant neighborhood in Bogotá. It was decorated with the best objects and materials money could buy—Sèvres porcelain from Paris, silk curtains from Italy, rugs from Istanbul. Baccarat glass filled at least two cabinets, and the three maids Régulo employed barely had enough time to shine all the silver in a day.

One evening after dinner, while we sat in his formal living room, Régulo talked to me about his wealth.

"I have gone from being a youth with no desire for possessions to owning all the trappings of a successful life," he said. "Sometimes I lie on the couch and imagine the whole house going up in smoke after a sudden fire."

"Don't you care about your wealth?"

"It could be gone tomorrow."

Régulo's life as a bachelor was a rich one. "I used to give dinner parties once a week," he told me as he smoked a cigarette while lying on the couch. "I invited no more than ten people and treated them to a seven-course meal accompanied by the finest wines I could find."

"One of the maids told me that your soirees lasted well into the late hours of the night," I commented.

"They did."

I took a sip of Brunello. It reminded me of my first visit to Alessandro's house. At the moment, he seemed so far away.

"How did you learn so much about wine?" I asked Régulo. He drank some cognac.

"I educated myself. I own one of the most envied cellars in Bogotá; my house has become a frequent stop for Spaniards, Italians, Belgians, and the French. Here they find good food, good wine and, as a result, good conversation. It's funny," Régulo added after another sip of cognac, "someone once told me they consider themselves privileged if I ask them to dinner more than once."

"I suppose women are especially interested in getting to know you," I said.

Régulo smiled playfully and took a strand of my hair. "Now that I have you," he said, "I'm not eager to entertain. What man would not trade a busy social life for a quiet existence with the woman he loves?"

I could think of one who hadn't.

Régulo stood up. "Come," he said, "I'd like to show you my library." He took my hand and led me down a hallway to the back of the house. As we walked into the room, I noticed the light through three large windows. There were Persian rugs and walls covered with books. He had a desk, a reading chair, a lamp on a table next to it, and a sofa.

"What a beautiful room!" I exclaimed. "You should have been a writer, an intellectual instead of a businessman."

Régulo smiled. "Inés," he said, "you are the first woman to see my favorite room in the house."

I walked around Régulo's library and saw that he had a history section, one for philosophy, another one for novels, and, on a separate wall, his poetry collection.

"You must spend a great deal of time reading," I commented.

"Yes. I inherited my father's love of words," he replied.

A collection of Garcilaso de la Vega's poetry made me pause. My mind returned to the day when I read his sonnets in Paipa before Alessandro played the guitar and sang. I felt ashamed. How could I have fallen for him so easily?

Régulo interrupted my thoughts. "Why are you shaking your head?" he asked. "Don't you like Garcilaso?"

"I do," I replied, returning to the present. "I studied his sonnets with my tutor in Paipa, even memorized some of them. I was just remembering the time I read several of his poems to guests at a social gathering. Alessandro was there. I had just met him. When I think about those early days, I get mad at myself for being so naïve."

Régulo placed a hand on my shoulder. "Don't blame yourself, Inés," he said. "You were young and inexperienced, like Alfonsina Storni, one of my favorite poets. She fell in love with a married man. Have you heard of her?"

"I've read some of her work," I replied. "She's very outspoken."

"The French philosopher Charles Fourier would call Alfonsina a *féministe*," Régulo mused. "She believes men and women should be equal."

"So do I," I replied. "But I don't know if that will ever happen."

"It may take time," Régulo said, "but it will happen." He sounded so convinced, I felt a wave of love for him. I turned around and kissed him. He took a couple of books from the shelf and beckoned me to join him on the sofa.

"Why don't we take turns reading poems?" he asked. "Our own private poetry reading."

"I would love that!" I said, settling next to him.

"You read first," Régulo suggested, giving me Storni's *Languidez.*

"It's one of her early works," he explained, "published in 1920."

"How do you know?" I asked.

"I've read it."

"I had no idea you liked poetry so much," I commented, flipping to the dedication page and reading *"To those who, like me, didn't attain even one of their dreams."*

"How sad," I said.

"I told you," Régulo said, "Alfonsina has had a hard life, not only as a woman, but also as an artist and a single mother."

"She's a mother?"

"Yes, she had a son at twenty," Régulo replied. "Her married lover didn't help her at all."

"I can relate to that," I commented. "It's hard enough to be a female artist in a man's world. To have children and a husband or a lover on top of that makes it practically impossible. But tell me," I said, turning to face Régulo. "When do you have time to read poems?"

"I read a poem every night before I fall asleep," he explained.

"Which is your favorite poem in this book?" I asked, glancing at the table of contents.

"My favorite poem by Storni is in another book," Régulo replied. He stood up and started looking through the poetry section. "Here it is!" he said. "'Capricho.' It's included in this brief volume published early in her career."

"I like 'Hombre pequeñito,'" I commented.

"So you are familiar with her work!" Régulo concluded enthusiastically.

"Yes," I replied. "I like her use of irony and admire her courage—the way she writes about taboo subjects and tries to break free from the mold that female writers before her and those of her generation have been subjected to."

Régulo raised his index finger and shook it. "You've been keeping your love of poetry from me!"

I laughed. "Who is your favorite poet?"

"At present, César Vallejo," he replied.

"The Peruvian writer who lives in Paris?"

"Yes. I'm interested in his work more than in his political views, though," Régulo commented.

"Have you heard his poem 'Los heraldos negros'?"

"Who hasn't?" he asked before beginning to recite the first lines. "*Hay golpes en la vida, tan fuertes . . . Yo no sé!* Some blows in life, they're so heavy . . . I don't know." We went on together. "Blows as if dealt by God's own wrath, as if, ahead, / the rip of every single thing we'd ever suffered / had pooled inside our souls . . . I don't know."

"These lines always make me cry," I said.

Régulo wiped a tear from my cheek and kissed me.

~

My love for Alessandro seemed like another lifetime. I wondered what had brought Régulo and me together. How could I have loved two men and have lain in their arms and still feel so differently toward them? I admired Alessandro's artistic ability, his music, and his knowledge of the world. Régulo had worked hard and traveled widely. His sophistication came through when he spoke and when he chose a wine or a gourmet dish.

What I had had with Alessandro, I now knew, had been a strong attraction. Perhaps I had loved him, but not in the passionate way in which I now loved Régulo.

On the surface Alessandro would always come out the winner. He was the more handsome of the two, the most dashing, charismatic, witty, and refined. His family had strong ties to Italian culture, and he had studied briefly at the university.

Régulo had never been to a university. He came from a family that was far from being pure European stock and did not initially strike a person as witty or refined. Yet he had gone far in a short time. He was successful in his field, gifted in languages, and self-educated. Besides, his personality had an intensity that never went unnoticed. He was passionate about life, and I became passionate about him. What I liked most about Régulo, though, was the way he tilted his head to the side and listened when I spoke. I knew Alessandro had never heard me, and if he had never heard me, how could he have loved me? Régulo's love was silent and profound. He looked upon me as his equal, and that made me immensely happy.

Chapter Thirty-Seven

After making love, Régulo and I would spend hours talking. Every day I discovered something new about him while I lay in his arms.

He grew up in a privileged household in his hometown, just like I did in Paipa. He was born in Somondoco, Boyacá, in 1904. Gregorio Vaca, Régulo's father, was Somondoco's mayor and its most prominent citizen. His greatest claim to fame was that he married into the wealthiest family in town, no small accomplishment for a "foreigner," an outsider from Garagoa.

I looked at Régulo on the bed, his black wavy hair tousled. His dark eyes turned to glance at me.

"Do you look like your father?"

"From him I inherited my dark skin and eyes. My mother had European blood." Régulo took a last drag from his cigarette, extinguished what was left into an ashtray, and lay down on his side, facing me. For a while we looked at each other. The sunlight filtering through the curtains brightened parts of his face. His high cheekbones had the faintest color on them. He raised his hand to stroke my hair. We did not speak. His fingers touched my lips and I was lost to him again.

I had never made love with anyone but Alessandro, nor had

I lain in bed during the day, the bright light of the sun streaming through the windows. I knew about the nuances of ardor by candlelight with my husband, but until that day I had been unaware that desire and passion do not require late hours, candlelight, or marriage. In me they bloomed not like a tender rose from my mother's garden, but like an orchid growing as an epiphyte on a forest tree, wild and fragrant in the warm tropical forest. It was altogether different to be lying in Régulo's arms, as if I had done so a thousand times before in a thousand different countries during a thousand different lives. In Régulo's arms, I became a woman.

I lay on my belly on the bed, wondering how it could be that Régulo and I felt so comfortable in each other's presence. We had met recently, and yet he understood my body as well as a mountain climber who has been down the same path countless times. He knew where to find the plants that grow and flourish and where to avoid the spiny ones, which way to turn, and how many steps to take before discovering the brook with icy water, the breathtaking view of snow-covered peaks.

It surprised me to think that I had never felt the longing, the desire, in my husband's presence that I now felt for Régulo. As the angel in the cornfield had predicted, I had loved and also suffered, and I was now learning that the shades of heartache are many, that being betrayed and abandoned is great cause for grief, but that when the heart chooses, it will not be dissuaded.

~

I don't know if it is true that Gregorio Vaca read every book he was lucky enough to find, but I believed Régulo when he told me that the more his father read, the more his passion grew.

According to Régulo, when Gregorio decided to marry, his calculation was not based on how much land he would have or how many cows he would own, but on how many books he would be able to afford with his wife's dowry.

"My mother's family had a vast library with books in Latin, Greek, Spanish, Italian, French, and German," Régulo said. "The library captured Father's heart. No one knew much about my father when he started courting Mother, but his flair and his imagination won her over. He impressed her by reciting whole passages from works by Herodotus, Cicero, and Plato. After their marriage, she financed his political career and filled his pockets."

"That reminds me of my father," I said. "He also liked to read and sat for hours in my mother's rose garden with a book in his hands. After he married my mother, he quit working. He didn't need to earn a living, given her wealth."

"Father has never had to work a day in his life," Régulo went on. "Following Mother's death, he inherited her fortune and continued leading a comfortable existence. Whenever he ran out of money, he raised cash by selling a cow, a calf, a house, or a piece of land."

When I went to Somondoco the first time, Régulo took me to see his family home. It was a large pink house with a bright-green stripe around the bottom. Located in the center of the town square, it stood majestically next to the cathedral. A wooden veranda wrapped around the second floor, adorned with orchids and colorful *mecedoras*, similar to rocking chairs.

As we stood outside the house, Régulo pointed at the veranda. "It was from this spot," he said, "that I first learned to watch the world and the people in it. My sisters told me that before I turned two, I would climb on one of the *mecedoras*, get comfortable, and observe the citizens of Somondoco as they went to the market on

Thursdays, to church on Sundays, and for evening strolls around the plaza." He lit a cigarette and stood in silence for a minute.

I felt the warm equatorial sun on my back. "It's a lovely house," I said.

"It was also from this veranda that I first saw a man killed after a discussion about politics in that bar across the street," Régulo continued.

"What happened?"

"Father ran out when he heard the screams, but the wounded man was already on the ground, his enemy holding the bloody machete in his hand and speaking as if in a trance. 'These damn Liberals will ruin the country,' he said before cleaning the blood off his machete with his handkerchief, placing it back in the sheath, and walking away."

"How old were you?"

"Too young to witness death."

~

Régulo was the youngest child born to his parents. Having lost his mother at an early age, his sisters Ana Tulia and Fidelia took care of him. When I met them during my first visit to Somondoco, I could not help but notice how protective they were toward their brother.

"Did Régulo tell you that we nicknamed him Principito, little prince?" Ana Tulia asked me.

"No, he didn't," I replied. "Why little prince?"

"Because he's always been our little prince, and we treat him like one."

During my first visit the sisters organized a tea to introduce me to the prominent citizens of the town. I was expecting a simple event and was surprised to find out they had planned an elaborate party with more than a hundred guests. I offered to help, but Ana Tulia would not hear of it. Fidelia said I was their guest and should rest for the party. I was relieved when they sent me out for a walk with Régulo.

Fidelia and Ana Tulia were accomplished cooks and housekeepers, and with their mother's inheritance they opened the first hotel in Somondoco. I stayed there under Fidelia's watchful eye while Régulo remained in his family home.

Adjacent to the hotel was one of the best restaurants in the region of Boyacá, and it was also run by the sisters. They called it La Odisea in honor of Homer. The restaurant had its own bakery.

"As a boy, I woke up early in the morning to the aroma of fresh coffee," Régulo told me when I commented on how delicious breakfast was. "The bakery is the most successful part of the business." On the second day of my visit, Fidelia gave me a tour of the restaurant. Three large wooden tables in the kitchen were dedicated to kneading bread dough.

"Every morning at four I come down to knead dough among the hired bakers," she told me.

"They need my help," Fidelia insisted during dinner when Gregorio brought up the fact that she often ran into him in the dark hallway or found him reading by candlelight.

"I always shake a finger at her," Gregorio said, "but it doesn't make a difference." He turned to his daughter. "You're not fooling me. You're still baking *pan de yuca* for your brother. Both you and Ana Tulia have spoiled him. Inés, would you believe me if I told you that they send Régulo bread once a week? As if people in Bogotá did not know how to bake!"

"Father, you would complain, too, if you did not get fresh *almojábanas* and *pan de yuca* for breakfast," Ana Tulia interceded, "so we've spoiled you as well. Besides, you can't blame Fidelia for wanting to do things correctly around here." Her sister nodded in agreement.

~

By the time we traveled to Somondoco, Régulo and I were used to waiting for the sun to rise and the world to wake while we lay in each other's arms.

After three nights, we could not bear to be apart. Régulo decided he would join me at midnight when the last candle was blown out. There were times when he almost collided with someone in the hallway. Other times Fidelia would knock on my door to see if I needed anything, and I feared she would turn the knob and find it locked.

One night, while we lay in bed before the ritual of adieu, I talked to Régulo about my concerns.

"Don't be silly," he said. "My family adores you." He stroked my leg with one hand and held a cigarette in the other. "They can see I'm happy."

"Have you told them about Alessandro?" I ventured.

"Not yet, but I will."

"What about Julio and Lucy? Chata won't always be free to look after them. We were lucky this time."

"My sisters visit me in Bogotá twice a year. Sooner or later, they'll meet the children."

"Régulo," I said, holding his hand, "I'm older than you."

"Just a couple of years." He laughed. "You're the only woman for me, Inés. My family will have to get used to it."

~

In Somondoco, Fidelia and Ana Tulia told me many stories about Régulo's childhood. I wanted to know everything there was to know about his past.

"My brother was tutored during the early years of his life, just like Father, and he learned to read at an early age," Fidelia said one day while she was making tamales. "Upon his graduation from elementary school, Father's best friend, Eusebio Vargas, gave Régulo a beautiful scented bar of soap from Florence."

"I remember that!" Ana Tulia interrupted while she handed her sister more chicken for the tamales.

"Even before he opened it," Fidelia went on, "we all knew it was the most delicious-smelling soap we would ever use to wash our hands. The bar was in a dark-green box with an elaborate design on it and an inscription that read, *Vellutina, Crema di Sapone*. Velvet soap.

"As Régulo opened the box, Eusebio explained that he had bought it in one of the oldest pharmacies in the world, Santa Maria Novella, located behind the train station since the 1700s.

"Inside the green box, there was a delicate soap wrapped in transparent white paper and sealed with a golden emblem. Régulo took the soap out. He closed his eyes and inhaled its aroma. Remember what he said?" Fidelia asked her sister.

"No, I don't."

"He said he wanted to travel. He wanted to go to Florence and buy more soap at Santa Maria Novella," Fidelia recited.

Ana Tulia laughed. "Eusebio also gave Régulo Dante's *Divine Comedy*."

Fidelia took a handkerchief from her sleeve and wiped her forehead. She had dark hair and eyes like her brother, but her skin was lighter. "Régulo finished reading the *Inferno* on the same day he used up his last morsel of soap. It left a lingering scent in the bathroom for a month," she continued.

"Did he ever get another bar of soap?" I asked.

"Years later, when he traveled through Florence, he went to Santa Maria Novella and bought more velvet soap," Fidelia answered.

Chapter Thirty-Eight

It was difficult for me to believe that at one time, Régulo and his family had moved to the capital. I saw the sisters settled in their home in Somondoco and in their restaurant, I observed his father sitting on the veranda while reading, and I could not imagine them living in the heart of Bogotá. I begged Régulo to tell me how their move had come about.

"When he had too much to drink, my father went down to the river to burn money," Régulo told me.

"Why?"

"He enjoyed it. After my mother's death, Father got drunk in the local bar, engaged in a political discussion, and realized he could end up dead. He put his machete away, stopped by the house to fetch me, and went down to the river to burn bills. The aroma of burning money always relaxed him. After the last piece of paper had been scattered by the wind, Father decided that we would all move to Bogotá. For a long time, he watched the ashes of his fortune. Then he lit his pipe.

"I waited for him to finish smoking. He took my hand and we walked back to town. Hours later, Father gathered the family around the dinner table and announced that we were moving to the capital."

"Did he tell your sisters that his life was in danger?"

"He said that Somondoco was not for us. Bogotá was brimming with opportunities. 'I'm not thinking about myself as much as I'm thinking about you,' he told Fidelia and Ana Tulia. 'If we stay here, I may see one of my daughters married to a Conservative. That would be a sin. This country needs more political parties; we can't continue to murder each other for our ideals.'

"Father decided not to sell the house. It took us a month to pack and make travel arrangements. We placed our belongings in wooden boxes and stored them in the attic. The windows were shut, the furniture was covered with linen sheets, and the food not needed for the trip was donated to the help. I was so excited about the prospect of going to the capital that I forgot to pack," he added.

I laughed. "It must have been hard for you to leave your town, though, your home. It was hard for me to sell my childhood home and leave Paipa."

"For me it was more like an adventure," Régulo said. "But it was difficult for my sisters."

"Well, you were young, and you probably didn't understand how that move would change your lives."

"That's true. On the final day, Father took an old trumpet out of its case, dusted it off, and played the national anthem. Then he stood straight and made his solemn announcement.

"'I will be locking the doors in a couple of minutes.'

"It was then that I realized my mistake. 'Wait!' I shouted. 'I'm not packed yet.'

"'There's room for one more box,' Father said as he lit his pipe. 'If you didn't think of it, it's not important. You can help carry those,' he added, pointing to a bunch of boxes in the corner packed with gold. 'One should travel light with luggage and loaded with money, and that we are, thanks to your dear mother, may she rest in peace.' Father raised the pipe to his mouth and inhaled deeply.

"'Régulo, let me pack your books in my suitcase,' Ana Tulia pleaded. 'I'm putting it in the carriage.'

"'We have no more room in there,' Father exhaled. 'We'll have to take turns riding and walking.'

"I handed the books to my sister. Father watched her open her suitcase in the middle of the road.

"'You'll get tired of Dante just like I did of politics,' he told me. 'You should have brought Cervantes. He would keep you better company.'"

"Your father was right," I agreed.

~

Régulo went down to the kitchen, made some coffee for us, and brought it up to the bedroom.

"Are you sure no one heard you?" I asked. He kissed me softly and continued with his story.

"Halfway through the journey, my leather shoes had to come off and be replaced with farmers' alpargatas. They made my swollen feet feel better." He stirred sugar into his coffee.

"How long did it take you to get to Bogotá?" I tried to imagine Régulo in alpargatas.

"A week later around dusk, we spotted the first city buildings in the distance. Everyone grew silent. Father stopped and lit his pipe.

"'I feel like a king with his court about to enter into an ancient city,' he said. 'Pity we do not have walls or gates to pass. The streets are not strewn with flowers, and no musicians play. What a reception.' I wondered if all that reading had gone to his head. Soon he would be seeing windmills.

"Fidelia and Ana Tulia sat on their suitcases. I unwrapped my leather shoes and forced my swollen feet into them.

"'Why are you doing that?' Father asked.

"'I don't want to walk into the city in alpargatas,' I told him."

"So even as a young boy, you were a dandy!" I ran my fingers through his hair. "Then what happened?"

"No one spoke. We all sensed the beginning of a new life."

Chapter Thirty-Nine

When Gregorio and his family arrived in Bogotá, they went to the historic district, La Candelaria neighborhood, not far from Rosa's house.

"Father pointed to a house across from the cathedral and lit his pipe," Régulo told me. "Fidelia, Ana Tulia, and I looked at each other while Father stood smoking, deep in thought. He turned to me. 'Régulo, go knock on the door and ask to speak to the owner. Then tell him I want to buy his house furnished.' I had to knock several times before a maid in uniform appeared, followed by an elderly gentleman. When he stepped out, I assumed he was the owner."

"And what did you say?"

"I said, 'Hello, sir. My name is Régulo Vaca. I was wondering if you would like to sell your house furnished.' He laughed and asked if I had the money to pay for it. I pointed across the street to the trunks loaded with gold. We moved in two days later."

~

The sun was gone. In the dusk, Régulo's face was hardly visible.

Our arms and limbs, wrapped around each other, were impossible to distinguish and separate.

"Are you hungry?" Régulo asked me.

"Yes."

"There's a tiny Italian restaurant around the corner. All we have to do is go down the stairs and turn. I'll continue with the story while we get dressed."

It was a cool evening. I took Régulo's arm, and we walked at a leisurely pace.

"Six months after we moved to Bogotá, a man in a three-piece suit with a Stetson hat and a gold cane knocked on the door. When Fidelia opened the door, the stranger said he wanted to speak with Don Gregorio.

"'Don Gregorio is taking a nap and does not want to be disturbed,' my sister answered without asking him in.

"'He'd want to see me,' the gentleman insisted. 'We go back a long time.'

"'That's funny,' my sister replied. 'I go back a long time too, and I don't remember you. What's your name?'

"'Ovidio Lopez. I left Somondoco years before you were born.'

"'If you want to wait for Father to wake up, you're welcome to stay,' my sister replied.

"Ovidio accepted, and when my father woke up from his nap, he took his afternoon bath and went down to greet him.

"Señor Lopez and Father had grown up together in Garagoa. Ovidio followed Father to Somondoco. After marrying a Bogotana, he moved to the capital and studied law.

"Following the customary greetings, Señor Lopez told Father that he had a client interested in his land in Somondoco. He offered Father a whole block of La Candelaria in exchange for his land in our hometown.

"'My client is from there. You might know him. Remember the Alarcón kids?'

"All Father remembered about them was that they wore no shoes to school. Ovidio was amused. 'Alvaro discovered a gold mine about ten years ago,' he told us. 'His ambition is to own Somondoco, just like he owns a part of Bogotá.' It was during that time that the new rich started cropping up like mushrooms," Régulo added. "I'm glad my father did not sell."

Gregorio Vaca refused Alvaro Alarcón's offer, and most of the family returned to Somondoco. Deciphering the universe and its meaning was easier in Somondoco than in Bogotá; besides, Gregorio was a man of simple tastes. He could not understand why city people had so many uses for money. Money he could burn.

Chapter Forty

When I met him during my first trip to Somondoco, Régulo's father told me he didn't like the fancy ways of city folk. I could not picture Gregorio anywhere else in the world except on his veranda with a book on his lap. No one could blame him for returning to Somondoco, where he had become accustomed to his life as a dandy and mayor.

Régulo stopped in front of the Italian restaurant. "Here we are," he said. "Let's forget about the past and enjoy the present. Do you like lasagna?"

"I do. But wait," I added. "I have one last question. Did you go back with your father to Somondoco?"

"Ana Tulia and Fidelia did; I stayed."

"How old were you?"

"Seventeen."

We walked into the restaurant, a small dark room with colorful tablecloths. The owner gave us a table by the corner, lit a candle, and placed a bottle of Chianti with two glasses in front of us. Régulo ordered, took my hand, and caressed my fingers one by one. He poured Chianti and raised his glass.

"To our life together."

His words reminded me that there was a world beyond the

restaurant walls, a world that might not welcome our love with enthusiasm. I raised my glass, inhaled the aroma, closed my eyes, and took a sip of wine.

Sitting at a corner table in the Italian restaurant and listening to *La Traviata*, Régulo and I did not feel the urgency to lie in each other's arms. A glance, a word, brought us together for a moment I would always remember. That night I understood what intimacy was.

I begged Régulo to continue with his story. He lit a cigarette.

"Before leaving, Father gave me a box full of gold. 'When you run out, send for more,' he told me."

"Did you?"

"No. I thanked him, but I wanted to work to earn a living."

~

Régulo's first job was in a French store named Claudel, a combination of paper, liquor, candy, and cigarette store. *Boutique* might be a better term for it, since the items they sold were imported and expensive. Glenmorangie from Scotland, Belgian chocolates, English tea, and beluga caviar. I remembered walking by the store with Chata and marveling at the delicacies in the window. Liquor we'd never seen before, pink almonds strewn about, and beautiful boxes of chocolates wrapped in red bows impressive enough to tie braids.

At Claudel, Régulo did not limit himself to delivering merchandise. He also spoke with the clients and befriended them.

"I dressed impeccably. My white shirt was properly starched just in case I had to meet an important client," Régulo told me. He was always dressed so; I couldn't imagine him any other way.

"During one of my deliveries, a client greeted me in French.

"'Bonjour,' he said.

"'Bonjour, monsieur,' I replied as I carried in a case of Dom Pérignon.

"'You speak French?'

"'I have been studying it at night.'

"'Have you learned the subjunctive?'

"'Not yet, but I will,' I told him. He handed me a generous tip.

"French became useful six months later, when I was offered a job at the railroad company owned and run by the Belgians in Colombia."

~

The restaurant was now crowded. Couples sat, drinking wine and eating. A round table in the back was filled with Italian men celebrating someone's birthday. As they sang, I remembered Florence.

For dessert, Régulo and I ordered a cake made with almonds and cream called *torta della nonna*, grandmother's cake. We shared the piece and drank *spumante* while he finished his story.

"I started as a supervisor at one of the local train stations, and for a year continued to learn French," Régulo told me. "Then I received a promotion and another one, and before long I was running the whole company for the Belgians. I travel to Europe twice a year and have the opportunity to learn Italian as well." He took the last bite of cake. "Now English is gaining ground."

"Do you speak English?"

"I study the language in private, but I never speak it."

"Why?" I could not envision what it was like to come to know the universe in other languages, to see and understand it in English or in French.

"Something about English makes me feel uncomfortable," Régulo answered. "I just can't imagine anyone expressing their feelings in that language."

"Try," I suggested. "Tell me you love me in English."

Régulo took my hand. "You are a bold woman, Inés Scala."

"Please call me Inés Camargo," I said. "That last name has brought me nothing but bad luck. I don't want to be reminded of my past."

He kissed my fingers. "*Te amo* in English is 'I love you,' Inés Camargo."

"Now say it in French."

His eyes had the same expression, but the words were more melodious.

"Je t'aime," Régulo pronounced as he brought his face close to mine. *"Ti amo, te amo."* He reached my lips.

"You're the bold one." I laughed. "Kissing me in public!"

Chapter Forty-One

Helena went back to Paipa and begged Father Rossi to write me a letter admonishing me to leave Régulo. After reading the letter, I decided to get advice from Reverend Minder. I had no luck finding him and gave up after two weeks, wondering if he had left the country without discovering El Dorado.

Rosa and Helena were not the only ones who considered my relationship with Régulo a mistake. Fidelia wrote me a letter.

Inés,

How shocking to discover that you are married and have two children. Think about what you are doing. We begged Régulo to end it, but he won't listen. You will never be accepted into our family.

Fidelia

Gregorio Vaca died unexpectedly that year. "I know in my heart," Régulo told me, "that Father would understand our situation. He welcomed you with open arms in Somondoco. It was clear he appreciated your beauty, your style, your intelligence, and the air of mystery that surrounds you."

As for Fidelia and Ana Tulia, both sisters had worked hard all their lives to protect Régulo. I was two years older than him and officially married to Alessandro Scala. They could not comprehend how their brother, an intelligent and promising young man, had managed to ruin his future through his foolish choice. Not to mention the children. If Régulo and I had any, they would be born out of wedlock. Lucy and Julio were a heavy load.

"They'll do nothing but bring you down," Fidelia told her brother when she showed up at his house unannounced and found us there, having lunch.

Régulo was aware of his sisters' opinions. He couldn't understand their blind judgment and their adamant refusal to accept me. For my part, I was saddened by the rift I had caused between them, but I had my own troubles to think about: a failed marriage, two children, and little money left after paying off Alessandro's debts. My own family looked upon me as an unnecessary burden. All these things I knew. And yet, Régulo's love had given me the strength to face my fears and get on with my life. I chose to accept what he had so generously offered and make the best of it.

My delicate features and sensuality had captivated Régulo. I was beautiful still, maybe even more so after motherhood. Carrying two children had softened my lines and added a little weight, which suited me well. My skin was as soft as ever, my light-brown hair had a healthy shine, and my eyes were still mysterious.

One morning, while I sat in my boudoir after Régulo had left for work, I remembered Rosa's condemnation. "You don't deserve to be a Catholic," she had said. I looked in the mirror and felt inundated with guilt for living with Régulo, for having "stolen" him from Helena, as Rosa implied, for not being able to keep Alessandro, and for failing my children.

I went to church and prayed to God, confessed my sins, and

said my Our Fathers, and still I could not overcome the feeling of guilt that had taken hold of me, shaking my life and my whole foundation.

Chapter Forty-Two

I settled in the house Régulo rented for us with Lucy and Julio and went about trying to organize my life and theirs.

Although like my mother, Aura, I am not inclined to structure, I did my best to come up with a reasonable compromise between artistic pursuits and serious family matters. In my world, playing the guitar, singing, dancing, and painting took precedence. Determined to expose Julio and Lucy to art, I bought oils and during my free time sat outside and painted.

Régulo had an appreciation for art as well, but he had decided to build an empire and spent countless hours thinking about ways in which he could make it come about. He did not mind my artistic temperament, but sometimes I got the impression that he would have preferred a more practical approach to life from me.

A few days after we moved, we hired a maid to cook and clean. With the maid, there was time to take the children out, go shopping, read a book, or play. Régulo came to the house for lunch and dinner and gradually started spending more time with us. Some evenings he was too tired to return home. Others, he had no desire to sleep alone.

One morning, Fidelia traveled from Somondoco to see me.

I was in my room, still combing my hair, and greeted Régulo's sister while I braided it.

"Régulo went to work," I told her.

"It's not him I want to see." Fidelia looked at the unmade bed disapprovingly. "It's you."

"What do you want from me?" I tied a ribbon around my braid.

"I want to know why you insist on dragging him down. Do you realize what this is doing to his career?"

"I don't think it's any of your business," I said, turning to look in the mirror.

"Régulo did not go home last night," Fidelia informed me. "I was there waiting for him. People know he spends many nights here."

"That's his choice. He's a grown man."

"*This* is a Catholic country. *You* are a married woman. He can't marry you. Your union will never be accepted. If you do love him, think of that."

Fidelia's words had the desired effect on me. For the rest of the day, I wondered if I was being fair to Régulo. I was aware of the passion I inspired in him, and I found it flattering that such an accomplished man had changed his life to be with me.

Having loved Alessandro, I was familiar with the suffering love can cause. Yet, from the first time Régulo touched my skin, I knew that my relationship with him was meant to be—that regardless of life's situations and inconveniences or people's opinions and condemnations, Régulo and I would be together and perhaps one day discover why fate had joined us.

For his part, Régulo knew I was troubled, but he was determined to change that; he would win me over, he said, as if he hadn't already.

Régulo took good care of me and showered as much attention on Julio and Lucy as he could. However, sometimes his enthusiasm vanished.

"Your love for me will never equal mine for you," he'd say.

"What makes you think that, darling?"

"There's no logic behind it," he would answer. "Love is irrational."

I made an effort to reassure him, but there was a part of him I could not reach, no matter how hard I tried.

~

Our intimate conversations took place either in bed or at the dinner table after the children had gone to sleep. During those moments, we would share a cognac and talk.

"How can you measure love?" I asked Régulo one evening. "It's not made up of chips."

"Maybe you can't measure it the way you would measure money, but there are other ways," he replied. "A comment here, a look there, a feeling in your gut that tells you it would be impossible to live without that other person . . . knowing you love too much." Régulo lit a cigarette and inhaled.

"Can you love too much?"

"Yes."

"When?"

"When it ends for one but not the other," he answered.

"Is love finite?" I pressed on. "Is it bound to end, or is our ability to withstand it finite?"

Régulo glanced at the maid clearing the table. "All around us we are bound by the finite, but we search for the infinite," he said. "That's why religion is important."

"I thought it was our sense of guilt that made it important."

Régulo laughed. "You should know; you carry your guilt everywhere you go."

Régulo couldn't blame me for feeling guilty. My sisters were watching and waiting for me to continue making mistakes. They talked of excommunication, of sin, of burning in hell.

~

As a director of the railroad company, Régulo could not afford a scandal. Living with a married woman and her children would give his enemies the opportunity to destroy his reputation.

When he worked long hours, Régulo did not make it back in time for lunch or dinner. Sometimes I went looking for him and brought him a meal, but we couldn't talk in front of his colleagues. Helena had been spreading rumors about us and had already told her supervisor, hoping that Régulo would be let go. Fortunately, Régulo's boss was very fond of him and decided to warn him.

"Your personal life is your business, Régulo," the man went on, "but don't let it ruin your career."

After Régulo told me about the meeting with his supervisor, I went less frequently to his office for the sake of peace. Even though Régulo said his boss was not terribly religious and didn't seem to mind our relationship, I thought we should keep in mind that we lived in a Catholic country where marriage and love were looked upon as synonyms.

"What about kindness and charity?" Régulo asked me. "Your sister seems to lack both. Spending all that time in church with Rosa doesn't seem to help at all. I guess she thinks the Gospel is for others, not for her."

I didn't laugh. I wasn't in the mood to joke about my sisters. How could Helena be so petty and selfish? It was clear she didn't care about me—that she was jealous, like Isabel. But going after Régulo, trying to ruin his reputation and get him fired, was unforgivable.

Consequently, Régulo and I did not have the life of a regular couple. I did not attend the social functions organized at the railroad company, and after Helena's attempt to ruin our relationship, I stopped going to see him at the office. I could never be Régulo's official partner; the Catholic Church would not allow it. *If only Father Rossi had stood his ground and refused to marry me to Alessandro,* I sometimes thought. But then I remembered the angel, and my mother's words: "There are no accidents."

~

The passion I felt for Régulo came upon me so suddenly, I did not know how to adjust to it. For the first time, I understood what it felt like to learn a foreign language and one day discover that the world is somehow different and richer because of a new vocabulary to describe the self and those around it. Now I knew why Mother wrote poetry, why she tended her rose garden with such care. Beauty, like love, must have its caretakers.

My previous life with Alessandro appeared weak and shallow. I realized I had not loved my husband; his betrayal had not meant as much to me as I had imagined.

My love for Régulo gave me strength. It had already led me to do things I never thought I would—to leave my family behind, to stop caring about public opinion, to reconcile to my fate as a fallen Catholic. Still, I had not managed to eliminate the sense of guilt that took hold of me periodically. Perhaps one day.

Without my sisters, I felt isolated. But I am not jealous by nature and got on with my life.

Chapter Forty-Three

Régulo looked forward to having dinner with the children and me, but his desire was not triggered by any of the elaborate dishes I sometimes prepared since I had learned to cook. Sitting around the dining room table with Lucy and Julio reminded him of his childhood in Somondoco.

"You are a beautiful woman, Inés Camargo," he said when I greeted him in the study with his aperitif.

"I hope you'll always think that," I replied, kissing him. "Even after time has filled my face with wrinkles and made my bones brittle."

Julio's favorite food was bread. He never got enough of it. During the evening meal, he ate four or five rolls, and often someone was left without.

One night, after Julio continued to take rolls out of the basket, Régulo flew into a rage. He ordered the maid to buy more bread and sent Julio to his room, saying, "Don't come out until you finish the whole bag."

I was quiet the rest of the evening. After dinner, Régulo tried to talk to me.

"Julio needs to eat other things besides bread."

"You didn't have to get so angry."

"You're right," he admitted. "It's not Julio. I'm just worried about the future. There's nothing I would like more than to marry you, walk arm in arm with you, and introduce you as my love, my wife."

"We've already discussed that," I reminded him gently.

"I have an idea," Régulo said. "Listen to me. We could go to Ecuador and get married over there."

"We could."

"I'll start getting the paperwork ready."

~

At night, after we closed our bedroom door, the fears, the ghosts, and the past were left behind, and Régulo and I looked at each other as we had that first day when he unbuttoned my blouse. Regardless of our situation, I was happy.

During the day, I dedicated my time to Julio and Lucy. We mounted a little wooden theater in the patio and spent many afternoons performing plays. I sewed the costumes and helped with the dialogue. When singing and dancing were called for, I would bring out the small guitar from my Paipa days.

On these occasions, Régulo was quick to laugh. When I picked up the guitar, he smiled. "You were born to sing and play," Régulo would say. "I feel privileged to have an artist for a partner, even if I don't understand you."

"What man can understand a woman?"

~

Although he lived with me, shared the same dinner table and bed, loved me passionately, and made love to me with the same passion, Régulo always felt that there was a part of me I did not reveal. How could he understand that what had happened with Alessandro had hurt me in a way that I might never get over, or that after Alessandro and Isabel had broken my heart, I had trouble trusting anyone else? Isabel's betrayal and my sisters' disapproval had taken a toll on me. Deep down I sensed that our love would survive, but daily I struggled to remain open and optimistic, to give part of myself away while at the same time staying true to my art. How could I be available and willing to listen, run a household, and take care of the children while also devoting time to my painting? Sometimes I felt that being a mother, a lover, and a household manager could consume me, and I fought hard to keep a little bit of myself private so that I would have something that was only mine, a source of my creativity. For although I thought having children was a creative act in the true meaning of the word, and bringing children into this world meant being selfless for a period and devoting yourself to raising them, I wondered why men didn't seem to have to make these choices—even if, like Alessandro, they were not the breadwinners. I was always trying to conserve some energy until the next time I could pick up my paintbrush and stand in front of a canvas, dreaming.

"Inés, you're a mysterious woman," Régulo would tell me as he looked at me, as if trying to read my mind. I smiled and did not deny what I knew to be true. "I was your second choice," he said when he was feeling gloomy.

"What lover wouldn't want to be the only one?" I asked.

Régulo had a jealous nature, and when he thought about my previous life with Alessandro, bitterness took hold of him, and he had to fight hard to keep it from enveloping him. I seldom spoke about my childhood in Paipa and my marriage to Alessandro. I sensed I was treading on dangerous soil.

My aloofness both tormented and captivated Régulo. He savored the moment when I rose from bed to put my clothes on and watched me as I bent to gather my stockings around my ankles before pulling them up.

"Why must you always get dressed so soon?" he asked as he lay in bed smoking a cigarette.

"Being naked is a sin," I answered as I pulled up my stocking.

Régulo laughed. "According to whom?"

"Father Rossi."

"For all you know, he's dead. You're beautiful naked, Inés Camargo. If I could paint like Goya, *La Maja Desnuda* would have competition."

I buttoned my skirt.

Chapter Forty-Four

When Gregorio died, Fidelia and Ana Tulia kept the restaurant and the hotel, but they decided to sell the family home. They informed Régulo about their decision once the papers had been signed. First he was outraged, then he remembered a farm outside of town that his father had owned. Régulo approached his sisters and asked them to name a price. Buying the farm made up for the disillusionment he went through over losing his family home.

One year after he set me up in the new house in Bogotá, Régulo and I traveled to Somondoco and stayed at his father's farmhouse outside of town. From then on, we always spent the holidays there.

Our travel ritual included a four-hour journey on a bumpy road. Once Lucy was old enough, she and Julio rode in the back of the truck on top of sacks of grain. Régulo and I sat in front with the driver. I grew to enjoy the ride to Somondoco. The landscape reminded me of Paipa.

As soon as we left Bogotá, the temperature dropped, and Julio and Lucy wrapped themselves in coats and blankets. Dark-brown mountains pierced the sky, and broken fences surrounded dirty fields with cows grazing. We passed the clotheslines and shacks at the outskirts.

When we were getting closer, we felt the warm air. We passed banana trees and peasants taking pigs to town. After two or three sharp turns, we spotted a guava tree, a light-blue house, and a row of wooden crosses commemorating deaths on that dangerous road. Then we saw the orange trees and our house with white stucco walls and dark-green wood trimming, standing like a monument by the road.

The house was two stories high with verandas on both floors. Its windows had no glass, but wooden shutters kept light and heat from invading the rooms.

~

In Somondoco we went to bed after sunset, got up at dawn with the children, and walked to the stables to drink fresh milk. Later, while the children played and I planned the daily meals, Régulo stood on the veranda and greeted everyone as they walked by, or sat on a rocking chair and read.

Once the children were asleep in the next room, Régulo and I lit a candle, pulled out a bottle of brandy, and made love by candlelight. Afterward, we drank brandy and talked.

During those nights in Somondoco, I felt close to Régulo, as I had at the beginning, before our families meddled in our lives. I was able to love him without guilt, remorse, or fear. As we lay in each other's arms, I felt without a doubt that we were meant for each other.

One night, as I lay in bed sipping brandy, an idea came to me. "I'm ready for a new taste," I told Régulo. "Why don't you make wine from oranges?"

Régulo sat up. I offered him a sip of my brandy. He reached across the night table and took an orange.

"I saved this for tonight," he said.

I peeled the orange and held it first to his nose and then to mine. Its rich aroma filled my nostrils. I fed Régulo a piece. He shut his eyes and ate.

"Why orange wine?"

"Oranges can be sweet or sour," I answered. "Like love."

"Oh, I don't know," he replied. "Fruit eventually ripens. Why orange wine?" Régulo asked again.

"I had a dream about it shortly after we met. You had just made some orange wine and you poured it into a silver goblet for me to taste. It was slightly bitter on my tongue, but as I drank it, a sense of well-being spread down to my belly. All my regrets came pouring forth. And then my fears, my hopes, my intuitions. Deep sadness took hold of my heart and squeezed it so hard I could not breathe. I remembered Alessandro's departure and felt my broken heart swell in my chest and hurt and hurt and hurt with pain too hard to bear."

Régulo held me in his arms and stroked my back and my hair. I cried. "But then," I went on, "my heart was filled with love for you."

Régulo took another sip of brandy and looked at me for a while. Then he dipped the last piece of orange in the drink and squeezed the drops onto my tongue.

"An elixir of orange wine—I suppose it could be done," he said before blowing out the candle and gathering me to him.

ORANGE WINE

Chapter Forty-Five

When Régulo found out that the railroad company was being sold to the Colombian government, he vowed to get out. “I would rather starve than become a government employee,” he told me.

Following that day, life with Régulo was marked by silence and hard work. He was not a social person by nature, and once he became an entrepreneur, he dedicated most of his time to developing new ideas.

“I’m glad I don’t have to entertain as in the old railroad days,” he commented. “I have no desire to do so.”

It was just as well, since people had started snubbing us when we moved in together. I wasn’t sure anyone would attend one of our parties.

After leaving the railroad, Régulo invested his time and savings in a series of activities that filled his heart with joy and made him rich. For his first business venture, Régulo chose a childhood friend, an architect named Araque, for a partner. One of their experiments involved making bobby pins. Together they made about a hundred. Fortunately, they realized that their methods were too rustic and that the century would come to an end before they could manage to mass-produce them.

The day after they had an explosion on the patio, Régulo

decided to try another venture. I inherited the bobby pins and used them to create innovative hairstyles that other women tried to copy.

Their next project was selling material from town to town. Régulo and Araque bought the cloth in Bogotá and traveled to the provinces to sell it. They each carried two suitcases full of cotton, silk, and wool, and sometimes had to climb mountains to reach a village. On one of these occasions, Régulo came home empty-handed.

"I traded my suitcases for a farm in Sumapaz," he explained when I asked what had happened to the merchandise.

Araque came up with their third project. It involved selling shoes, which they imported from a factory in Ecuador. Following the arrival of each shipment, Régulo and his partner went around to stores and houses to sell. They gave up after receiving a shipment of right shoes only. For several years Julio and Lucy wore right-foot shoes on both feet.

Once the railroad company had been sold to the Colombian government, many of the train routes were eliminated, and eventually train service stopped altogether.

"I told you," Régulo said, "our government is incapable of running a railroad, let alone a country." As many of the railroad tracks were disassembled and sold, Régulo and his partner bought the iron and sold it at a higher price.

Perhaps because he was tired of selling door to door, Régulo decided to open a store. After much thinking, planning, and investing, he came up with a business that sold threads, material, and needles for embroidery and European silk. The store was closed before it folded.

"What's the use of trying to sell fine lace to people who cannot see the difference?" he complained.

Régulo always managed to get out before he lost all his money. I tried to be helpful, but I must confess that sometimes his business dealings got on my nerves. He always seemed to be in the middle of building something, borrowing from the bank so he could pay the bills, or talking to his customers about delivery dates. I never understood how he could keep it all straight in his head, and I resented the many evenings he came home and talked about his problems at work.

I felt that way although I understood that Régulo's work gave us the opportunity to live well. But sometimes I thought we had forgotten why we had come together in the first place, what our shared beliefs and our objectives were. As time went on, our evening conversations became discussions about the problems Régulo was having with employees, the government, or taxes. He seemed so caught up in building an empire—for what, for whom, I did not know, but I was certain that if I posed the question, he would insist it was for me. I had my doubts, and yet, I knew deep within myself that Régulo could act no differently, that he had his own path to follow, his lessons to learn.

~

On mild nights I went to the backyard and lay in my hammock. While the children played around me, I gazed at the sky and counted my blessings as I counted stars. When I got to ten I made a wish. Sometimes I wished I could make Régulo happy. At other times, I asked for a studio and the ability to put on canvas all the paintings I had in my head. I wanted to allow my spirit, my creative force, to have expression. Sitting in front of a canvas, paintbrush in hand, I forgot all the pain Alessandro and my sisters had caused me, all my daily concerns, my regrets. Time ceased to exist. As my brushstrokes covered the surface with color, my imagination soared.

I bought more brushes and paints, had a local painter stretch canvases for me, and started frequenting Virgilio Suarez's atelier. Suarez had just returned from his first European exhibition and was beginning to receive some recognition for his talent. Soon students from all over the country wanted to take classes with him. He turned most of them away. When I finally managed to get an appointment, Suarez sent a brief note requesting that I bring one of my paintings along to the interview.

I had a handful of paintings ready but didn't know which one to choose. They all seemed imperfect now that Virgilio Suarez was going to determine whether to accept me as his student based on a single canvas. I decided to ask Régulo for his opinion.

"Which painting should I take to my interview with Suarez?" I yelled from the kitchen.

"Take them all," he yelled back.

"I can only take one."

"Then I vote for *Self-Portrait*."

His choice surprised me. "Really? Why?"

"Because it's bold, unique, and vibrant. It's you."

I walked into the bedroom-turned-studio and looked at my self-portrait, wondering what had possessed me to use so much red. My crimson mouth was slightly open, as if I were about to say something. I had to admit Régulo was right, though. Despite such boldness, the composition worked. I decided to take the self-portrait instead of one of the still lifes I had recently completed. No doubt Suarez had seen enough paintings of plazas, roses in crystal vases, and pears in porcelain bowls.

Looking at my colorful self-portrait, I realized it had little resemblance to the art I had seen in the museums in Florence or to Modigliani's geometrical lady in Alessandro's home in Paipa. In my painting I stood next to a window, observing the viewer. Beyond the window you could see a garden, red roses blooming. My face and my loosely gathered hair were bathed in light. The red curtains, a shade lighter than my lipstick, framed the scene.

Later that afternoon, I sat in Suarez's living room trying to remain calm. The master spent a long time studying my canvas. I was afraid he would never speak.

"I like this composition," he finally said. "All that red, all that passion."

"Thank you, Maestro Suarez," I replied, my heart beating fast.

"You should call me Virgilio now that you'll be joining my atelier, Inés," he said. "I insist."

I was thrilled.

"Have you given it a title?"

"*Self-Portrait.*"

"*Rouge,*" he said. "The title should be *Rouge.*" Virgilio stood up and walked around the room without losing sight of the canvas. "*Rouge* it is, then," he repeated, as if he had painted it. He stopped in front of me and took my hand.

"I'm putting together an exhibition that will be shown in Paris at the end of the year," he said. "I would like to include your painting. The French will love it."

I was speechless. Virgilio held on to my hand. When I tried to pull it away, he squeezed it harder.

"I devote most mornings to my work," he went on, crushing my fingers. "Students start showing up at three. See you on Monday. Come ready to paint," he added, leading me toward the front door without letting go. "I almost forgot," he said. "Once a month I collect money to purchase supplies." Virgilio opened the door with his free hand and kissed mine before releasing it. I left Suarez's house with the address to his studio.

"Guess who will be exhibiting her work in Paris?" I asked Régulo.

He embraced me. "What did I tell you, Inés?" he remarked. "That painting is extraordinary. You are not aware of your own talent. We'll travel to Paris for the opening of the show!"

"Promise?" I asked.

"I promise," he replied.

Unfortunately, we didn't make it to Paris or to the art show. In order to finance our trip, Régulo was counting on being repaid for a loan he had made to his friend Araque, but he never got the money.

"Without that money we won't be able to travel to France," he told me one evening.

"I understand," I replied. "It's not your fault." But as hard as I tried, part of me resented not being able to go. I had told Régulo I understood to appease him. I didn't want him to feel guilty for breaking his promise. But the truth was I felt frustrated, even angry. I decided to go for a walk to calm down before I said something I would regret. I had been dreaming about this trip to Paris for months, picturing us visiting the museums and the parks, strolling down the boulevards arm in arm. Virgilio had put me in touch with a French painter, and we had agreed to meet at his atelier in Paris. "Perhaps he'll let you attend some of his classes while you are there," my mentor had said. "He uses a unique painting technique that may serve you well. His students rave about him. I'm planning a trip to Paris as well. We can all meet there." Now I would have to tell Virgilio I wouldn't be able to meet the French painter or join him in the French capital, after he had taken the trouble to introduce me to the French master. It was embarrassing, but I was more disappointed than embarrassed. I had an opportunity and it had vanished.

After his return from France, Suarez asked me to meet him at his house. As soon as I walked in, he opened a bottle of French champagne, poured some into two glasses, handed me one, took the other one, and raised it.

"I want to make a toast to you, Inés, and to art, beauty, and artists!"

"Salud," I replied as our glasses touched. Virgilio emptied his flute in one motion and poured himself another drink.

"I have something for you," he said after his second glass. He went over to his desk and took a red silk bag out of it, walked over to me, and handed me the bag.

"I thought red silk would be appropriate," he said. "It's yours. Come, open it."

It was heavy. I sat down and opened it. To my amazement, I discovered it was full of money.

"That's your part for the sale of *Rouge*," Virgilio explained. "I already took my commission. Oh, and you paid for this fine champagne, too, so drink another glass!" he said, pouring more champagne in our flutes.

"The French gentleman who bought *Rouge* asked me to tell you that if you ever make it to Paris, you are invited to go see your painting at his gallery," Virgilio said. "He loves it."

I walked home a little tipsy and elated about my first sale.

~

A few days later while I was working in his atelier, I sensed Virgilio's presence behind me.

"You are an exceptional artist, Inés," he said.

I put my brush down and turned. "Thank you," I replied.

"How long have you been painting?"

"A few years."

"One day you'll have your own solo show," he said.

I felt myself blushing.

"Mark my word," he concluded.

"That's very kind of you," I replied.

"I'm not here to pay you compliments," Virgilio explained. "I mean it." He looked straight into my eyes.

I felt a tremor. The intensity of his gaze unsettled me.

~

Suarez belonged to a group of avant-garde artists in Bogotá that included poets, painters, and novelists. Once a week they met for dinner at a restaurant in La Candelaria. All evening they talked about art and life while drinking and smoking until the early morning hours. The one time I was able to join them, Virgilio sat across the table from me. He poured some red wine in my glass.

"Inés, you must make your art a priority," he said.

"I'm trying," I replied, "but it's hard, with children and a household to run."

"Don't you have help at home?"

"We've had to cut back since Régulo left the Belgian railroad company," I explained. "We let go of two maids, and frankly, the one we kept is not very good. I've had to cook more often. I also have to go to the market every morning while she's cleaning and doing the laundry."

"I'm sorry to hear that," Virgilio said. "But you still owe it to yourself and to the world."

“That’s why artists should never marry,” someone at the end of the table joked.

“Is that true?” one of the women in the group asked. I had heard she was a Russian aristocrat and a poet.

“Unless you are a man and find a wife to take care of everything!” another poet chimed in.

“If you are independently wealthy and don’t need a man to support you, you’ll be fine,” a different woman at the table exclaimed. The daughter of a wealthy local merchant, she was also studying under Virgilio.

Everyone laughed, but I thought about the truth in that statement. I was the only woman in Virgilio’s atelier with children, a household to run, and a “husband.”

~

When I got home late that night, I found Régulo outside, smoking a cigarette and pacing back and forth.

“I don’t think I can do this, Inés,” he said.

“But you agreed I should go!” I exclaimed. “This was my first dinner.”

“I thought I could do it, but I spent all evening wondering where you were and with whom.”

“You knew I was in a restaurant in La Candelaria with Virgilio and the others,” I insisted.

“Yes, but they’re all free spirits, artists, with no family obligations. I’ve heard they change lovers often, and that they are all fine with it.”

“Where did you hear that?” I asked Régulo, though I didn’t wait for his answer. I was tired. My only desire was to go to bed. I didn't have the energy to reassure him. After opening the door, I climbed the stairs quietly so as not to wake the children.

At times I had been aware of Régulo's jealousy concerning other artists and my spending too much time in Virgilio's atelier. I knew he wanted me to have my independence and time for my own work, but I was also aware of the fact that he felt insecure because he was not an artist but an entrepreneur, and although he admired art immensely, he couldn't participate in it as an artist, only as an observer.

"But entrepreneurs are also creative," I pointed out during one of our conversations on that topic.

"Yes," he agreed, "but not in the same way you artists are."

"What is it that bothers you about my painting?" I asked him. "Surely it's not the time I devote to it, since that never interferes with our daily routine or our time together," I added.

"No, it's not that," Régulo replied. "Sometimes when you are talking about art or about one of your classes or meetings with other artists, I feel left out. I know it's irrational, but I can't control it. I just don't want to lose you."

"You are not going to lose me, *mi amor*," I reassured him. Régulo came across as self-possessed and confident. I often forgot that he had insecurities concerning me.

"You are so talented, Inés," he said, "and so beautiful, intelligent, and sophisticated. I feel you could go off to Europe with one of those painters and live a great life there without giving it a second thought. You see, I couldn't do that. . . ."

"I wouldn't leave you or the children," I replied.

"I know, it's not rational, but I see your potential and it makes me nervous. I would never want to hold you back."

The next day, I decided to sell the emerald necklace and the beautiful stones Father had given me when I married Alessandro.

The earrings and the ring that Roberto Risi had made for me in Florence would pay for my painting supplies and for Virgilio's lessons; this in turn would give me peace of mind and more freedom. I didn't want to ask Régulo to fund my artistic career.

Part of me felt bitter about selling my beautiful jewelry. The other part knew I had no choice. Money had been tight since Régulo had quit his job at the railroad company. He supported me and the children and paid for the house. I didn't feel comfortable asking him to pay for my art lessons as well, especially now that he had started feeling jealous about my colleagues. I would become more independent.

Chapter Forty-Six

Régulo was between ventures when he received a letter from his sister Fidelia.

Dear Régulo,

Our hotel is busier than ever. People from Chocontá, Guateque, and Bogotá come and stay for months. There are rumors of an emerald mine close by. I think you ought to return to Somondoco to investigate.

Yours,

Fidelia

Régulo showed me the letter, gathered a change of clothes, and made plans for the trip. He did not intend to stay long.

Upon his arrival in Somondoco, Fidelia informed him that a local man had discovered emeralds in a mine three kilometers from their house. It seemed to be a promising business. The mine was on land that once belonged to their mother.

"If Father had not sold it so he could continue burning money by the river, that mine would be ours," Fidelia told her brother.

During that visit to Somondoco, Régulo became an emerald trader. His new profession took him to places he had never been before—Beirut, Paris, Rome, Madrid, Geneva, and New York. He met some of the finest jewelers in those cities, found sophisticated clients, and fulfilled his dream of traveling around the world.

"My great-great-grandmother was right," he said the first time he traveled to Europe. "She predicted that one of her family members would stumble upon a treasure close to home." Precious stones changed his life, and mine, too, as a result.

Selling emeralds was Régulo's favorite career. He always kept ten or fifteen stones neatly tucked in his vest. Periodically, he would take the paper wrapping out and unfold it to glance at the gems. Sometimes I would touch them. They were beautiful. It baffled me to think that one of those stones could be exchanged for a house or a carriage.

Even after he got out of the emerald business, Régulo still relished keeping stones in his pocket. He sat admiring them for a long time and meditated on their color, size, shape, luminosity, and fragility.

When he found a perfect emerald, he would hold it up for me to see.

"Inés, this is like our love," he told me once while showing me a three-karat stone. "Beautiful, luminous, and delicate." During those moments, it seemed to me that he felt a connection with beauty the way I felt a connection with art.

~

"Mi amor," I said one afternoon when we were out walking. "Now that you've started traveling to faraway places, perhaps I could join you on one of your trips? I'd love to go to Paris with you."

"What about the children?" Régulo asked.

"Chata could keep them," I replied. "I never got to see my painting at the art exhibit in Paris. I would love to see the gallery where it's hanging."

"I know," Régulo said. "I'm sorry I couldn't keep my promise to take you there for the show, Inés. I was sure Araque would pay back the loan."

"It wasn't your fault," I replied. "But why did you keep it from me? Why didn't you tell me?" I insisted.

"I didn't want to disappoint you."

I remembered the times I had spent daydreaming about the trip, choosing outfits, shoes, and hats. My countless excursions to meet with the seamstress. The new hat I had purchased was still in the box. I couldn't bring myself to wear it. I stopped walking and turned to face Régulo.

"Please tell me, will we ever travel to Paris together?"

"We will, my love, we will," he said, his voice full of conviction. "I promise."

My eyes welled up with tears. Better start walking again. I didn't want him to see me cry.

~

A few months after Régulo realized that the mining trade was becoming dangerous, he decided it was time to change professions.

One of his Colombian clients owed him a vast amount of money. As payment, he offered Régulo some cash and a large piece of land in Somondoco. Régulo abandoned the emerald trade, hired local farmers to dig up trees from his family's ancient orange groves—the same ones his great-great-grandmother had blessed—and re-planted them, next to hundreds of orange trees, on his new land.

Chapter Forty-Seven

Régulo and I had managed to create a life together. He treated Julio and Lucy as his own children, and we lived our lives as a regular family. We had dinner together as often as possible, and on Sundays we took the children to the park. Lucy was a calm child, often playing with her dolls or with the tea set Régulo had bought for her. Julio was more restless, more curious. Some Saturday afternoons Régulo took the boy with him to play chess downtown. He had been playing chess in the same café with the same friend for years. Julio loved going with Régulo. He sat quietly watching the men play, until he learned most of the rules and many moves of the game. When Régulo noticed that the boy had learned to play by watching him, he decided to teach him everything he knew about the game. He was the perfect teacher for my son and had the patience to sit with Julio and show him different moves on the board, explaining why some led to victory while others ended up in defeat. I loved watching Régulo and my son playing chess. Régulo never let him win. If Julio won, it was because he earned it.

"You know," I heard Régulo tell Julio one day, "chess mirrors life. That's why I enjoy it so much."

Régulo was impressed by Julio's intelligence, by his ability to learn. “I think he could become an excellent chess player, Inés,” he told me one day. “He could compete in tournaments.”

“But he’s only a child,” I replied, “and I want him to enjoy his childhood. He’s already gone through a lot.”

“But he’s very intelligent and curious,” Régulo insisted. “If he doesn’t want to compete, he doesn’t have to do it, but I think we should give him the chance.”

One day Régulo came home with a present for Julio. The large box was wrapped in red paper and had a bow on it. Julio was delighted.

“Can I open it, Papá Régulo?”

“Yes, but first try to guess what it is,” Régulo replied.

Julio stared at the narrow box for a little while. “A rifle,” he finally answered.

“Good guess,” Régulo said encouragingly. “Why don’t you open it and see?”

With his sister’s help, Julio tore the paper off and opened the box.

“What is it?” I asked.

Julio used both hands to lift a sword out of the box. It was shiny and beautiful. Made of steel, and heavy as a result. My son could lift it, but he couldn’t swing it very well. In fact, the first time he tried to swing it, he almost knocked over a porcelain flower vase I had on the coffee table.

“Careful!” I said, half annoyed at Régulo for getting Julio such a dangerous present. “Do you think that’s an appropriate gift for a boy?” I asked him.

“I do,” Régulo replied, “but I’m afraid you don’t.”

“I just don’t want him to get hurt,” I said. “Maybe we can put it away until he’s older. . . . He’s only seven.”

"It's a toy sword," Régulo replied. "Lighter than the real weapon and not as long."

Julio turned to me. "Mamá, please, please let me keep it! I promise I'll be careful."

I couldn't say no to my son. The eagerness in his eyes and his enthusiasm won me over. "Fine," I finally replied. "But you can only play with it when someone is supervising you."

"I promise I won't play with it when I'm alone!" he said as he ran over to hug me and kiss me.

"Where did you get the sword?" I asked Régulo.

"A friend of mine who traveled to Toledo, Spain, brought it back for me. People have been making swords in Toledo since before Christ was born. It's the sword capital of the world."

"Now you are exaggerating," I said. "You are just trying to make me laugh."

Ever since that day, Julio took the sword out of its case as often as he could. He'd lift it with both hands and raise it slowly. Every time I watched him do that, I held my breath. I felt uncomfortable watching my son as he held a weapon, even if it was a toy replica.

"You know, Julio, a sword is a weapon," I explained one day. "It could kill someone."

"I'll never use it to kill anyone, Mamá," Julio promised.

One afternoon while I was painting in my studio downstairs, I heard a loud noise and a scream. I rushed upstairs and found Julio sitting on the floor holding the sword, crying, the balcony doors wide open. My heart started beating so fast I thought it would burst. I ran to my son and hugged him.

"What happened?" I asked him after he calmed down.

"I have been telling Fernando about my new sword, and he

wanted to see it, so we agreed that I would show it to him from the balcony," my son explained. "But when I tried to hold it up so he could see it better, I lost my balance."

"Oh my God!" I said. "You could have gotten hurt. Promise me you'll never do that again."

"I'm sorry, Mamá, I won't do it again. I promise," Julio said, his voice shaky and the tears still running down his face.

A few weeks later Julio climbed up to the balcony, chasing a canary that had escaped from the neighbor's house. The maid was cooking lunch, and I was trying on a new dress while Lucy played on the floor next to me. I thought Julio was in the kitchen helping with lunch, as he liked to do. Instead, my little boy was very close to catching the bird, which sat on the sill in the balcony and sang.

Thousands of times I've imagined the scene. Julio reached over and managed to grab the bird by its tiny yellow tail but had to let go when he lost his balance. The iron railing was not secured. It gave, and my son fell to his death. If he had never gotten that sword, I thought, he would not have opened the balcony doors to show it to his friend, and he would have forgotten about the bird. Instead, Régulo had bought him a sword, and that sword had changed our lives forever. I blamed Régulo for the sword, and I blamed myself for letting Julio keep it. I knew my anger and my sense of guilt wouldn't bring my son back, but I couldn't help myself.

Régulo did not know how to comfort me. Perhaps my sisters were right, after all. Perhaps Julio's accident was God's punishment for all my sins. I couldn't forgive myself. Maybe I did not deserve to be happy, to live with a man who adored me and to have a family.

After Julio's death, I cried every day while staring at the

unfinished painting I had of my son. Six months earlier, Julio had sat on the living room sofa while I stood in the middle of the room, paintbrush in hand, observing. During that time, I became familiar with all my son's features, not as a mother but as a painter. I never tired of studying his large eyes, his button nose.

Régulo gave Julio a regal funeral with a horse carriage, dozens of white roses, and new clothes for me and Lucy. Half of Bogotá attended. All those people who had snubbed us before now stood with somber dignity in the church. As I looked around at the crowd dressed in their fine black clothes, sporting elegant hats and gloves and witnessing my despair with morbid curiosity, I remembered the ladies of high society in Paipa whispering behind my back after Alessandro's departure.

How many times had I dreamed of going out with Régulo, arm in arm, to a social function or just to walk around the city on a Sunday afternoon? Daydreaming, I had thought about the dress I would be wearing, the shoes, the hat, the way people would greet us with respect. On the day of Julio's funeral, our first official outing, I could not have cared less what I wore, what my hair looked like, and how people greeted me.

We rode in the carriage to the cemetery and tossed sprigs of white roses on the small white casket as it was lowered. Women I had never noticed came to pay their condolences and embraced me. Rosa, Chata, and Helena attended the funeral, but they sat at the back of the church. When I saw them, I walked over to their pew. Chata gave me a long embrace as we both wept. Helena and Rosa nodded. For a moment, I thought Rosa was about to open her arms, but she seemed to change her mind. I felt my heart hurt and decided not to approach her or Helena. A rejection from them at this moment would have been devastating for me. I had to keep myself together.

Julio's funeral helped me cope with the pain of losing him, but I found no outlet for the sorrow that I felt at seeing my first child disappear from my life.

For years after Julio's death, I could not get rid of the haunting memory of his fall. During the day, I managed, by keeping busy, by pretending to go on with my life, to prevent the horrid image from resurfacing. But once night fell and I lay on my bed, the picture of him lying lifeless on the ground, the color gone from his once rosy cheeks, his eyes forever shut, came vividly into the fore. It was more than I could bear. Every corner of the house was filled with memories of Julio. Sometimes I thought I heard his laughter.

One night, in desperation, I went to the bathroom and emptied all the medicine bottles I could find, but, alas, I was not meant to join my son. Régulo called the doctor and had him nurse me back to life. I had no choice. I had to face the pain. My heart felt heavy and pulled my body down, much like it had in my dream about the orange wine. Oh, how I wished that there was something I could do, a medicine I could drink that would take the pain away.

In my despair, I started attending mass and confession early every morning and twice on Sundays.

"How can you pray to God?" Régulo wondered. "He took Julio away from us."

~

I had a little room in the rear of the house, behind the patio, and I dedicated it to prayer. Statues of the Virgin Mary and Saint Martin de Porres adorned it.

The saints' room became my escape, the place where I felt I

belonged. On special occasions, I took Lucy into my retreat and showed her my collection of saints, including statuettes of Saint Mary Magdalene and Saint Gabriel the Archangel.

My daughter sat in silence and watched me pass the beads of my rosary while muttering Hail Marys and Our Fathers. One day I noticed, as I put my rosary away, that Lucy sat in her usual chair, crying. My heart grew heavy with sorrow.

"What's wrong, child?" I asked her.

"You never play with me now that my brother's gone," Lucy said. I held her in my arms for the first time since Julio's death.

From that day forward, I was always willing to put aside my prayers and chores to play with my daughter and to spend time making dresses for her dolls. I remember the prettiest party dress I made from silk embroidered the color of gold, a rich, sensuous fabric that others might think would be wasted on a doll. As I painted a portrait of Lucy and her doll—my daughter with auburn curls and green eyes, her baby with white-blond hair, wearing the golden dress and no shoes—I cried.

~

In the corner of my prayer room, I kept a wooden chest. It contained the old-fashioned lilac silk dress I wore when I met Alessandro, my father's edition of *Don Quixote de la Mancha* with one of my mother's roses in it, and a lock of Julio's hair.

Sometimes I would shut myself in the room and look at Julio's hair for hours. On those days, the burden of my child's death became a weight too terrible to bear. I had to fight with all my strength to stay afloat.

Chapter Forty-Eight

When I became pregnant with Régulo's child, the news filled him with immense pleasure.

"It's a miracle!" he exclaimed. He took my hands, held them for a long time, looked into my eyes, and kissed me on the lips.

"I'll be right back," Régulo finally said as he ran toward the door. A little while later he came back, carrying the largest bouquet of roses I had ever seen.

"You have no idea how long I've been dreaming of having a child with you, Inés," Régulo whispered as he handed me the flowers. Yellow, pink, white, and red roses. Their fragrance reminded me of my childhood in Paipa, of my *agua de rosas.* I buried my nose in the flowers and decided I would make a special edition of my perfume using petals from this bouquet, and I would call it Aura in honor of my mother.

Régulo's love, along with Lucy's excitement and my own desire to begin a new chapter in my life, gave me the strength to ignore the voices in my head. Soon, I stopped imagining what Rosa and Helena would say, what Fidelia's initial reaction would be. By the time our daughter was born, I had already chosen a name for her.

"Rosario," I told Régulo. "If she's a girl, we will call her Rosario."

"What makes you think we are having a girl?" he asked.

I shrugged. "It's just a feeling . . . but I think I'm right."

"Why Rosario?" Régulo wanted to know.

"Because the word reminds me of my mother's roses in Paipa, of the beautiful bouquet you gave me, and of the rosary I've been using to pray for Julio ever since he died," I replied.

"You know," Régulo commented, "Rosario comes from the Latin *rosarium*, meaning rosary."

"I knew it!" I said, delighted. "This child will be a blessing to us, a healer to many."

"I wouldn't want your sister Rosa to think we named the baby after her, though," Régulo commented. "She's caused you so much pain."

"Think of Rosa as a single flower shriveling in a desert of her own creation," I replied. "Rosario brings to mind abundance, not one rose, but many, just as the beads of the rosary are many, and color and perfume. She'll give us what my sister tried to steal from us—happiness."

Régulo's comment about Rosa made me realize I wanted to leave the past behind and dissolve the bitterness that hung around us like a shadow. I spent all night staring at the ceiling and decided to get up when I witnessed the first light of dawn through the sheer curtains. As I looked at the sleepy city from my bedroom window, a new name came to me.

"I thought about what you said yesterday," I told Régulo that morning during breakfast. "You're right. We don't want to give our daughter a name that resembles Rosa's. Alba—her name will be Alba, *el despertar del sol*, the sun's awakening. It describes her more appropriately."

Régulo smiled. "Alba it is, then," he said. "Our daughter will be named Alba."

Six months after Alba was born, Régulo decided we should move. The new house was located on Sixty-Sixth Street, close to a bus station. We wanted to open a business that would benefit from its proximity to the station. With this in mind, Régulo bought a small two-story building annexed to the house. A restaurant was on the second floor and a store on the first. We hired a French cook to help with the restaurant. Régulo put all his knowledge of food and wine to good use. He came up with perfect dishes and superb wines.

Besides candy and cigarettes, the store carried beer, wine, whiskey, rice, lentils, bread, and butter. After a year and a half, we closed the restaurant as it proved to be too expensive. I ran the store for a long time afterward.

Although our new house, the store, and our new child kept me busy, I missed my sisters. Julio's death had opened a wound that I didn't seem to be able to heal alone. I thought of Mother and of all of us growing up in Paipa, how we used to play hide-and-seek in the garden, drink our chocolate in the afternoon with Mother and Father in the library, and tell each other stories before we fell asleep. Now I was alone with my pain. I would have loved to reach out to Chata, but I was afraid Rosa would not let her communicate with me. It was sad. I felt alone in the world.

Whenever I tried to talk to Régulo about it, he grew impatient. "How can you miss them?" he would ask. "They have been so unkind to you." I envied Régulo for being able to live without family and religious crutches and wished my world were as clearly defined as his.

"I miss Chata. She hasn't seen the baby."

"Don't you meet people in the store?"

"Yes, and I enjoy contact with the public," I said. "I meet interesting people, but they're not family. I have no family left."

"Give it time. Give it time," Régulo insisted.

At the store, I came to know everyone by name and after a while developed a following of loyal customers. It was through the store that Alessandro found me.

Chapter Forty-Nine

"What do you have to do to get a beer around here?" he asked.

I was behind the counter talking to Lucy and recognized his voice. My heart stopped. I opened the bottle, poured the drink, and looked at him. He was still incredibly handsome.

"Inés!" Alessandro exclaimed. "How long has it been?" He lit a cigarette.

"Ten years."

"Ten long years," he whispered as he exhaled. "Have you lived in Bogotá all this time?"

"For the most part." I poured some sherry in a glass, set it down, and asked, "How is Isabel?"

"Who?"

"My sister."

"I wouldn't know," he answered as if we were discussing a stranger. "She's your sister. Don't you keep in touch with her?"

"Now and then she writes to Chata and Helena, but we haven't communicated in years." *Not since she betrayed me with you,* I wanted to add, but I didn't.

"How about you?" Alessandro glanced at me through the cigarette smoke.

"I can't complain."

Lucy walked behind the counter, carrying her baby sister. I handed her a bottle.

"I see you've been busy," Alessandro commented. He lit another cigarette and waited for an answer.

"Inés!" Régulo called from the house. I turned to go, but Alessandro grabbed my wrist.

"Wait. When can I see you again?"

"I'm here every day except Sundays. But I don't think we have much to talk about. It's been so long," I added as I moved my hand away.

Alessandro looked at me, the cigarette still in his mouth. "You could never forget our life together, darling, even if you wanted to—the most promising couple in Paipa," he said.

I thought about our life. He seemed to read my mind. "I know, babe, we both made a lot of promises we didn't keep. But you and I were good together. I wish I had never walked out on you."

"People wish many things."

"What do you wish?" he asked.

I remembered the night I saw him dancing in the café with Isabel. I turned to leave.

"Remember," Alessandro shouted as I walked away, "we're still married. I'm still your husband."

I felt sick to my stomach. Once outside the store, I leaned on the wall for a minute. When Régulo caught up with me, I was in the bathroom.

"Could you be with child again?" he asked.

~

Since that day, Alessandro showed up periodically for a beer and a chat, as if nothing had ever happened between us to prevent it.

He was still living in Paipa, no longer with Isabel. His wandering heart had moved on. I found out he had been disinherited, did not hold a regular job, and continued playing his guitar here and there when the occasion arose.

"How are Donatella and Carlo doing?" I inquired one day as I poured his beer. My hand shook. I worried that Régulo would walk in, see Alessandro, and misunderstand.

"You haven't heard?" Alessandro took a sip. "My mother jumped off a cliff, wheelchair and all."

"Oh my God! I didn't know. And your father?"

"He's still living in the house, but he's lost his mind. Luisa, our old maid, takes care of him. I don't see him very often."

"That's very sad."

"I know, and now there's no chance he'll change his testament." My husband lit a cigarette and exhaled the smoke thoughtfully. "I bet Father Rossi had something to do with it."

I was annoyed by Alessandro's selfishness and his lack of sensitivity, and I wondered why I had fallen in love with him in the first place.

"How can you think about a will now?" I asked.

"I've never been as saintly as you, darling." Alessandro laughed. "Thanks to Reverend Minder, I'm a fallen Catholic."

I poured myself a glass of red wine and sat on a stool for a moment.

"Years ago, I tried to find Minder," I said.

"Why were you looking for the reverend?" Alessandro asked. "Don't tell me you have decided to become a Protestant!"

I looked the other way. I did not want him to know about my fears.

"Minder's no longer in Bogotá," Alessandro informed me.

"He moved to the Amazon jungle to learn about healing practices from the Indians."

"Did he give up on El Dorado?"

"No, he found hallucinogenic mushrooms and a wife instead. Last I heard, he was running around the jungle in a thong and had his own plot of cannabis."

I couldn't help but laugh. The thought of Reverend Minder running around the jungle naked was too much to bear.

Alessandro put his drink on the counter and looked at me. "Inés, you look beautiful when you laugh," he said.

~

Sometimes Alessandro brought Lucy candy and gave it to her as he would to any child—as if it made no difference that he was her father. I wondered if he would ever inquire about Julio.

"Where's your brother?" he finally asked Lucy one day. My daughter looked at me, a blank expression on her face.

"He died," I answered as I wiped the counter clean. My eyes welled up with tears, and I leaned on the bar, trying to regain some composure. Alessandro took my hand. I looked at him, and for the first time saw an expression of sorrow on his face. I cried for Julio.

"He was our firstborn," Alessandro whispered. "I don't deserve you or the children. I never have."

Chapter Fifty

Alessandro often forgot to pay for his beer. I noticed that his shirt cuffs were frayed and his shoes old and worn. When I could, I would put together a bundle of Régulo's old clothes for him, which were still newer than what he wore.

Soon Alessandro's shadow started looming over my life with Régulo; our household felt the impact of his presence. Sometimes Régulo would ask me what I was thinking, and I could not bear to tell him that I was remembering my previous life. But I've never been a good liar, and Régulo knew I was keeping something from him. I didn't want Alessandro to disrupt the peaceful balance I had managed to create with Régulo. My time was often divided between the children and Régulo, and I didn't want to upset Régulo by talking about Alessandro. It was as if we lived in a microcosm far away from the world, and any possibility of that universe being disrupted made me anxious. I knew, from experience, that while he appeared self-confident and open-minded, Régulo had a hard time accepting my bohemian colleagues and the lifestyles they led. I had experienced Régulo's jealousy first-hand with my art teacher Virgilio, and I didn't want to witness that again.

On one occasion, I gave Alessandro Régulo's favorite hat by

mistake. Régulo missed it the next day, and when he asked for it, Lucy mentioned her father.

Régulo flew into a rage. “If you’d rather be with Alessandro, I’m not going to stand in the way,” he said.

Although he was not one to make accusations or to threaten, his sadness and anger left me feeling helpless. After he calmed down, Régulo packed his suitcase and his books.

On his way out, he found me sitting at the kitchen table smoking a cigarette.

“I’m leaving,” he said.

“You’re overreacting.”

“I can’t let that man barge into our lives and destroy what we have.”

I took a drag from my cigarette. “It was a mistake. I feel sorry for Alessandro. I don’t love him.”

“How can you feel compassion for someone who has hurt you?” Régulo asked impatiently.

“He’s miserable. He has no family, no future.”

“He had all that,” Régulo insisted, “but gave it up. I didn’t know you smoked,” he added when he noticed my cigarette for the first time.

“I don’t. I’m just nervous.”

Régulo put his suitcase down and lit his own cigarette. We both smoked in silence.

“You mean to tell me you’re leaving me because of a hat?” I asked.

“No. I’m leaving because I can’t stand that man insinuating himself into your life again,” Régulo explained. “It’s clear to me that he still haunts you. I cannot tell you what to do, but I refuse to stand here and watch.”

I took a bottle of Bordeaux from the counter and poured a

glass of wine for me and one for Régulo. Then I offered him another cigarette. He hesitated.

"I should be going," he said.

"Let's talk about it."

Régulo sat down and lit the cigarette. He took a sip of wine and glanced at the table. A bowl of peeled potatoes sat next to a chicken on a platter, waiting to be seasoned. Chopped onions, yucca, and plantains had been prepared.

"What are we having for dinner?" he asked. I knew then he was not leaving.

Chapter Fifty-One

I had promised myself never to return to Paipa, and I had no desire to set foot in my hometown again, but I broke my promise a year later and traveled there to find Father Rossi, the only person who could help me with the process of annulling my marriage to Alessandro. While in Paipa I heard Isabel was living in a small house by the river, and I went to look for her, found the front door open, and let myself in.

The house was well furnished. As I walked around the foyer, I wondered if Alessandro was taking care of my sister. In the living room I noticed a boy reading.

"Good morning," I said. He looked up from his book.

"Good morning. *Mamá* is in the kitchen."

"My name is Inés. What's yours?"

"Raul." He went back to the book.

"Pleased to meet you, Raul. I'm your aunt."

He shut the book and looked at me, surprised. "Pleased to meet you too," my nephew finally stammered.

I found Isabel in the kitchen making soup. For a while, we looked at each other in silence.

I spoke first. "I didn't know you had a son."

"Would you like something to drink?" She walked toward the cupboard.

"No, thank you. I won't stay long. I just wanted to see you."

Isabel stopped in front of the cupboard and turned to look at me. "Why on earth would you want to see me?"

"It's been too long. I've missed you. Is the boy Alessandro's?"

"What difference does it make?" she countered.

"None; it's just that he looks like him."

"He is."

"At least Alessandro is taking care of you," I said soothingly. I wanted to add that Alessandro loved her. God knew I longed to see my sister happy, but I couldn't lie to her.

"What makes you think he's taking care of me?" Isabel asked. The expression on her face betrayed the truth.

"This is a nice house," I answered. "Don't misunderstand me, Isabel," I tried to reassure her, "I think Alessandro should take care of you. It's his responsibility."

"Well, it's not him," she said impatiently. "Remember Giles, the Belgian gentleman who bought the mansion?"

"Yes. He was married."

"He still is," Isabel answered while she chopped an onion. "But he's been good to me." My sister turned to face me. "He wanted you."

That day Isabel asked me to forgive her for her betrayal. I cried for my sister's unhappiness, for Alessandro and his inability to be constant, and for Isabel's lost youth and broken home.

~

Later in the week I visited the garden in the mansion. I wanted to see my roses, but Giles told me that they had dried up inexplicably.

Only one bush remained where I had stood and cried years before. A red rose had just bloomed. It reminded me of the passion I once felt for Alessandro, in another lifetime, oh, so long ago.

Chapter Fifty-Two

When the time came for our cousin Gustavo to work in the first parish to which he had been assigned, Rosa wrote me a letter, entreating me to abandon my life of sin and go back to Alessandro.

Inés,

Helena and I are convinced that the church will investigate our family before Gustavo takes over the parish. Your sinful life with Régulo would destroy his future and his chance of becoming a bishop one day. Go back to Paipa and to your lawful husband. If you care nothing about human decency, do it for your family. You've already put us through enough shame and suffering.

Rosa

After reading Rosa's letter, I couldn't find any peace anywhere, not even with the saints. *When will the past stop haunting me?* I wondered. Why was I expected to change my life so that a cousin I hardly remembered could fulfill his role as a priest? And what about Isabel? Why was Rosa not lecturing her also? After Isabel cut ties with us, I thought she would regret it. Now I felt she had made a good decision. After all, she had run off with a married man who also happened to be my husband. *My husband.* That sounded worse than what Régulo and I had done. Rosa and Helena had often shown how little they cared about me, my life, my children, and my future. Now they expected me to give up my relationship with Régulo just because it was inconvenient! I should confront them, I thought, tell them how I felt, express my anger. And, no matter how much time had passed, I still couldn't forgive myself for Julio's death. Sometimes, at the worst moments, when I couldn't control my heart or my mind, I came to the conclusion that my son's death was my punishment for finding love with Régulo, for defying society's rules, for following my heart.

Régulo and I were still not married. The possibility of a wedding in Ecuador had evaporated when we had failed to produce a copy of the annulment of my marriage to Alessandro. Father Rossi had refused to help me, and without him I didn't know where to go or who to ask. The annulment had never been filed, even though Alessandro had assured me that it would be. Missing the exhibit in Paris had been devastating, a once-in-a-lifetime opportunity that I feared would never come again. I was tired of feeling like a misfit, tired of fighting for my art, my love for Régulo, and my children. As a man, Régulo would never understand what I was going through, no matter how much he loved me. I had to accept that. I was certain of one thing, though. I didn't want my love for him to turn into bitterness.

Following a week of sleepless nights, I packed my bags and left the house with Lucy and Alba while Régulo was at work, without writing a note or leaving a forwarding address.

~

Once we arrived in Paipa, my daughters and I went straight to

Alessandro's house. He was in bed, drunk; with Lucy's help I cleaned the place up. By the time my husband awoke, I had prepared soup, and we were all sitting at the table waiting for him. Alessandro was surprised to see us.

"Why the hell did you come back?" he yelled.

"My cousin is about to get his first parish as a priest, and Helena and Rosa are worried that my situation could create problems if the church decides to investigate his family."

Alessandro swallowed his drink in one gulp.

"To make my sisters happy," I continued.

A sneer swept across his handsome face. "They've never cared about you. Look at Isabel."

"I forgave both of you," I said with resolution.

"Well, I don't need your pity or your compassion," he told me. "If you came here to save my soul, you're wasting your time and mine." Alessandro poured himself another shot of aguardiente.

"So, let me see if I understand correctly," he went on. "They asked you to leave that poor bastard who has been taking care of you and your little beasts and to come running to me, *to me*, who cannot even take care of myself?" He lit a cigarette and paused for a moment to exhale. "God knows I loved you once, Inés, but now things have changed. I have someone else."

My eyes focused on a dirty spot between my suede shoes. I tried not to blink.

"Look at me," Alessandro said. He poured another drink. "There's nothing left for us. You can stay for a week, maybe two, while your cousin is crowned a saint. But you better be gone after the ceremony."

~

From that moment on, my husband waged a war against me that did not respect the bounds of decency Rosa and Helena had been so eager to point out.

"If you're going to live here, I expect you to act as my wife," he said.

Once again, I slept in Alessandro's arms and felt his flesh next to mine at night. Long after he had gone to sleep, exhausted by drink and after lovemaking, I kept the candle lit. I could not comprehend how I had once loved him. What was it, I tried to understand, that made the act of love seem right, and brought us fleeting happiness on this earth? And where had it all gone? Why could I not bring it forth at will and recall the thrill and the emotion I once felt? It was sheer torture to be with Alessandro while thinking of my love for Régulo, to wish for Régulo's touch, to miss the passion in his eyes as we made love. I felt I didn't deserve Régulo; I didn't deserve his love. It had been so hard to overcome all the obstacles that we had to face. His sisters didn't love me, and my sisters didn't seem to love me either. Helena and Rosa didn't approve of our relationship, and Julio's death had been devastating for both of us. Destruction seemed to be a theme in our lives. How could we fix that?

Alessandro had wasted his family fortune. He had never been a proper father to his children, and now he was ruining his health with drink.

"To see you," he said, "the woman who gave her life to me without a second thought, the woman I betrayed with her own sister, sitting at my table and looking at me, is revolting. Your forgiveness is revolting."

That night after we went to bed, I cried silently until I fell asleep from exhaustion. Just as I was drifting off, I heard a voice close to my ear. "You will overcome all the pain and destruction because your fate is to live and to love, to celebrate life with Régulo. Don't give up." I remembered the angel in the cornfield, and I wanted to believe the voice, but I still couldn't stop crying.

Chapter Fifty-Three

Lucy wrote Régulo a letter, begging him to send for us.

Dear Papá Régulo,

I can no longer live with that monster. He is my father, I know, but he has never been a father to me.

When he first appeared at the store, I secretly wished that everything I had heard about him was not true. I hoped he would tell my mother he had a fine job and a house for us and that we were welcome to go and live with him. I just wanted that sad part of my mother's life to be right so that her sisters would love her again and love me too.

The second time he came to the store, Father asked Mother to get someone else to fill in for her while he took us for a walk downtown. It was close to Christmas and people were everywhere. He took me into a toy store and told me I could choose anything I wanted. "I would like a doll," I said. The saleslady lined dolls up on the counter. I chose the biggest one of all, with blue eyes that closed when you rocked her. Remember when you asked where I had gotten that doll? It's the only thing my father ever gave me, but that's not why I love her. I love her because she reminds me that for one afternoon, I was important to him. Please come get us.

Lucy

I learned later that after reading Lucy's letter, Régulo had gotten on the first train to Paipa. He had found a hotel room, had taken a shower and shaved, and had gone looking for Alessandro's house.

Alessandro opened the door. Régulo stood at the threshold.

"I'm here to take Inés and the girls back to Bogotá with me," he said.

My husband laughed. "In case you didn't know," he answered, "Inés left you. She's done being a sinner. She wants to be a good Catholic now."

Lucy and I stood in the dining room, waiting. Régulo did not move. Alessandro did not ask him in. I took Lucy's hand and squeezed it. I wanted to push Alessandro out of the way and embrace Régulo, shut the door, and run with my daughters and my true love. My heart was pounding so hard I could hardly hear myself thinking. I would have to go upstairs to fetch Alba.

"Inés!" my husband finally yelled. "Come over here and tell your lover that he wasted the trip." Alessandro turned around to look for me. "You can have her," he said to Régulo. "Her time is almost up."

I walked to the door. My heart kept beating furiously. "How did you know where I was?" I asked Régulo, trying to keep my voice steady.

"That's not important," he replied, annoyed. "Are you coming with me or not?" Alessandro stood between us. I saw him close his hands into fists, ready to punch Régulo. I felt afraid. I knew

Alessandro had a gun hidden in the house, and for a moment, I saw him grabbing it and shooting Régulo.

"I can't," I pleaded. "I promised Rosa and Helena I would stay in Paipa until our cousin gets his parish."

"See?" Alessandro interrupted. "She doesn't know what's best for her."

"What about Lucy and Alba?" Régulo asked. "I think they would be better off with me."

"I want to go back to Bogotá," Lucy said as firmly as she could.

"Suit yourself, you little traitor," Alessandro sneered.

"Go get your bag," Régulo told her. Then he turned to face me. "I'm taking the girls." His sad eyes lingered on me for a moment. It broke my heart.

Alessandro laughed. Régulo pushed hard on the door. "I warn you," he shouted. "If anything happens to Inés, I'll hold you responsible."

"Are you threatening me?" Alessandro raised his voice and his hands.

Régulo ignored him. He turned to me again. "I'll be in the hotel until tomorrow afternoon if you change your mind," he said as he turned to leave.

~

The following day I attended the seven thirty service and waited for Father Rossi afterward. He had aged quite a bit, but he recognized me and seemed pleased to see me. He took me into the confessional, and I described my dilemma.

"In the eyes of God, my child, Alessandro is your husband,

and therefore you should stay with him," the priest told me.

I walked out of the church, my heart sinking with every step. According to Father Rossi, in God's eyes I belonged with Alessandro. According to my sisters, I belonged with Alessandro, but my heart told me that my true home was with Régulo. That day I decided never to return to church.

How could I pray to a God who didn't seem to understand me, my feelings, what I was going through? As hard as I tried, I couldn't bring myself to think that God would want me to go back to a man who had betrayed me, who had never been a good husband to me or a good father to his children. Régulo was right. How could I accept a God who had taken my son away from me, from us? And yet, my determination to be with Régulo despite family disapproval and societal norms was growing weak. Father Rossi's advice and my sisters' condemnation had worn me down. It was too much, trying to build a life together while everyone looked upon us with disdain. No one wished us well. Chata, the only one who expressed her support for me in her letters, was economically dependent on Rosa and didn't dare speak up against our sister in public.

~

That afternoon I found Alessandro in the arms of a woman. I was glad, as I broke all the plates in the kitchen, that my daughters were gone. If I'd had a gun, I would've shot him. Alessandro grabbed my wrist. It hurt, but I still reached for glasses, plates, anything I could grab. He slapped me. My cheek was stinging, and my nose hurt. With my free hand I grabbed a knife and tried to hurt him, but his strength won. He pushed me hard and I fell, hitting my head on the hardwood floor. I ended up in the hospital. The doctor was brief.

"That fall injured your spinal cord. No more children."

"That's just as well," I replied.

I felt like asking Father Rossi if he thought Alessandro's behavior was acceptable in God's eyes.

From the hospital I walked to the highest hill in Paipa and stood at the top, my hand over my eyes, blocking the sun. The landscape reminded me of Somondoco and of my recaptured life with Régulo. I decided to leave for Bogotá.

Chapter Fifty-Four

During the train ride I realized I could not go back to Régulo. I had turned him down when he offered to help; I had made him suffer. I was ashamed of having taken Lucy and Alba away without leaving an address or a note. If I told Régulo what had happened between me and Alessandro, he would not hesitate to kill my husband.

I needed a fresh start, a new life far away from all those who wished me ill. Looking out the train window, I remembered the fortune teller at the circus in Paipa so many years ago, and I recalled that she had warned me about the *malocchio* and had told me to be careful. At the time, I had dismissed her comments. Now I wondered if she'd been right. Fidelia had made it clear many times that she thought I was holding her brother back, preventing him from succeeding. Why did it all have to be my fault? Hadn't Régulo made his own decisions? And yet, part of me wondered if I should set Régulo free. He needed freedom to pursue his dreams, just as I needed peace of mind and time to pursue mine. All that bickering, all that back-and-forth with our relatives, along with strict societal norms and accepted conventions, had worn us both out. Looking at the beautiful green hills and the tall guava trees, I decided that leaving Régulo was the only choice I had, the only way I could protect our love for each other. If I left now, before things got worse, at least we would remember the beautiful moments spent in each other's arms, our family meals, our conversations—not our fights and arguments. I had enough memories of those with Alessandro.

After my arrival in Bogotá, I rented a small house in Chapinero. I wanted to live in peace, for once in my life, without thinking about the needs and desires of others. Once I had settled down, I sent for my daughters. Régulo did not ask me for any explanations.

Months later, Fidelia surprised me with a visit. She was as cordial as ever, but I could not figure out why she was there. I was no longer a threat to her or her family. Then she mentioned, in passing, that Régulo had recently gotten married. I felt my heart break. Fidelia went on.

"Her name is Maria. I think he hoped to make you jealous."

"What is she like?" I asked.

"Neither interesting nor pretty. We both know Régulo did not marry for love," Fidelia said as she glanced at me. "In all fairness to the girl," she continued, "she has some good traits. I like her delicate hands and long fingers. She has a fragile neck and a petite frame."

"Have they known each other long?"

"I don't think so." Fidelia took a sip of tea. "Régulo told me he invited her out a couple of times. Before he knew it, he had met her family and they were engaged. He did not intend to marry her, but I think he hoped she would help him get over you."

A week later, Régulo came to visit Lucy and Alba and to tell me about his marriage.

I congratulated him. "You deserve a family of your own," I said. "I've created nothing but problems for you."

Régulo sat for a while, thinking. "What problems did you create for me?" he asked. "I learned to love you more than life itself. I experienced a passion I'll never feel again. Those are the problems you created for me, Inés, and for those problems I will always be grateful to you. But you had to make your choices, and if your love for me is but a shadow of what I feel for you, that is a problem without a possible solution."

"You're wrong, Régulo. I love you."

"I know," he answered. "I should not have married Maria. It's not fair to her. It's not her fault."

I turned to look at him. "I have always loved you, Régulo, and from the moment you first touched me, my love has never changed. But I also felt that I was holding you back, that you should be free. After Julio's death a sense of guilt overpowered me. I didn't think I deserved you."

"I was hoping to make you jealous," he said sadly.

"I'll always be jealous of any woman who sleeps by your side," I replied, "but I want you to be happy. If marrying Maria will make you happy, then I'm glad you did."

Régulo slammed the door on his way out. I thought then that I had lost him.

~

I decided to get on with my life, raise my girls, and sell my paintings to pay the rent and to put food on the table. As I looked around the room, I noticed a bowl of oranges. I picked one up, peeled it, and inhaled its aroma. It took me back to Somondoco, to my life with Régulo, to his arms. I wanted to cherish that memory forever. I decided then that I would make orange soap, so when I used it on my skin, it would remind me of my love.

That afternoon I set up a lab in the house, rounded up the ingredients, and got to work. It was grueling and my hands suffered, but in a few months I had produced enough soap bars to take them around to the perfumeries in the city. I sold out on the first day. More orders were placed, and I had to hire an assistant. People asked if I could make any other type of soap, but I was hesitant. I did, however, remember the rose fragrance I had made with Mother's roses many years earlier in Paipa, and I tried that again. It sold out as well. One of my customers traveled to Paris and took samples of my soap and my *agua de rosas* with her, and a couple of businesses placed orders. I had never imagined that a person could earn money doing something they enjoyed.

~

Régulo's marriage to Maria lasted fourteen months. During their honeymoon in Chile, they spent one day shopping for me, Lucy, and Alba. After their return, Régulo came to visit me and gave me a bottle of Chilean wine. We drank it together while he told me about Santiago and all the places he would like to take me.

Once the honeymoon was over, Régulo continued to visit me and my daughters. Maria became jealous. After one of her outbursts, Régulo agreed to stop seeing us. He wrote me letters instead.

Dear Inés,

Maria has started making friends. That doesn't bother me, except for the rumors. I don't know whether or not to believe the talk about her affairs with my employees. I heard that one of my drivers begged her to move in with him. If this is true, she probably turned him down because she does not want to leave her comfortable life. She comes from a large family, and she's never had the luxury of maids or fine china. Her closets are brimming with expensive clothes from Paris. In a few months, she has accumulated more shoes and purses than she would be able to use in a lifetime. Her jewelry box contains a vast array of earrings, brooches, and bracelets. She's easy to please. All I have to do is buy her new jewelry or a dress, and she'll be fine for weeks. I do not mind spending money on her; it makes me feel better for having married her.

I often marvel how two women can be so different from each other. I have never understood what makes you happy.

By the way, I saw one of your paintings at a gallery the other day. I recognized my bed. You have a wonderful sense of shape and color. I bought it. Why didn't you let me know you had started selling your art in local galleries? The gallery owner said you've had a couple of exhibits there already.

Yours,

Régulo

Dear Régulo,

I'm glad you like my painting. I'll let you know about the next exhibit. By the way, I've been making orange soap and agua de rosas. *The soap has a fancy French name, Savon a l'Orange. I'm sending you a sample. I miss you terribly in every sense.*

Fondly,

Inés

A month passed before I received another letter from Régulo.

Dear Inés,

Maria's lover finally showed up at my doorstep in the middle of the night, drunk. He started banging on the door and crying.

I took her back to her parents. "You can keep your daughter," I told them. Maria's family was outraged, and her two older brothers swore revenge. Initially, I did not take the threats seriously.

Two weeks later her brothers showed up with guns. I was standing with my back to the door, looking for a paper on my desk, when I felt a force push me to the left with such strength that I fell. Then I heard the shots. Each of the brothers fired three shots. They missed me every time, but they created a huge disturbance. I ended up buying a gun and challenging them to a duel. The authorities found out about it. I have been told I have to report to jail in three days. They plan to keep me there for a week. I've packed your orange soap and will take it with me. Every time I inhale its aroma, it takes me back to that night in Somondoco when we dreamed of making orange wine. I won't be allowed to bathe in prison, but I have a bottle of your agua de rosas *to keep me clean. Your scent brings back so many memories. I miss seeing you. I've started believing in guardian angels.*

Régulo

P.S. We're even. You've had Alessandro and I've had Maria, not that it's any comfort to me now.

During the time Régulo was in jail, I took him lunch every day. We would sit in his private cell and talk while he smoked cigarettes and I sketched on the pad I carried with me.

Once he was released, Régulo went back to his house, and he and I continued leading separate lives. Still, we saw each other during his visits to Lucy and Alba. Every time he visited the girls, I offered him a cup of coffee. If it wasn't raining, we sat outside watching the girls play in the garden and sharing our latest news. I liked to hear what books he was reading and what he thought about them, if he had discovered any new poets. Before leaving he always asked to see the painting I was working on.

One afternoon he stood in front of the canvas for a while, in silence.

"What are you thinking about?" I asked him.

"I wish I were a photographer so I could take a picture of you in front of your paintings," he mused. "They are so beautiful. The rest of the world deserves to see them."

Chapter Fifty-Five

After Régulo got out of jail, he needed time to sort things out, time to eliminate all traces of Maria's existence from his house and from his life. He wanted to go back to me and ask for another chance, but he didn't feel it was right to jump from his disastrous marriage to the love of his life.

"I just couldn't bring myself to approach you," he said when I asked him about it later, "to tell you I still loved you. Fear of rejection paralyzed me. Besides," he added, "it didn't feel right to go back to you after leaving a woman I had married on a whim, out of jealousy, and in an attempt to make you jealous."

I felt disappointed, but who was I to judge him? I had not handled things well either. I could have gone to Régulo, told him I loved him. But I didn't. I, too, was afraid of rejection. We were both to blame.

As the days went by, the more I thought about it, the more I imagined that Régulo didn't want to be with me. When he came to see the girls, we never spoke about the future.

During one of his visits, he mentioned that he had hired a woman named Augusta as a full-time housekeeper.

"I instructed her to get rid of all the clothes Maria had left behind," he said, "along with all her trinkets and the furniture she bought."

"Really?" I asked. "What did she say?"

"She asked me what I wanted her to do with the stuff. I said I didn't care. 'You can burn it if you'd like. I just want it out of my house.'"

Régulo told me that before she started working for him, Augusta had operated an elevator in the building where he rented an office on the third floor. She captured his attention one day, and during their daily conversations, they got to know each other. When Régulo offered her a job as his housekeeper, Augusta didn't hesitate to leave the office building. Apparently she had a good feeling about Régulo. Besides, he had offered to match her salary. Eventually, she ended up sharing his bed, evidently as she had planned.

Augusta resembled a Chinese porcelain statuette made in haste. She had a small face with sharply defined features, a thin neck, and a very large body that stood out especially when she wore bright colors. When I met her, Augusta showed me a picture of herself as a young woman, long before she became Régulo's mistress and her body expanded; she was wearing an old-fashioned suit and standing against a black Opel. She had left Ibagué and traveled to Bogotá with her slim body, sharp nose, and a suitcase of dreams. Shortly after her arrival, she met a tailor, and before she unpacked her suitcase in her boardinghouse, he gave her a tour of his shop. Nine months later the birth of their daughter changed Augusta's plans. The tailor never married her.

I was surprised when Régulo told me that he was sleeping with Augusta.

"She keeps me warm at night," he confided in me. "You know

I've never liked sleeping alone. When morning comes, she's out of bed before dawn."

"Maybe she knows it's not her place," I ventured.

"She knows about you," he replied. "You scare her. While looking through my papers the other day, she found out that we had applied for a marriage license in Ecuador. 'Thank God this is a Catholic country,' she told me. 'Inés will never be able to marry you. What does she want another husband for?'"

Clearly, Augusta failed to notice that my affection for Régulo transcended defined boundaries and social propriety.

A year after Régulo returned Maria to her parents, he found out through his lawyer that she had had a daughter by the name of Fannie. She claimed that the daughter was his and demanded that he include Fannie in his will. Régulo agreed to it as long as she cooperated with his efforts to get the Vatican to annul the marriage.

Chapter Fifty-Six

After Régulo and I ceased thinking that we would be sharing each other's lives, he started spending part of the year in Somondoco. He had never cared for Bogotá. Somondoco was his passion. Régulo went there every holiday to the same house where we had found happiness. When I thought about it, I wondered how he could share his bed and his daily meals with Augusta and at the same time write me letters mentioning his love for me.

Dear Inés,

I go to bed early so I can savor a moment alone. When I cannot sleep at night, I pass the hours reading a book, and then, beat by my own tiredness, I blow the candle out and sleep and half dream, until the moment when, in total darkness, I gain consciousness of my existence, of those around me, and of the objects that I have come to know by the habit of touching them.

In the dark I am more acutely aware of smells. The candle smoke, the wooden floors, the cherry wax that I always insist on. Cherry-scented floor wax has become difficult to find and quite expensive for a small town, but if they run out of it during the week, I ask Augusta's niece, Magdalena, to walk three kilometers to buy it. The young girl does not know, as she walks toward the town in her rugged shoes, mumbling to herself, that early in the morning while the world lies half asleep, the smell of cherry wax takes me back to my childhood when I lived in the main square of Somondoco with my family, and that it reminds me of the lovely, passionate nights I spent with you.

After lying in bed for a while, I rise slowly, gather my slippers and my housecoat, and head out to the veranda. From my mecedora *I stare at the firmament and think of you. The stars seem so close that sometimes I think it's true what they say about them influencing our future.*

I wonder, as I glance at the firmament, if you and I have shared another, happier lifetime and if we will see each other again during this one. God knows I long to see you and to hold you in my arms again. Perhaps it is this longing that has brought me back to Somondoco. We shared such blissful nights in this room. As I sit in my chair at dawn, I miss you.

Régulo

Inés,

I brought your orange soap and agua de rosas *with me, and I inhale their aromas when I'm thinking of you. I bathe every night with your soap. It feels like velvet on my skin.*

Last night, as I lay awake in the dark, thinking about our evenings with brandy and candlelight, I remembered your idea about orange wine. "Make wine from oranges," you said.

As I sat in my mecedora, *witnessing dawn, I decided you're right—if wine can be made with grapes, it can be made with oranges as well. I have the orange trees. I will make orange wine.*

Looking forward to the day we toast with orange wine,

Régulo

P.S. I'm sending you some oranges so you can make more soap.

~

It took Régulo six months to explain to his workers how to go about making wine from oranges. Afterward, there was always orange wine production in Somondoco.

Dear Inés,

The first bottle was ready today. I toasted you. I'm drinking another glass as I write. The color is a little murky, the aroma strong, and the taste similar to that of a Chianti. Here's to you, Inés, unforgettable Inés. You inspired me to create something new. Only you could do that. In vino veritas, I will always love you.

Régulo

For Régulo, the pleasure of producing orange wine seemed to surpass the satisfaction of building an empire. It also proved to be a wise investment. He sent barrels of his wine to relatives and friends. Fidelia and Ana Tulia served it at their restaurant.

The repercussions of the Depression in Colombia were devastating. In Somondoco, all the emerald mines shut down, and overnight, the wealth and prosperity that had come with mining disappeared. Local people lost their jobs, and hotels and restaurants went bankrupt.

Inés,

A town meeting was organized to discuss the dire situation in Somondoco. The mayor, Fidelia's son, described the crisis in full detail. "Gentlemen," he said, "the emeralds are gone. The gold is gone. Even our priest has left. We must find a way out of this crisis. Our young people are traveling to the city in search of opportunities, but they're coming back empty-handed. We need a solution, an idea, a miracle." Everyone sat in silence, hats on their laps. After a while, I spoke.

"Orange wine."

"What?"

"Orange wine. I have been making it at my farm," I said, "and I have perfected the process. We will become the Rioja region of South America."

Everyone stood and clapped. Over the last few months, Somondoco has become famous for its orange wine. Even the president of the republic wrote me a note praising my wine and wits. Some claim that the wine has miraculous powers. Supposedly, it heals people from their disappointments in love. Many have traveled from Bogotá to have a taste of it and heal their wounds. I will send you a bottle. It may heal you too.

Yours,

Régulo

P.S. It hasn't worked for me. I still miss you terribly.

Chapter Fifty-Seven

Alessandro was found lying face down with a dagger in his back. The news of his murder was published in all the local newspapers in the Colombian capital. The investigation took four months to complete, and at the end, Isabel confessed that she had poisoned him before using the dagger.

"I hate that man for what he did to me and to Inés," she concluded after her confession. My sister was sent to jail and her son, Raul, placed in an orphanage.

~

I was sitting in the garden putting the finishing touches to a painting when a bottle of orange wine arrived. Along with the wine, Régulo included a clipping of the newspaper article describing Alessandro's murder. He wrote *Now you're free* on the bottom.

I opened the package, uncorked the bottle, smelled the aroma, and took a sip. Initially, it felt bitter on my tongue, but then its sweetness sprang forth and overwhelmed me. I cried for Julio, for Alessandro, for Isabel, for Mother and Father. But my sorrow left just as quickly as it had come, and my passion for

Régulo erupted. I felt the empty space he had left inside of me and longed to have him fill it once again. That day, I vowed to return to Somondoco to find Régulo. I decided to buy a bus ticket for the next day. I was walking out the door when the postman arrived with another letter from Régulo.

Dearest Inés,

I have not been able to forgive myself for not taking you to Paris. I consider it one of the biggest mistakes of my life. Even though you didn't complain about it when I had to cancel the trip, I knew how deeply disappointed you were. Perhaps you have forgiven me, but I can't let it go. When I told you we wouldn't be able to travel, I probably came across as someone who didn't care about your art or your artistic career. Please believe me when I tell you nothing could be further from the truth. I feel such admiration for you—love too. All this time, I've been searching for a way to make it up to you. I think I finally found it.

I have great news: Our orange wine will be crossing the ocean! A winery in La Rioja has agreed to purchase one thousand barrels a year. I had reached out to several wineries in Spain, and one of them responded. The owners decided to travel to Somondoco to "taste this orange wine you rave about in your letter," they replied. They stayed a few days with me, observing how the wine is made. After their visit I received another letter stating that they were committed and asking me to get back to them as soon as possible. "I'm sure you know how special your orange wine is," Señor Gonzales, the main owner, wrote. "It can change your life. Our wines are excellent, but they don't have that power."

I am to travel there in a month to sign the contract, and I told them that my partner, Inés Camargo, must be included in that contract. Half of the earnings will go to you. After all, it was your idea to make orange wine. I've asked my lawyer to draft a separate contract for us. We will be equal partners. The Spaniards agreed to my terms and want to meet with you as well. I've taken the liberty of purchasing two tickets for Spain aboard the Altamira, *and of handling reservations for our stay over there. I hope you will agree to come. It could be the honeymoon we never had. I thought you could also bring samples of your orange soap and rose water. We can drop them off at the perfumeries in Madrid.*

If you are concerned about Lucy and Alba, I want you to know that I have asked Chata if she would stay with them while we are gone. She agreed wholeheartedly. She's going to tell Rosa that she has a religious retreat, and she'll go stay at your house instead. "It will be more like a children's retreat," Chata joked. The religious excuse was her idea. She said she's delighted she'll be able to spend some time away from Rosa. I hope you don't mind that I took the initiative to ask your sister for her help.

Love you, as always,
Régulo

I reread the letter again and again and grew happier each time. I had never been to Spain and had always dreamed of seeing the landscape Cervantes describes in such detail in *Don Quixote de la Mancha. How could I reject Régulo's offer? He made me his business partner! I will finally have a stable income. We are going to Spain. . . . We are going to Spain!* I sang and danced around the room before sitting down to write my brief reply.

Yes, yes, yes!
Love,
Inés

~

Régulo asked my permission to put together an itinerary. I agreed, and we started meeting a couple of times a week so he could bring me up to date.

"I admire Miguel de Unamuno's writing," Régulo said one afternoon, "and I've always wanted to visit Salamanca, the city where he lives."

"I'd love to go," I replied. "My mother often spoke about Salamanca and its famous plaza, the most beautiful in Spain, according to her."

"Perfect!" Régulo exclaimed. "I think we should spend a couple of months in Madrid and then stop in Salamanca for a little while before heading over to La Rioja."

Chapter Fifty-Eight

A month after I received his letter inviting me to join him, Régulo and I embarked on the journey that would take us to Spain for four months.

We took a ship from Cartagena to Málaga. During our stay there, we visited the fortress built in the eleventh century by the third Berber king of the Taifa of Granada. It was magnificent, worth the challenge of climbing up those hills to reach it. From the fortress we went to the cathedral, built between the sixteenth and eighteenth centuries. The climate was ideal, and the sun and the warm temperatures were so different from the cloudy and rainy Bogotá weather. We walked on the beach, soaked up the sun, and found local restaurants serving delicious fish dishes including fried sardines and anchovies, a cold garlic soup that we were told had been brought to Spain by the Greeks, and local wines. Of all the wines we tried, muscatel left the sweetest taste in our mouths. Régulo was delighted to discover that Málaga's wine culture had its roots in the Phoenicians, who founded the city, and that besides their garlic soup, the Greeks had also brought olive oil to the Iberian Peninsula. Walking along ancient streets, we caught glimpses of courtyards with pink and fuchsia peonies, roses, and orange and lemon trees planted in large terra-cotta pots.

"So that's where the scent of orange and lemon I smell every-where comes from," Régulo said.

"I've been smelling the roses too," I added.

"Of course you have!" Régulo teased. "You are a master per-fumer; you have a keen sense of smell."

"I wish I had brought some of my painting materials," I mused. "There are so many beautiful spots here I would love to paint."

"We'll find some supplies for you," Régulo said. "You can make the sketches here and finish them when we get to Madrid. You'll find everything you need there." That afternoon Régulo gave me a sketch pad and a box of pencils. I was overcome with joy.

"Where did you find these?" I asked as I turned the blank pages one by one, imagining what I would draw on each one.

"I asked the hotel owner," he replied. "Draw," he added. "Capture what you are seeing, and you'll have sketches you can use in paintings later on."

From Málaga we traveled to Córdoba, a city with a mixture of Roman, Arab, Jewish, and Spanish cultures, but with an iden-tity all its own. Drier than Málaga, but like that city, warm and full of sunshine, Córdoba was a walker's paradise. Régulo and I strode along the city streets all the way to the Guadalquivir River and crossed the splendid Roman bridge built in the first century BC. We spent hours meandering along small, narrow streets looking at shops, restaurants, and cafés, and stopped to admire the courtyards of houses with beautiful gardens brimming with flowers and orange and lemon trees. But the biggest surprises were the large orange trees along the streets, which we were told had been planted in the city by caliphs during the fifteenth century to decorate around the Great Mosque of Córdoba, which was started in 785 to 786. The oranges, large and bright, brought color to the city like the pink geraniums and red carnations hanging in colorful pots outside the white buildings.

We spent several afternoons in the mosque and its adjacent cathedral. Régulo hired a private tour guide to tell us about the history of the buildings and how they came together as the two religions they represented coexisted in the city. The guide then took us to visit the synagogue in the Jewish quarter, built in the fourteenth century. I found it amazing that these different cultures and their religions had been living in peace until the Reconquista, when the Catholic monarchs decided to recapture territory from the Muslims who had occupied most of the Iberian Peninsula since the eighth century.

We sat for hours at outdoor restaurants enjoying local dishes and talking about all the discoveries we were making. We tasted eggplant with honey for the first time, and it became one of our favorite dishes. We also had a soup that had just been prepared, a dish called *salmorejo,* served cold like the garlic soup in Málaga, but consisting of bread, tomato, and olive oil.

All around the city we heard guitar music and singing, in taverns and in places called *tablaos,* where you could experience flamenco. We spent several evenings in *tablaos,* fascinated by the music, the song, and the dance. As we discovered, people stayed up late in Spain, and they didn't hold back, celebrating life and love. Régulo and I were free to do as we pleased, we could stay up late and sleep late if we wanted, and we could take our time making love. During our time in Spain, we rekindled our passion for each other. Our love grew.

I was sad to leave Andalusia for Castilla and Madrid, but Régulo reassured me.

"You'll find things to love there as well, *mi amor.* Madrid is a vibrant city, full of artists, intellectuals, and sophisticated people," he told me. He was right.

In Madrid we lived for two months in a hotel located close to La Castellana Boulevard, a busy street filled with cafés, restaurants, and flaneurs, Baudelaire's casual strollers. Like them, we walked through the boulevards and streets, ate at taverns and restaurants, visited the Prado Museum, and walked through El Retiro Park. During one of our walks at El Retiro, we saw Ricardo Bellver's masterpiece, *Fuente del Ángel Caído,* the *Fountain of the Fallen Angel,* inspired by lines in Milton's *Paradise Lost.* Bellver's angel looked so proud and angry, but also beautiful, like the angel I had encountered in the cornfield in Paipa.

On Sundays, we sat at a café in Plaza Mayor and watched families with children and young men and women dressed in church clothes stroll around the plaza. They had so much life, so much *salero,* meaning elegance and grace. In fact, the women walked as straight as if they had all taken ballet lessons during their childhood. Régulo and I loved the Castilian accent, the way Spaniards pronounced their *c*'s and *z*'s.

Remembering my visit to Florence, I had packed stylish, comfortable shoes for my trip to Spain. After returning from Italy, I had had a local shoe cobbler copy the models I had brought from Florence. Fortunately, they were classic shoes that would never go out of fashion, but by the time we arrived in Madrid, the three pairs of shoes I had brought with me were worn out. I went shopping and bought a new pair of handmade suede pumps and a beautiful black box-shaped calf purse at Loewe, the Spanish high-fashion store. Régulo was right; I fell in love with Madrid as well. Bigger than Málaga and Córdoba, it reminded me more of Bogotá, except more sophisticated. I loved shopping in Madrid. The salespeople were knowledgeable, respectful, and attentive. I visited the shop of a seamstress recommended by a saleslady at Loewe and ordered several new dresses.

"We can have a fitting before you leave for Salamanca," she said. "I'll have them ready when you come back to Madrid after visiting La Rioja."

I walked around Madrid admiring the architecture, so different from that of Florence and Bogotá. Madrid's streets were wider, and the sculptures and paintings in the Prado were astounding. I also loved the churches. My favorite one among them was Los Jerónimos, built in Gothic style in the early sixteenth century. Standing outside this magnificent building, I recalled the day in Paipa when I had vowed never to return to church, but as I entered the monastery, a feeling of peace came over me. Since that afternoon I made it a habit of going in any time I was in the area and praying for Chata, Lucy, Alba, and Julio. The façade of the church looked as delicate as embroidery. I wanted to paint it. Everywhere in the city I saw scenes I wanted to paint. Fortunately, I found an art shop close to Puerta del Sol and bought watercolors, more pencils, and a handmade notebook with paper thick enough for watercolors.

Régulo spent the mornings reading while I worked on my drawings. After a leisurely lunch, we would walk to one of the parks or to a museum. We spent hours meandering the streets of Madrid, sitting at cafés, and talking about our lives, our plans. One of our favorite destinations was Café Gijón in Paseo de Recoletos. We walked there in the afternoons for *café con leche* or a glass of wine and to watch the writers, artists, and intellectuals who participated in social gatherings or *tertulias*.

Evenings were long and sweet. After dinner we sat on our hotel terrace, listening to the crowds below, sharing our impressions of the day. Nights, we slept in each other's arms. Making love in Madrid and Málaga and Córdoba was as wonderful as it had been in Bogotá and in Somondoco, except now we didn't have to worry about our families or anybody else. It truly felt like a honeymoon. No matter how much time had passed, our passion had not diminished. On the contrary.

"I got us tickets for a zarzuela," Régulo said one evening. "Tomorrow's performance of *El rey que rabió* begins at eight p.m."

"That's wonderful!" I exclaimed. "I've never seen a zarzuela on stage."

"I think you'll like this one," he replied. "It's a love story with mistaken identities and a king who falls in love. The music is excellent."

"Will they also have singing and dancing?"

"But of course!" Régulo assured me. "I think you'll find it more entertaining than Italian opera, even though opera originated a century before the zarzuela and has its own merits."

"My Spanish is better than my Italian, though," I joked. "I'll be able to understand the dialogue and the songs."

Régulo and I went to the Prado at least once a week. There we saw Diego Velázquez's painting *Las Meninas*, as well as his *Crucified Christ*, and some of Goya's work. We also traveled to Toledo to visit El Greco's house and to see his paintings.

However, the painting that impressed me the most during our time in Spain was *The Childhood of the Virgin* by Francisco de Zurbarán. In it, Zurbarán painted the Virgin Mary as a young girl, with her parents next to her. The colors in the painting—the reds and whites, framed by a dark background—were exquisite.

The little girl in the center of the canvas looks up, her face full of hope and illuminated with potential. Zurbarán's magnificent work of art brought tears to my eyes.

One early morning we left for Salamanca. I sat by the train window thinking of Don Quixote, watching the Castilian landscape, and knowing how fortunate I was to be there with Régulo. He had booked a hotel close to Plaza Mayor. We dropped our bags off and went to have lunch in the plaza. The city, smaller than Madrid, with narrower streets, was still impressive. We took the stairs to one of the entrances to the plaza. As we climbed the steps, neither one of us was prepared for the beautiful square we would find at the top. We stepped through an arch into the square. Régulo took my hand. For a while, we stood admiring the beautiful buildings, the arches surrounding the plaza, and the cafés. Mother had been right. It was exquisite, so stunning it took my breath away. Smaller than Madrid's Plaza Mayor, and built in the same baroque style, Salamanca was by far the prettier of the two. We found a table at Café Novelty, famous for its literary *tertulias*, and sat down, happy to spend an afternoon in this lovely part of the world.

During our week in Salamanca, Régulo and I visited La Catedral Vieja de Santa María, dating back to the twelfth century, and La Catedral Nueva, which was started in 1513. We also took walks on the Roman bridge, toured the university, and tried as many restaurants as we possibly could. Café Novelty became our afternoon spot. Soon after we started going there, the artists and intellectuals who sat in the back for their *tertulias* invited us to participate in their conversations. We were delighted. Unamuno showed up once and got into a serious discussion about religion with Régulo. Listening to them, I was reminded of Régulo's vast reading and his intelligence.

During our tour of the university, I learned that Christopher Columbus had visited the city and met with university geographers before leaving for the New World.

"Are there any famous people who haven't been here?" I asked Régulo.

"Not many," he replied.

Those days in Salamanca were unforgettable for both of us. Now we had memories of four lovely cities in Spain, four places to return to one day.

We took an evening train from Salamanca to La Rioja and arrived in Logroño midmorning the next day.

Chapter Fifty-Nine

In Logroño we stayed in a small hotel located in the main plaza. After Madrid and Salamanca, this town in La Rioja seemed more tranquil. From the hotel balcony we could see rows and rows of grapevines far in the distance. The owners of the winery had invited us to join them for dinner and sent a car to fetch us. The restaurant was located outside of town. As the car rode up a hill, we saw an imposing villa surrounded by vineyards and olive trees. There were a few men standing outside.

"Señor Gonzales is waiting for us," Régulo said. "He's the one in the middle." The gentleman approached our car and shook Régulo's hand as soon as we got out. He then turned to me and kissed me on both cheeks, which I found surprising.

"Inés, please forgive me for being so friendly," he said. "I feel like I know you, like we've already met. Régulo told me so much about you when I visited Somondoco. My only regret is that I didn't get to meet you then."

I was taken aback by his candor, but I felt it was genuine. "It's a pleasure to meet you, Señor Gonzales," I said. "I'm delighted to be here."

"Please call me Miguel," he replied. "Let's go in and join the others. We are throwing a party in your honor." He showed us the way.

"Really?" I asked. "But why?"

"Because you and Régulo have created a special wine that will bring us all wealth and happiness," he replied.

We joined a large group of people inside the restaurant and were led to a private room and invited to sit at the main table with Miguel and the other owners. I had Régulo to my left and Miguel to my right. The meal started with cava, cheese, and *jamón serrano,* similar to prosciutto. After the introductions and a speech by Miguel celebrating our partnership, we were served a series of local dishes, which included potatoes Rioja style; *caparrones,* a Spanish bean stew made with chorizo sausage; quail with white beans; cod with a delicious tomato sauce; and other delicacies. A different Rioja wine accompanied every dish.

"I hope you like our local cuisine," Miguel said. "It was such a delight to try some of your Colombian dishes when I was in Somondoco."

"It's nice to hear you liked our food," I replied. "You have such wonderful wines in Spain."

"I'm glad you like our wines," he commented, "though none are as good as your orange wine."

"Do you really believe that?" I asked, surprised.

"Why, yes, our finest wine may be able to transport you to paradise for a moment, but it cannot make you feel the way your orange wine does. Drinking this Rioja," he said, lifting the glass to his lips and taking a sip, "is very pleasant, but you don't relive past experiences the way you do with your orange wine. Our wines don't heal. Yours does."

I realized then that what I had considered my own

subjective thoughts about the wine were actual characteristics that it possessed.

We were scheduled to sign the contract the next day. That morning Régulo took a package out of his bag and started unwrapping it.

"When we sign the contract, I want us to toast with our wine," he said, showing me two bottles of orange wine. "They made it! We'll take them to the winery."

In the evening, after a tour of the vineyards and a tasting of local wines, we signed the contract with Miguel and the owners of the winery. Régulo uncorked a bottle of orange wine.

"To our partnership," he said, raising his glass. "May it last a long time, and may it bring us all success."

"Chin-chin," everyone in the room repeated at once.

"Thank you for this special treat, Régulo," one of the owners said.

I turned to him. "Can I ask you a question?"

"Yes, of course, Inés," Miguel replied.

"You have such fine wines in Spain," I said. "The Riojas we tasted last night and a minute ago are delightful. Our orange wine is a bit bitter and doesn't match your best wines in quality. I'm curious to know why you would be interested in importing our wine, when you could figure out how to make it here. What made you decide to buy it from us?"

"Mi querida señora, my dear lady," one of Miguel's colleagues said. "I'm glad to hear you appreciate our wines; they are fine wines indeed. But there is one ingredient in your wine that I don't think we would ever be able to replicate in ours. Hence our interest in your orange wine. If it didn't have this ingredient, we would not be investing in your company."

"And what ingredient is that?" Régulo asked.

The man shrugged. “We don’t know,” he said. “But what we do know is that it’s a mysterious, magical ingredient. We noticed it when we were in Somondoco and you organized the wine tasting, Régulo. After drinking your wine my colleagues and I felt immediately better, as if a burden had been lifted from our shoulders.” He looked first at Régulo and then at me. Miguel nodded. “You must both be aware of the fact that your wine heals people. In fact, I’ve been dying to ask you. What is your secret?”

Régulo smiled. I took another sip of wine. The Spaniard was right. One felt better after drinking it.

“Well,” Régulo said, “it’s a combination of things. The orange groves in Somondoco are special. They were started by one of my ancestors who moved from Valencia to Boyacá.”

“Of course, that makes sense,” the wine producer commented. “The best oranges come from Valencia. I should have thought of it. But the origin doesn’t explain everything. Otherwise, we would be able to make it here. I confess we tried but didn’t succeed.”

“The other part is a bit more complicated to explain,” Régulo went on. “Some of my ancestors had the gift of seeing.”

“What do you mean, ‘the gift of seeing’?” one of the employees asked.

“They were clairvoyant. This gift has been passed down through the women in the family. When the first orange trees appeared, my great-great-grandmother sat in the middle of the orange grove and blessed the trees and their fruit. She then predicted that a special nectar would one day be made from their oranges, and that this nectar would have magical powers to heal people, not only physically, but also spiritually.”

Everyone in the room fell silent.

“What else?” someone asked.

"It would mend broken hearts, dissolve jealousy and envy, and protect those who drank it."

"That's amazing!" Miguel said. "Why didn't you tell us this when we were in Somondoco?"

"Because I wanted you to find out for yourselves. If you heard it from me, you might assume I was making it all up to sell our wine."

Several people extended their glasses for refills. Régulo uncorked the second bottle of wine and started pouring.

"Furthermore," Régulo added, "my great-great-grandmother also predicted that a woman with the letter *i* in her name would be the one to come up with the idea of the nectar, and of other healing potions."

Everyone looked at me. I felt warm, with color on my cheeks. My legs grew weak.

"Inés Camargo!" one of the three owners exclaimed. "Did you know that?"

They were all staring at me. Someone brought a chair. I sat down without speaking.

"In all fairness to Inés," Régulo went on, "I had not told her about the prophecy."

"But why not?" another owner asked.

"Because my great-great-grandmother also said that this person would suffer in love, and suffer loss, and that going through that suffering would give her the understanding she would need to heal herself and others, but only when she acted with love and a pure heart. I had forgotten about the prophecy until I met Inés, and then, when I remembered it, I feared that if I told her that one of my relatives had predicted we would meet and that I thought she was the person they had described, she would think

I was crazy. Also, how could I tell her she would have to suffer in order to express her gifts as a healer?"

"You can't play with destiny," one of the women said.

"Beautiful señora," an owner addressed me, "what do you think of all this?"

"I don't know what to say," I replied. "At first, when Régulo mentioned his great-great-grandmother's notebook, I thought he was joking, but now that he looks so serious, I actually think it does exist. I'd love to see it."

"And what other healing potions have you concocted?"

"She has *agua de rosas* and orange soap," Régulo answered.

"Did you bring samples?"

"I did," I replied, "but I ran out in Madrid."

"That's too bad. We have connections here and overseas," the gentleman said. "We could help you sell and distribute them in Europe."

"Actually, I put some samples aside to bring today." Régulo opened his briefcase and took two orange soaps and a small bottle of rose water out and handed them to the man. I couldn't believe my good fortune. The gentleman took the soap and the rose water, inhaled their aromas, and passed them around for the others to do the same.

"Exquisite!" he pronounced. "You make a good team," he told Régulo. "She's the creative spirit behind the enterprise, and you, Régulo—you are the businessman who puts the deals together. What an amazing couple!"

Chapter Sixty

After our stay in La Rioja, we stopped in Madrid for a week. There we stayed at the same hotel and walked to Café Gijón in the afternoon for the *tertulia*. A few days after our arrival, as I was leaving for the seamstress's shop, Régulo stopped me at the door and kissed me.

"I made reservations for tonight at a very special restaurant," he said. "Perhaps you should wear one of your new dresses for the occasion."

I was intrigued. "We've already been to many special restaurants," I replied. "I can't imagine what would make this one more special."

"You'll see." Régulo winked.

As requested, I selected one of my new dresses to wear. It fit me perfectly. Looking in the mirror, I had to admit the color suited me. I had been reluctant when the seamstress had first recommended a red silk for the dress I had in mind, but now I could see she had been right. I added a pearl necklace and earrings I had bought in a local jewelry store and went to show Régulo.

"Inés!" he exclaimed when I walked into the room. "You look stunning!"

"Thank you, *mi amor*," I replied. "Which shoes do you think I should wear? Will we do a lot of walking?"

"You can wear any shoes you'd like," Régulo said. "I hired a driver to take us to the restaurant."

We rode through the city streets all the way to Plaza Mayor in a lovely car. Watching the city and the Madrileños, I daydreamed about living in Spain with Régulo. Perhaps one day.

"We are here," the driver finally announced as he pulled up by the restaurant. "Calle de Cuchilleros 17." Régulo opened the restaurant door for me and followed me in.

"Good evening. Welcome to Casa Botín," the host remarked. "Have you been here before?"

"I have," Régulo replied, "but the lady hasn't."

"Wonderful!" he said, turning to me. "I get to tell you a little about our history. Rumor has it that ours is the oldest restaurant in the world."

"Really?" I asked.

"Yes. It was founded in 1725," he said. "Since then, we've been serving kings and queens, artists, writers, politicians, actors, and discriminating people. We are famous for our lamb and our *cochinillo*," he explained. "I recommend you try them both." The host continued talking as he led us down the stairs. "The restaurant has remained in the same family since the beginning. Have you heard of Francisco Goya?"

"Yes," I replied, "we saw his paintings in the Prado."

"Then you'll be happy to hear that he worked here at Casa Botín as a waiter while waiting to be accepted to the Royal Academy of Fine Arts."

"That's amazing," I replied. "Was he a good waiter?"

"I have no idea," the host confessed. "But I imagine he was

better at painting than at waiting on tables. He looks a bit crazy in his self-portraits, right?"

Régulo and I laughed.

He pointed to a corner table. "The table you requested, señor," he said to Régulo.

It was a magical evening. Régulo and I talked, savoring the specialties of the house, including the *cochinillo asado* and the lamb that the host recommended. The wine, a red Rioja we had tasted during our visit to that region a few days earlier, was superb. Most tables were full, and people were enjoying lively conversations. At one point, everyone grew quiet as a man was shown to his table. He was tall and had an imposing figure. Our waiter informed us that it was a famous American émigré writer.

After dessert, Régulo ordered coffee and cognac. As I sipped my cognac, I watched him take a box out of his pocket. It was wrapped in beautiful blue paper. He handed it to me.

"Inés," he whispered, "I want you to know that regardless of what happens between us after our return to Bogotá, I would like you to keep this token of my love for you."

"You sound so serious," I replied, unwrapping the box and opening it to find an emerald-and-diamond ring. It took my breath away.

"Régulo," I said, "it's beautiful."

"Try it on," he insisted.

I slid the ring on my finger. It fit perfectly.

"I brought the stones with me and had it made by a jeweler here," Régulo explained. "Please keep it on, Inés. Nothing would make me happier than to see you wearing it." He put the empty box back in his pocket and lit a cigarette.

I looked at my ring while Régulo smoked. The emerald was

large and dark, with so much radiance. The diamonds next to it made it shine brighter.

"Is this an engagement ring?" I asked.

"I would like it to be an engagement ring, *mi amor*." Régulo took my hand in his. "But if you are not ready to say yes, I still want you to keep it and to wear it when you feel like it, as a reminder of my love for you, which will never change no matter what life brings our way," he added, kissing my fingers.

"Where did you find the emerald?" I asked.

"I've had it for a long time," he replied. "It belonged to my great-great-grandmother, who gave it to my grandmother, who then gave it to me before she died. 'Régulo,' she said, 'use it to make a ring and give it to the woman you wish to marry, and it will happen.' Obviously, she didn't know it would be so complicated. Or . . . perhaps she did."

"If she was clairvoyant she did," I said. "You know, the emerald is the stone of the seers."

"Yes," Régulo replied. "And a symbol of truth and love."

"It's also supposed to bring success in creative endeavors."

"That's right, *mi amor*," Régulo said as he blew the smoke out. "And you are an exceptional artist. This reminds me of something I recently read. Have you ever heard of duende?"

"What do you mean? The little magical beings?" I asked. "Many years ago, in Paipa, I saw one in a field. Remember? I told you the story."

"I remember. You are fortunate to have seen one," Régulo said, "but that's not what I meant. I'm talking about García Lorca's duende, the creative spirit that some people personify."

"I have never heard that definition of duende," I said.

"It describes a mysterious power that a work of art embodies and its capacity to move someone profoundly."

"Really?"

"Yes, duende is also the ability an artist has, whether she is a singer, dancer, musician, or a painter, like you, to fill the stage with her sole presence and to move the public through the expression of her art. Remember the flamenco performance we saw when we first arrived in Madrid?"

"Yes. It was incredible. But what does it have to do with duende and with García Lorca?" I asked.

"Last year Lorca gave a lecture in Buenos Aires titled 'Juego y Teoría del Duende.' He's interested in popular culture and popular art, and he's been studying both. I read the script and found it fascinating. But I'm telling you all this because I've been thinking that you have duende."

"Me?"

"Yes, you," Régulo replied, laughing.

Not knowing what to say, I looked around the restaurant. The American writer caught my eye. He was smiling, as if he had been eavesdropping on our conversation. His Spanish must have been better than I thought.

A few minutes later a waiter approached our table. "The señor sitting over there asked if you would like to join him for an after-dinner drink," he said.

Régulo and I looked at each other and then at the famous writer. He raised his arm and beckoned us over. The waiters were already moving another table next to his.

"*Perfecto,* señores," the headwaiter announced. "Now you'll have more room. What can I bring you?" he asked.

I noticed the small milky-looking liqueur in the writer's hand.

"What are you drinking, señor?" I asked.

"Crema de orujo," he replied. "Have you ever tasted it?"

I shook my head.

"You should try it," he said. "It's made from the leftover skin of the grape after it's been crushed and macerated to make wine."

"So, it's sort of like a grappa?" Régulo asked.

"Yes, but much sweeter," the writer explained. "It comes from Galicia. Legend has it that a monk invented it, used it to cure the sick, and added honey to it. It also contains a bit of caramel, which makes it taste even sweeter." He took a sip before handing me the glass. "Would you like to try it?"

I took a small sip. "It's delightful," I exclaimed. All at once, flavors of honey and caramel spread throughout my mouth. Régulo ordered two of them.

"Tell me about you," the writer said after we toasted with the *orujo*. "Have you been to Madrid before?"

"I have," Régulo replied, "but it's Inés's first time. Do you come here often?"

"Yes, as often as I can," he answered. "I love Spain. I carry it in my veins. Where's your home?"

"Bogotá, Colombia," Régulo answered. "Have you been there?"

"No," he said, "but I would like to go. I visited Cuba on my way to Key West a few years ago. It's charming. I plan to return. Do you know it?"

We shook our heads.

"How many times have you visited Madrid?" he asked Régulo.

"I came here twice when I was an emerald dealer and sold stones to jewelers all over Europe," he answered.

"What a fascinating profession!" the writer exclaimed. "A bit like writing. I imagine you look at the stones as I look at words, trying to find the perfect one, the one that captures an idea or a feeling the way an emerald captures the light. My job is to make this happen in as simple and honest a manner as possible."

"Exactly," Régulo agreed.

I noticed a notebook and two pencils on the table. "Are you writing a novel?" I asked.

He picked up the notebook and flipped through the pages. "I'm working on paragraphs, describing scenes I plan to include in a future novel or short story," he replied. "They are memories, personal experiences I write down before I forget all the details. I save them until I'm ready to use them." He added a period after a sentence and closed the notebook.

Régulo pulled out two emeralds from his vest pocket and placed them in the palm of the writer's large hand.

The author studied them. "So, you came back to Spain to sell emeralds?" he asked Régulo.

"No," I replied, "we came here to sell orange wine."

"Really?" He looked at me.

The waiter poured water in our water glasses. He had been listening to our conversation. "Orange wine?" he asked. "You know, *señor* is a wine expert. He knows more about wine than our sommelier."

The writer smiled. He opened his notebook once more, found a page, and read aloud a paragraph praising wine—its sophistication, delicious flavors, natural qualities, and the pleasure we experience while drinking it.

"I agree!" Régulo said.

"Tell me about your orange wine," the writer requested.

Régulo and I described our wine and mentioned some stories about its healing properties and the winery in La Rioja.

"That's fascinating!" the American commented. "I would like to try this orange wine. You can describe wine only after you have tasted it. Each wine requires different words. I'm wondering which words would suit your orange wine."

"Really?" I was intrigued.

"Yes," he continued, "I'll show you what I mean." He opened his notebook again and started flipping through the pages until he found what he was looking for.

I sat mesmerized, paying attention as he described a dinner of seafood paella paired with a bottle of Verdejo wine, a delightful combination of flavors. Listening to his words, I pictured him pouring a glass of Verdejo, inhaling its aroma, and taking in the notes of laurel, hay, and almonds before drinking. In simple, straightforward language, the writer revealed how each sip of cold, crisp wine added surprising layers of savor to the cod, shrimp, mussels, and rice seasoned with saffron.

I was astounded. "That's absolutely beautiful," I exclaimed. "You are a master at capturing the sensory experience."

"Brilliant," Régulo agreed. "I hope you'll be inspired to write something as lovely after you taste our orange wine. If you give me your address, I'll send you a case."

"The safest thing would be to send it to the Ritz in Paris," the writer explained. "I'll be traveling there in a few weeks, and I plan to remain in Paris until the fall."

He looked at me. "What do you like most about Madrid?" he asked.

"The museums," I replied. "I could spend a whole day in the Prado studying Zurbarán's paintings."

"Ah, the Spanish Caravaggio," he exclaimed. "Are you a painter?"

I was about to reply, but Régulo answered for me.

"Her work has been exhibited in Paris," he said, his voice full of pride.

"Wonderful," the writer exclaimed. "You must give me the name of the gallery or the museum. I'll go see your art when I get there. Here, write it in my notebook," he said, handing me one of his pencils.

I wrote it on the last page.

"I love art," the American author mused, "almost as much as I love wine. Maybe more."

When I asked him who his favorite painter was, he said he liked the impressionists, especially Monet and Cézanne, and asked me if I was familiar with their work. I shook my head no.

"You should travel to Paris to see their paintings."

"Why?"

The American writer explained that he had learned from these French masters by studying their paintings and had gained a deeper understanding of writing by analyzing their work. He went on to say that during his stay in Paris, he finally understood the art of writing sparse, honest sentences that mirrored paintings he greatly admired and that he believed the impressionists taught him a great deal about the importance of simplicity and sincerity in art.

Régulo and I stared at the American, fascinated, waiting for him to say more.

He took another sip of the *orujo* and said that while living in Paris, he visited the Musée de l'Orangerie, the Louvre, and the Musée du Luxembourg, seeking inspiration. He used to go there during his lunch break to look at paintings instead of eating.

"You exchanged food for art?" I asked. "How could you concentrate on an empty stomach?"

He laughed.

"So, Monet's and Cézanne's art gave you a new way to approach your writing?" Régulo asked.

He nodded.

He was right, I thought. There is no substitute for simplicity, a measured tone, a straightforward style without subterfuge. I wanted to write down what this brilliant writer had just said. I wanted to learn from him just as he had learned from Cézanne. He seemed to be thinking about something.

"I learned to understand Cézanne much better and to see truly how he made landscapes when I was hungry," he continued. "I used to wonder if he were hungry, too, when he painted. . . . Later I thought Cézanne was probably hungry in a different way."

"Since we've been in Spain, Inés has been painting with watercolors," Régulo volunteered. "She has captured beautiful scenes in Madrid, Salamanca, and La Rioja."

"I'm afraid they're not very good," I said. "Nothing like Cézanne's."

"It's her first time using watercolors," Régulo explained. "I'm not an art critic, but I think they're excellent."

"Régulo!" I was going to ask him to stop talking, but the writer interrupted me.

"I would like to see them," he stated.

We agreed to meet for coffee at Café Gijón the next day so I could show him my drawings.

My new friend took his time looking at the watercolors. I had managed to paint a total of fifty or so drawings.

"Régulo is right," he finally said. "These are excellent, simple and true, like the best writing."

"I'm glad you like them," I replied, my heart beating fast.

"This one is my favorite," he added, pointing to a sketch of Plaza de Santa Ana. "Listen, Inés, if you are willing to trust me with these drawings, I'll take them to Paris. I have a friend who owns a gallery there. I think he'll want to buy them. I leave tomorrow."

"Why, of course!" I replied. "I would be honored."

Chapter Sixty-One

During our return trip on the *Altamira*, Régulo and I talked about the beautiful places we had visited, our good fortune with the Rioja winery, and our past and our present—but not about the future. We spent time in bed, sat on the ship's deck and watched the stars, and enjoyed lovely dinners and dance and song. One night, shortly before we were due to arrive in Cartagena, Régulo took my face in his hands.

"I would love to have you back in my life every day, Inés," he said. "You don't have to give me an answer now. Think about it after we get back. Take your time. I'm willing to wait for you."

"Are you sure you're not going to get yourself married *otra vez*, again?" I teased.

"I'm sure," Régulo said. "I've been cured."

"Completely?"

"Completely."

~

When we got back to Bogotá, Régulo sent the American writer a case of orange wine. Months later, we received a lovely note from him stating that the wine had arrived safely, all the bottles intact after the long journey. His letter chronicled how he chilled a bottle of our wine, opened it as soon as it felt cold enough, and chose to pair it with caviar. In his simple and exquisite style, the writer described spoonful after spoonful of caviar, followed by sips of orange wine that added a taste of tanginess. First the wine turned sweet, then dry like the finest champagne. The chilled wine with its crisp taste brought memories of his happiest moments, but he also relived his past mistakes and felt all the regrets he had been carrying inside and the deepest sadness, as if the wine were cleansing his mind and heart, healing his soul. And then he felt at peace, filled with hope.

In this letter the writer also mentioned that as soon as he arrived in Paris, he went to see my painting *Rouge*, which he described as a *capo lavoro*—as the Italians would say, a masterpiece. Quite different from my watercolors, he noted, but just as fascinating. I was thrilled to hear that he had sold the watercolors I left with him to his friend, the gallery owner, and that soon he would wire me the money. This gallery owner had decided to organize an exhibit for me, my first solo show, and he wanted me to ship my most recent drawings and paintings as soon as possible to his address in France. The last line of the writer's letter was a question: "When are you coming to Paris?"

~

I wanted to write him back right away and tell him that since my return to Bogotá, I had been painting almost every day. In fact, I painted when I wasn't taking care of Lucy and Alba or making my *agua de rosas* or my orange soap. Soon I had to hire more assistants and rent a larger space to produce my potions, as they were called in Spain. My daughters, my potions, and my art kept me so busy I didn't have time to think about my future with Régulo. My busy life gave me the excuse I needed to postpone making a decision about our future, since Régulo had put it in my hands.

One day when I was sitting in front of my canvas, working on a portrait of Lucy and Alba, Lucy started crying.

"What's wrong?" I asked my daughter.

"I miss Papá Régulo," she answered. I put my paintbrush down, walked over to her, and took her in my arms. Lucy's tears made me realize how much I missed Régulo too. I felt a deep longing to see him.

That afternoon I decided it was time to get my things in order and tell him I had made my decision. I wanted to be with him. I wanted us to rebuild our family. I asked Chata to stay with Lucy and Alba, bought a train ticket for Somondoco, and sent Régulo a telegram announcing the date of my arrival.

~

I took the train on a still morning in July. The sun was beginning to rise, but it seemed to linger for a moment beyond the mountain peaks. As I walked to the station with a small suitcase in my hand, I thought that perhaps at that moment, Régulo sat in deep thought on the veranda of his country home in a *mecedora*. Dawn had always been his favorite part of the day.

I couldn't wait to see him, to hold him, to kiss him on the lips. It was time to end our suffering and move forward in our lives together, with Alba and Lucy. I chose a window seat and looked at the landscape while thinking about the first time I had traveled from Paipa to Bogotá, not knowing what I would find or how my life would be impacted. Now I knew where I was going,

Somondoco, and why—to see the love of my life. We would start all over again. I glanced at the beautiful ring Régulo had given me in Madrid, my engagement ring. Yes, we would get married. Forget Ecuador. Our wedding would be in Bogotá, and our daughters would be the flower girls. Oh, I missed Julio so much. I wished he could be there with us and experience this new chapter in our lives.

Chapter Sixty-Two

As I rode on the crowded train, I tried to imagine what Augusta and Magdalena were doing in Somondoco. Through Régulo's letters, I had grown fond of the girl. I also felt compassion for Augusta, a woman I believed Régulo had never loved.

After the long journey, I got off the bus in front of the house, crossed the road, and walked around slowly, savoring every step. It had turned out to be a warm morning, and the sun was shining. The garden was as nice as I remembered it, with roses and orchids, banana trees, and a cactus in the middle. One solitary flower adorned the cactus tree, protected by the spines around it. I walked past the tree and up to the kitchen.

The light coming from the doorway darkened as I arrived at the kitchen door. It was probably difficult to see my face, but Augusta must have known as she looked up that it was me.

She had her hand suspended in midair, a piece of *pan de yuca* about to be stuck in her mouth. Before she could say or do anything, I greeted her.

"Hello, Augusta. How are you?"

She seemed unsure as to what to do. After a pause, she put the *pan de yuca* down, cleaned her hands on her apron, and received the hand I was offering her.

"I'm fine," she said. "Everything is the same around here."

"I see, and this señorita? She must be Magdalena." I glanced at her. She stared back at me.

"Magdalena is my niece," Augusta explained. "She helps me around the house."

"Nice to meet you," I said. Magdalena looked at the floor.

"You took an early bus," Augusta said abruptly. Her tone was as informative as it was condemning.

"Yes, I was eager to see Régulo."

Augusta's face tightened. "Well, he's upstairs," she mentioned before turning to her niece. "Magdalena, why don't you take her upstairs?"

"That won't be necessary," I insisted. "I know my way. Unless something has changed from when I used to come."

"I told you," Augusta repeated, "everything is the same. He has been waiting for you and refused to have breakfast until you came. It's ready. That bottle," she added, pointing, "is a special blend of his orange wine. He was waiting for your arrival to open it."

"Thanks, I'll let Régulo know I'm here."

"Wait!" Augusta shouted louder than was necessary. "Do you have any bags? Magdalena will take them upstairs for you."

"I only brought a small one," I said. "I can carry it."

Augusta seemed relieved. Obviously, she was hoping I would not stay long.

I took the stairs to the veranda. As I climbed, I could hear Régulo reciting a poem. He stopped and called my name.

"Inés?"

"It's me."

My voice and my presence became one as I turned the corner to find Régulo. I kissed him first on the head, my lips barely touching his hair, and then on his cheeks and eyes.

"I was wondering when you'd get here," he told me. "Come on, let's go downstairs to have some breakfast."

I watched Régulo as he rose from his *mecedora*, and I admired his small, agile frame, his dark skin, his high cheekbones, and his eyes, which were like pieces of coal burning furiously.

As I turned to go, I looked at the view from the veranda. The dirt road in front and beyond, green pastures, cows grazing, an orderly pattern formed by orange trees, and a guava tree down by the road, taller than the banana. This was the landscape I had remembered years before as I stood upon a hill in Paipa, glancing at the mountains far away. I had painted it many times over the years.

A few steps ahead Régulo was waiting for me. He lifted my hand to his lips, kissed it, and placed it in his.

"Inés, it took you long enough to find your way back," he said, "longer than I had hoped. But you returned, just as my great-great-grandmother had predicted."

"Really?" I stopped. "Where is her notebook? I'd like to read all her prophecies."

"I'll show it to you soon, *mi amor*," Régulo whispered, "but at present we have other things to do."

"Like what?"

"First, we'll have a toast with orange wine," he replied. "Then, we'll have breakfast, followed by our morning walk. In the afternoon we'll start planning our wedding and our honeymoon in Paris."

Acknowledgments

A very special thank-you to my grandfather, who inspired me to write about his life and who, when I took a pause, appeared to me in a dream, sat on my bed, and whispered, "Finish writing the novel." He taught me to love literature, and he predicted, when I was very young, that I would become a writer. Growing up with him and my grandmother and watching them interact, I became fascinated by their story. I'll never forget tasting my grandfather's orange wine, served with all our meals. Murky and bitter on the tongue, it gave me a sense of other worlds waiting to be discovered.

I would also like to thank my children for motivating me to write this novel so I could share stories about Colombia with them, descriptions of places where I—an immigrant writing in the second language I learned—grew up, so they could become familiar with the land of my ancestors and the eccentric cast of characters that once populated my life. Isabella, Stephany, and William, thank you for listening to my stories about that world. Your curiosity and your desire to hear more taught me that remembering is crucial and retelling magical.

A huge shout-out to the Bread Loaf Writers' Conference, where I initially shared an early draft of this novel. It was my first writers' conference, and I had no idea how important Bread Loaf would become in my life. I treasure the friendships I have made throughout the years in Vermont and Sicily and the fantastic colleagues I've been fortunate to work with during the Bread Loaf in Sicily conference.

A special thank-you to those who read earlier drafts of the novel and gave me feedback, and to the generous friends who have supported me and my writing throughout the years.

I would like to express my deepest gratitude to Madison Smartt Bell, remarkable literary agent, human being extraordinaire, and brilliant writer, for his encouragement and support and for offering invaluable advice concerning writing, editing, publishing, and beyond. I'll always be grateful to you for this and always glad our paths crossed in Sicily.

My heartfelt thanks to Meghan Harvey and Matt Kaye for welcoming me into the Bindery community. As one of those writers whose work doesn't fit "onto a predefined shelf," I am thrilled that my novel found the perfect home at Bindery Books. Your innovative approach to publishing, combined with the high level of professionalism and superb teamwork you foster, render you truly unique pioneers who are changing the publishing landscape.

I am genuinely grateful to be working with the amazing Marines Alvarez. Your passion for books and your enthusiasm for stories are uplifting, not to mention your sense of humor, discriminating taste, and ability to analyze literature and share your insights with readers in profound and intelligent ways. You are keeping stories alive and building meaningful bridges between writers and readers.

My sincere appreciation to the wonderful Kim Kent, for managing all the different aspects of the publication process. Gracious and patient, you have made it look easy and have kept everyone on track. Thank you for sharing your knowledge, and for answering all my questions with unwavering enthusiasm. Warmest thanks to Megan McKeever as well. You read my work with great care and gave me excellent suggestions. Your keen observations and thoughtful comments were incredibly helpful. I am also grateful to CJ Alberts for her marketing expertise, Charlotte Strick for her vision for a beautiful cover that captures the essence of the novel, and Kylee Hayes, who made sure everything concerning the final editing fell into place. Every single one of you has passionately and assiduously taken care of a million details in order to make this the best book it could possibly be. I feel incredibly lucky to be working with such a talented team.

Among all the exceptional people I have been fortunate to encounter during my life, my beloved deserves outstanding recognition. A rare individual who combines integrity and gentleness with intelligence, humor, and resilience, John has been my greatest supporter throughout the years, embracing all my creative projects and some outlandish ideas. Thank you for believing in me and for reminding me that there is goodness in the world.

Lastly, to my mother and brother, my deepest thanks for being who you are, for your love, and for being patient when I get carried away with words.

Notes

Terms:

Salero: While the traditional meaning is saltshaker, and *tener salero* means "to have a saltshaker" in Spain, *tener salero* also signifies "to have charm, charisma, or a lively personality, to be very engaging and attractive." It's considered a positive attribute, especially in regions like Andalusia in southern Spain.

Gustavo Adolfo Bécquer:

Britannica, "Gustavo Adolfo Bécquer," last updated December 18, 2024, https://www.britannica.com/biography/Gustavo-Adolfo-Becquer

"25 poems by Gustavo Adolfo Bécquer," La Belle Seville, December 7, 2022, https://www.labelleseville.com/en/25-poems-of-gustavo-adolfo-becquer/

Federico García Lorca:

Federico García Lorca, *In Search of Duende* (New Directions Books, 1999).

Alfonsina Storni:

Alfonsina Storni, *Languidez versos,* Cooperativa Editorial, 1920. https://upload.wikimedia.org/wikipedia/commons/e/e7/Languidez_-_Alfonsina_Storni.pdf

César Vallejo:

César Vallejo, "The Black Heralds," trans. Yvette Siegert, Poets.org, accessed January 25, 2025, https://poets.org/poem/black-heralds.

Garcilaso de la Vega:

Garcilaso de la Vega *The Works of Garcilasso de la Vega*, trans. by J. H. Wiffen (1823; Project Gutenberg), 343, 348, 349, https://www.gutenberg.org/files/49410/49410-h/49410-h.htm.

Thank You

This book would not have been possible without the support from the Mareas Books community, with a special thank-you to the Producer members:

Amy Church
Audrey Quinn
Brittney Cornelius
Cadence Rochlen
Caitlin Vanasse
Calliyanna
Cristina B
Dawn May-Christ
Eric Calamari
Heather Hulscher
Jennifer Down
Jenny McEldoon
Kayla Chapman
Kia Borner
Margaret R Camp
Megan K
Meredith Hackerson
Reads with Rachel
Ruaridh K
Sara Conrad
Sarah Sharfi
Sarah Tucker
Suzanne Wdowik
pawsitivevibes
Fortunesdear
Leaf
Ramona
melodygrant
alana
watalienaite
velosigraptor
bookwyrmbella

About the Author

ESPERANZA HOPE SNYDER was born and raised in Bogotá, Colombia, and has lived in the US, Italy, and Spain. She is the author of a poetry collection, *Esperanza and Hope* (Sheep Meadow Press, 2018), and two plays, *Lullaby for George* and *The Backroom*, the latter of which is being adapted to film. *Delicates*, her cotranslation of Wendy Guerra's poetry collection (Seagull Books, 2023), was noted in *The New York Times* and was long listed for the 2024 National Translation Award. Esperanza has also been assistant director of Bread Loaf in Sicily and co-coordinator of the Lorca Prize. She lives in Shepherdstown, West Virginia. *Orange Wine* was inspired by the story of her grandparents.

Mareas Books is an imprint of Bindery, a book publisher powered by community.

We're inspired by the way book tastemakers have reinvigorated the publishing industry. With strong taste and direct connections with readers, book tastemakers have illuminated self-published, backlisted, and overlooked authors, rocketing many to bestseller lists and the big screen.

This book was chosen by Marines Alarez in close collaboration with the Mareas Books community on Bindery. By inviting tastemakers and their reading communities to participate in publishing, Bindery creates opportunities for deserving authors to reach readers who will love them.

Visit Mareas Books for a thriving bookish community and bonus content:

mareas.binderybooks.com

MARINES ALVAREZ has been creating content across a variety of platforms since 2011, building a vibrant and engaged community of story lovers. Profiled by *Rolling Stone* and *Vulture*, Marines is a community builder on- and offline, crafting reviews that invite readers to think critically about media and representation. She is also the cofounder of BookNet Fest, a yearly bookish event that brings together readers, authors, and reviewers around a shared love of books.

@MYNAMEISMARINES (IG AND TIKTOK)